Praise for *The Dark Cove Theatre Society*

"With its lush, brooding setting and cast of ambitious young actors, *The Dark Cove Theatre Society* will enthrall theatre lovers and dark academia fans alike—along with anyone who's ever battled anxiety or perfectionism in the cutthroat world of the arts."
—Olivia Worley, author of *The Debutantes*

"A captivating boarding school story that will leave you laughing, crying, and cheering for Vi. With its interwoven letters and found texts, this is the perfect read for every theatre kid at heart."
—Tatiana Schlote-Bonne, author of *Such Lovely Skin*

"Stylish and candid, full of sharp observations about a young artist's growing pains."
—Curtis Campbell, author of *Dragging Mason County*

"A new queer gothic classic set on an island that every reader will long to visit."
—Kevin Alves, *Yellowjackets*

"Set in a lush, eerie world, *The Dark Cove Theatre Society* is an expertly told story that explores the nature of privilege and elitism in the arts. I fell in love with Violet, who at times seems to be simultaneously amused and intimidated by her surroundings, which feels highly relatable. If you love dark academia and spooky settings full of sapphics, this book is for you."
—E. Latimer, author of *Witches of Ash and Ruin*

"What a ride! Sierra has an incredible talent for pulling you straight into her world. I was completely captivated by the eerie, intriguing universe of *The Dark Cove Theatre Society*—every page offered new clues that kept me hooked. Before I knew it, I was completely immersed in Vi's world. The characters felt real, the story was full of twists, and it kept me on edge right up until the end. I couldn't put the book down and read it in one sitting. If you're looking for a gripping mystery you're going to love this book!"
—Ashley Leggat, *Life With Derek*

"A thrilling mix of ambition, mystery, and secrets. Sierra Riley delivers a story that is impossible to put down."
—Alexander Elliot, Hulu's *The Hardy Boys*

"Riley expertly blends the moodiness of dark academia with the poignant anxieties of modern adolescence to create a punchy, engaging, and relatable story for today's teens. Readers will root for Violet as she struggles to find herself in this world of cutthroat drama students and lofty professors. Finally, dark academia drama for all the anxious theatre nerds."
—Matteo L. Cerilli, author of *Lockjaw*

The Dark Cove Theatre Society

Sierra Marilyn Riley

The Dark Cove Theatre Society

Cover designed by Rachel Nam
Interior designed by Rafael Chimicatti
Edited by Jieun Lee
Copy edited by Anne Fullerton
Proofread by Linda Pruessen
Expert read by Nancy Cooper

Cover image credits:
Crow: Epine / Shutterstock. Castle: Vlada Young / Shutterstock. Trees: iStock.com/Tatyana Goncharuk.

This book is funded in part by the Government of Canada. *Ce livre est financé en partie par le gouvernement du Canada*. We acknowledge the support of the Canada Council for the Arts. *Nous remercions le Conseil des arts du Canada de son soutien*. We would like to acknowledge the funding support of the Ontario Arts Council (OAC) and the Government of Ontario for their support. We also acknowledge the support of the Government of Ontario through the Ontario Book Publishing Tax Credit, and through Ontario Creates.

Conseil des arts du Canada

Canada

Library and Archives Canada Cataloguing in Publication
Title: The Dark Cove Theatre Society / Sierra Marilyn Riley.
Names: Riley, Sierra Marilyn, author.
Identifiers: Canadiana (print) 20250117959 | Canadiana (ebook) 20250118092 | ISBN 9781834020082 (hardcover) | ISBN 9781834020099 (softcover) | ISBN 9781834020105 (EPUB) | ISBN 9781834020112 (PDF)
Subjects: LCGFT: Novels.
Classification: LCC PS8635.I538 D37 2025 | DDC jC813/.6—dc23

Published in the U.S.A. by Annick Press (U.S.) Ltd.
Distributed in Canada by University of Toronto Press.
Distributed in the U.S.A. by Publishers Group West.

Printed in Canada

annickpress.com | sierramarilynriley.com

To all my crushes and castmates
but most of all to Quinn, the very best of both.

CAMPSITE
BOYS' DORM
ACCOLADE NORTH
MT. CALIBAN
WINCROFT THEATRE
RAVEN LAKE
LIBRARY
RUTGERS DINING HALL
ACCOLADE SOUTH
DARK COVE
FERRY TERMINAL
TRACK
GIRLS' DORM
TENNIS COURTS
N
FLECK BEACH
FOOTPATH
ROAD
CLIFF

Appendix A

Excerpt, Dark Cove Arts Academy brochure

Welcome to Dark Cove Arts Academy

Since its founding in 1892, Dark Cove Arts Academy has accumulated a far-reaching reputation for academic excellence, consistently ranking as a top art school at an international level. Here, traditional wisdom blends with visionary curricula. Through its provision of classical, gender-segregated training in Dance, Music, Theatre, and Visual Art for young men and women, the Academy provides students with the tools and facilities they need in order to become masters of their respective craft.

Our campus, a designated heritage site, is located on a forested island roughly eighty nautical miles off the north coast of British Columbia, Canada. Rich in historical significance for both settler and Indigenous peoples, Dark Cove Island's resplendent environment is conducive to the rigorous, creative teachings of the Academy. Facilities include two schoolhouses designed in the Gothic tradition by Vincent DuMaurier, a large communal library, a dining hall, two darkrooms, two state-of-the-art recording booths, ten rehearsal studios, a two-hundred-seat proscenium stage theatre, and boutique boarding accommodations with views of Raven Lake.

Guided by the values of persistence, courage, and excellence, Dark Cove's first headmaster, Frederick Stine, recognized dedicated artistic education as a keystone to the development of the world's future leaders. During Stine's incumbency, young men and women were instructed to choose a path to which they could dedicate themselves fully, no matter how dark the night, no matter how difficult the course might reveal itself to be. They would act as their own guiding lights, and this would be their legacy. Though the curriculum has been updated since Stine's tenure, that tenet holds true. Graduates of the Academy's three-year program leave the island with highly specialized skills, a comprehensive understanding of the creative industries at large, and a vast network of alumni at their fingertips.

Countless cultural pioneers have passed through these halls, each one taking a piece of the island with them, each one leaving a piece of themselves behind, forever tethered in spirit to the Academy. Once a Covie, always a Covie!

in tenebris lucem creamus

Chapter 1

A foghorn blares as the six a.m. ferry casts away from the mainland. It takes less than a minute at sea for me to realize I have neither the stomach nor the focus to get any reading done here. The front of the boat, already heaving on choppy water, is an apparently irresistible photo op. I tuck *Jane Eyre* into my satchel, gulp down my seasickness, and make for the main deck—anything to distance myself from the feral mass of students snapping pictures at the helm. Soon, social media feeds will be deluged with pretty girls kicking up their Duke + Dexters in front of an ominous white wall—the mist out here is *Silent Hill* thick. It's not exactly ideal photo-shoot weather, but this is our last chance to post, text, or call before losing signal. Once we get to the island, we won't even be able to send an e-mail without the help of a microwave-sized desktop computer at the campus library. I pull out my cell (down to two bars already) and wipe the sea spray off the screen with my sleeve. Among the still-there droplets, one new message:

KAY: where r u?

I type: ujnj ippppp

Okay. Writing a reply on this stubbornly wet phone, like reading Brontë at the bow, is a fool's errand. I set out to find the sender instead. Wind thrums in my ears and mist needles my face as I thread through reunited friend groups. Even on our co-ed nautical voyage, the school populace separates into gendered blocs, subdivided by areas of study and interest. For each Dark Cove Arts Academy major, there are different specializations and, as a result, innumerable Covie cliques.

I pass brooding poets, giddy vocalists, a conglomeration of film bros shouting "let's go" for no discernible reason, a tight cluster of hush-toned ballerinas, philosopher types, a bunch of photographers comparing lenses or whatever, and then, of course, there's the Dark Cove Theatre Society, the most exclusive club on campus.

The Society is known for its talented elite, illustrious drama productions, general snobbery, and, these days, notoriously debaucherous, very illicit parties. There is no shortage of rumors and lore attached to it—everything I know about the Society I've learned against my will—but its inner workings are unknowable. Fact cannot be separated from fiction, at least not from my position on the outside. All the theatre kids swirl around the Society members, a little fearful but mostly envious. The club's de facto rulers, a trio of gorgeous lesbian actresses,[1] stand at the eye of the storm: Magpie the Pugnacious, born with Angelina Jolie lips and a silver spoon in her mouth; Rue, whose shampoo-commercial hair and dewy complexion conceal the biggest brain on campus; and last but most certainly not least, there's Frankie Lin, our resident ingenue. If Dark Cove were a normal high school, Frankie Lin would be a cheerleader. At Dark Cove, she's the star actress. Pick any genre and she's the leading lady—she's Elle Woods, Sidney Prescott, Buffy the freakin' Vampire Slayer. Only somehow hotter than all of them put together and she knows it, wearing a baby-pink Fiorucci cherub tee and a pair of invisible angel wings to match.

I brush past swaths of silk, Egyptian cotton, and cashmere, tugging at the seams of my own clashy, ill-fitting outfit. It's an assortment of Value Village finds that looked relatively cool until I put them on this morning: a *The Exorcist* tee that simultaneously accentuates the roundness of my belly and makes my boobs look weirdly hexagonal, paired

1 Commonly referred to as the Dark Cove Lipstick Lesbians, the Thesbians, or the Gaykeepers. Though I am not proud to admit it, that third one was conceived of by yours truly.

with wedgie-inducing low-rise Levi's that I regret ever squeezing my body into and intend on burning immediately after use.

The back-to-school ferry ride is an annual fashion show of about two hundred student models. Soon enough, we'll all be forced into drab variations of the school uniform: knee-length kilts, cotton-blend button-ups, wool cardigans, Covie-green[2] rugby shirts, and—for formal curricular events[3]—tweed blazers with matching trousers. The ferry ride is an opportunity for students to assert their aesthetic identities and style sense (or, in my case, lack thereof).

A flash of cow print catches my eye from the back of the boat. It's Kay in a campy but chic Western getup, looking like a contestant on a themed episode of *America's Next Top Model.* They're typing something on their phone. I call their name. They don't hear me. My pocket buzzes. I'm wiggling my way between two clumps of flanneled guitarists when I accidentally collide with a six-foot someone who I quickly identify as Hunter Kinsey.

The golden boy. My not-ex. Ex-crush. Whatever. The seasickness comes back with a vengeance. "Sorry," I mumble.

"No prob, Vi." He smiles like a white-toothed Abercrombie ad, like it's nothing. His skin is a deep bronze and his eyes are the color of a well-watered lawn. The hair on his forearms glitters against his late-August tan. Summer has treated him well. Of course it has. "I see you didn't learn how to not be a klutz in the past few months, huh?"

When he winks at me, I want to throw myself overboard. I notice a whisper of stubble that wasn't there the last time we talked. "Yeah, no. Didn't end up getting that waitressing gig," I shout over the sound of crashing waves, fighting the nausea, desperately trying to seem breezy—failing, naturally. "Sold yoga pants to suburban moms instead."

"I dig it." He chuckles and my organs somersault. Funny how you can spend months getting over someone and then they laugh and destroy all that progress like a lost game of Jenga. "You know the Hollywood

---

2 A deep verdant.

3 Exams, school portraits, etc.

Forever Cemetery? I worked there—six feet above Burt Reynolds, Judy Garland, all of them—slinging stale popcorn. Totally legendary." As the son of some big producer at some big production company, Hunter's summer jobs are a rite of passage—a fun anecdote more than a necessity. I don't know what to say to him other than, "Oh, cool," which is what I say when the foghorn sounds, politely ending our conversation. Hunter's friend pod swallows him up and carries him away while chanting the school's Latin motto, which has nothing to do with anything right now. I am reminded that I don't like him anymore. It's easier to remember that you don't like someone when you don't have to look right into their ridiculously gorgeous face. I reroute myself to Kay, who's now just a few feet away. Their raven-black bob is pulled back by dozens of acrylic cow-print clips, face freckled with silver glitter.

"I came to save you from the compulsive flirter, but it looks like the bros did it first." They shudder, watching Hunter's group drift into the distance like a Nike-branded storm cloud. "The toxic masculinity is palpable."

"Is there such a thing as toxic femininity?" I dart my eyes at a giggling Frankie Lin. She flips her long, silky mane over her shoulder. The picture of perfection.

"Ah, not yet a day into the semester and the inquiring minds of Dark Cove Arts Academy are already engaging in gender discourse." Kay chortles, their eyes mascaraed and rolling. "Ready for another year stranded on an island with pretentious art students?"

"Sure," I say with a false air of amusement. "Our own personal *Lord of the Flies.*" The students around us may look chummy on this boat, but make no mistake, they are sharks.

Dark Cove Arts Academy is a century-old school with a serious reputation across the Pacific Northwest and beyond; the alumni pool is a who's who of industry greats. Graduates go on to achieve the highest of the high accolades—I'm talking Oscars, Tonys, Pulitzers, Grammys, and Golden Globes, among other pretty trophies that simultaneously mean everything and nothing. I'd be lying if I said I didn't have an acceptance speech already prepared. I'm sure everyone does, though they wouldn't admit it. You can't seem like you want commercial success too badly—that's gauche. All that's to say, the culture here is cutthroat. Both Kay and I are scholarship students, which means we have to maintain an absurdly high GPA to go here. And since the bell curve is a thing, that makes everyone our competition. Kay's a Music major (specializing in composition), and I'm in Theatre, so fortunately we aren't rivals. If we were, they'd win. They're basically a textbook prodigy, and I'm not just saying that because they're my best friend: they get straight As, they play something like ten instruments (including the saw), and they're in a buzzy indie band.[4] Kay's sorted.

My creative and academic future is less certain. As of whenever this ferry docks, my specialization at the Academy is officially changing from acting to playwriting. I may have come to Dark Cove with aspirations of one day starring in a Scorsese spectacular, but I've always been a poet, too. It's just . . . I thought of creative writing as an easy-A elective. A hobby. Acting was my future. "Was" being the operative word. All that changed at the Spring Showcase,[5] when I had a panic attack that altered the trajectory of my whole life. I blacked out most of it, but there lingers the memory of me sputtering the word "sorry" about fifty times before running to the bathroom in tears. No one came after me, but the whispers followed for a while. As much as Dark Cove loves a tortured artist, that only applies if your shadow self can actually help you *make* art. In this instance, my attempt at tapping into the ol' emotional reserves produced the opposite effect. It didn't endear me to my peers or professors, either. On the bright side, there weren't many rungs on the social ladder left for me to fall to; I merely went from invisible to the subject of gossip for a week. They called me names, most of them implying mental instability, which I'm kind of used to, coming from an ultra-conservative, suffocatingly small town. I've got all the prerequisites of a stereotypical outcast—clumsy, chubby, shy, quick to cry, a little

---

4 Elemental Dust's EP came out last spring; it's experimental but not inaccessible, mostly folk-forward with unexpected R&B undercurrents and lyrics that will tear you apart. The most-streamed track, "Frankenbaby," has fifty thousand hits.

5 Dark Cove Arts Academy's take on final exams; every June, each student must present a piece (which demonstrates their strengths and artistic growth) to all students and faculty of their respective department.

obsessive, not without my quirks—and it turns out those prerequisites are transferable even to a non-stereotypical high school like Dark Cove. Thinking that life on the island would be any different just because it's a world away from my hometown? That was a fantasy. The reality is I'm me wherever I go, and every school needs its designated freaks.

My public meltdown was a wake-up call, and what a world I woke up to: I got a failing grade that tanked my average; my scholarship was reduced; I was assigned a work-study weekend job in the Dark Cove archives to soften the monetary blow; and the school informed my mother that they'd be closely monitoring my performance this semester. Basically, I'm on paper-thin ice. So, I leaned into my strengths when curating my new timetable: English Literature II, Playwriting I, Textual Analysis, Latin (a requirement), Theatre History II (another requirement), and Theatre Practicum (last requirement). No more acting, thank you very much. I like writing better now, anyway. With writing, you can edit out your mistakes.

Today marks the start of my penultimate year on the island. My plan is to study hard, work hard, and stay under the radar. The only way I'll ever be a writer worth knowing is if I at least make it to graduation.

Kay takes my hand and leads me to the back of the boat, forcing their way through the chaos with a confidence that will never not amaze me. My palm's getting clammy, but they don't let go until we're in the clear.

"Thanks." I wipe the sweat off onto my evil jeans. "For the hand."

They shrug. "Got you, girl. I know how you get in crowds."

My death grip now fixes itself onto the rusted guardrail as ocean thrashes against stern. The ferry casts out milky waves that ripple out in a mesmeric pattern. Miles back, the British Columbia mountainside recedes then dissolves behind a curtain of fog. I'm not sure how long it is that Kay and I stand there without talking, the excited shrieks of gulls and schoolgirls replacing conversation, the heavy spread of the Pacific filling out the rest. Salt air pours into my lungs and I exhale everything that came before this. It dissolves in the water behind us.

I sense Dark Cove before I see it. After an hour of gossiping, comparing summers, and whatnot, everyone on the boat quiets collectively, instinctively, at once. The seafowl stop their squawking. The engine rumble dulls to a low hum. Even the water stills. There's a palpable shift, as though the vessel has passed through to another dimension. Then, out of the fog, like an apparition, it emerges: a castle of pine and rock and bone at the edge of the world.

There's the illusion that it is the island moving toward the ferry, not the other way around. Something other than the mechanics of the boat draws us in. As the distance between us closes, I spot the old, out-of-commission lighthouse and modest bell tower peeking over the dark green overstory. I feel changed by the summer—Kay and I watched romcoms and *Sex and the City* as a way to psych me into my new writer identity—but the beach appears unaffected by months of sun. It's just as harsh and unwelcoming as I remember it. According to the pictures, Dark Cove has always looked this way, eroded by nothing, not the ancient grunt of sea nor the earth's climbing temperatures. Somehow, time rolls over the school's fossilized world like a tidal breeze. I wonder when, if ever, reality will catch up to it. The foghorn blares once more, ruining the perfect quiet. An ecstatic murmur ripples across the vessel, so close to kissing the rocky shore. She docks.[6] We're here. The air is electric with the heady scent of damp earth, fuel, and salt. A mix of excitement and dread bubbles in my esophagus.

A few teachers bark instructions into megaphones to "DISEMBARK SLOWLY" and "FORM AN ORDERLY LINE," which everyone ignores, the chatter picking up again. Kay grabs my hand so we don't lose each other among the student body wriggling and bottlenecking at the ferry's exit. The battered pier creaks underfoot, too tired for yet another procession of young, entitled, loafer-wearing wannabes. Above, a wooden sign reads WELCOME, COVIES, the paint peeling off so it's barely legible. Dark Cove lore has it that this sign was hand-painted in the seventies by one of the school's most revered alumni, horror director

6 Is assigning she/her pronouns to a boat sexist? Discuss.

Sven Olsen. Purportedly, his high status is the reason why the sign hasn't been maintained or touched up in recent decades, to preserve the mark of a genius.[7]

From my position in the snaking crowd of next-gen geniuses, I spot Headmaster Henley. He's a wiry and balding man with a mustache like a thin white hedge on his upper lip. Despite his slight hunch, the headmaster stands tall in his tweed suit where the dock meets the land, a small convoy of golf carts behind him.[8] Brittle strands of hair peek out of his crooked, oversized nose as if to check that the coast is clear, which it almost never is on this island. A murder of crows squabbles around Dark Cove's ruler. Henley waits silently, gaunt face expressionless, until all of us (teens and birds) pick up on his cue. We settle down to a hush. The clouds thicken into a dark, cottony gray.

When he clears his throat, it just sounds like he's saying "Ahem" phonetically. "Thank you," he begins in his vaguely European accent.

Kay leans over to whisper in my ear. "Here we go . . ."

Henley gives the same speech every year. This is only my second time hearing it, but I expect a word-for-word repeat of what he said 365 days ago. "I have been headmaster of this school for over two decades," Henley announces, his voice booming over the cool gale coming off the water, "and in that time I have witnessed hundreds—thousands—of young people step onto this dock in September only to become unrecognizable to me by the time I see them off the following June. On this island, you will undergo total transformation. Creatively, academically, spiritually, and intellectually, you will be challenged. Figuratively

---

7 Several actors and crew members who worked on Olsen's seminal film *Blood Night* (1982) have come forward with accounts of an "unsafe working environment," which, given Olsen's eccentric public personality, is unsurprising. The straight, oddball white man is an identity often conflated with the concept of genius.

8 There is only one trail and one uneven, winding road that connects the campus to the ferry terminal, but it is not wide enough to accommodate any vehicle larger than a golf cart. The school has four of these, strictly reserved for staff and primarily used to transport luggage, set pieces, etc. At one time, there were ten buggies, sources say, but six have disappeared. Another one of Dark Cove's many mysteries.

and literally put to the test." He pauses here for dramatic effect. The word "challenged" makes me wince—at the ripe age of sixteen, I feel I've already had my fair share of tribulations.

Kay whispers, "And *this* is where he starts rambling on about time."

"At Dark Cove Arts Academy, you do not merely pass through time; rather, time passes through you. The island's temporal reality changes the student, and the student, in turn, alters the course of history, both the present and the tenuous thing of the future. Art, after all, has the ability to suspend and bend the hours, stretch it out and compress it. The years you spend here will feel like a grueling eternity before they become a mere blip in your life's course. Spend these seasons wisely. Woe betide you if you let them slip away. However you choose to occupy yourself on this island is indicative of the artist that you are. And yes, you are already an artist. We will treat you as such. If you crack under the pressure at the Academy, you will not fare well in the 'real world.'" He lifts his skeletal white hands into air quotes, a physical colloquialism that looks awkward on the old man. Again, I am reminded that here, unless transmuted into brilliance, emotional struggles are regarded as hamartia.[9] "If you don't like how we operate, catch the ferry home and spare yourself the spiritual and physical labor it takes to be an artist in a dark world such as this one."

Headmaster Henley claps his hands together, making a sound not unlike a gunshot that echoes across the jagged shore. At once, the crows take flight in perfect choreography, blackening the sky for a moment before gathering on an algae-coated outcrop. I watch as they shuck shells of their innards. A chill runs down my spine.

"Of course, there will be nights when the pressures of your art seize you, tempt you, shroud your sense of purpose." His voice lowers to a sort of growl. "Hold on to that purpose. Under the masks of talent, beauty, and intellect, purpose is the only real thing. The only real thing over which you'll ever have ownership. *In tenebris lucem creamus.*"[10]

---

9 Derived from a Greek term for "to miss the mark," *hamartia* is theatre-speak for a fatal flaw that ultimately leads to the demise of the hero.

10 The Latin school motto translates to "we create light in darkness."

"*In tenebris lucem creamus*," some students in the crowd mumble back. The first years look as petrified as I feel inside.

This is where the speech ended last year (and, presumably, every year before that), but Headmaster Henley lingers. "You may notice some unfamiliar faces around the island in the coming months," he continues. "The International Art School Association will be making their annual visit at the end of October to evaluate the Academy's pre-professional training programs. Contemporaneously, we will be hosting the Dark Cove Board of Governors, who will be observing student life, sitting in on midterm presentations, and conducting interviews with select students. It is a long journey here, as you know, which the Board endeavors gladly in order to foster the continuous growth and prosperity of this institution. These are venerable business and community leaders upon whom you would benefit to make a good impression; all the more reason to be on your best behavior, yes? Second and third years will likely recognize some of the Board who have previously visited for the Academy's Annual General Meeting in May. Others, you will have only heard of. The Board's newest member, Mrs. Tabitha Lin,[11] will be joining us from Taipei. A long way indeed. I expect you to welcome her as you would our other esteemed guests: with hospitality and tolerance."

On this casually racist note, the headmaster turns dramatically[12] and disappears into a dense thicket of pine. Replacing his post, a stone-faced Magpie Black shuffles up dressed in a fussy, frilly, first-day-of-school blouse that wouldn't be out of place in a pirate movie, tucked neatly into a silk slip skirt. Frankie Lin and Rue whoop excitedly.

"Who put *her* in charge?" I say, just loud enough for Kay to hear.

"It's an honor to stand before you," Magpie begins her address, "as the President of the Dark Cove Theatre Society."

---

11 Tabitha Lin, named one of *Forbes*' Most Powerful Women in the early 2000s, is Frankie's mother.

12 Henley was a theatre actor in his youth. Select credits include Torvald in a West End production of *A Doll's House*, Caesar in *Julius Caesar* at Teatro d'Europa, and Woyzeck in *Woyzeck* with the Berliner Ensemble.

"The heir apparent has ascended the throne," Kay says stoically.

"As if that really means anything," I mumble. Though the Society appears to be self-determined, it's actually governed by the faculty;[13] the faculty curates the season of shows, the faculty holds the auditions, the *faculty* picks the President. And even so, the President's just a figurehead. The only functions they seem to serve are the tallying of votes in the Society's bizarre council election,[14] the occasional taking of attendance, and the leading of orientation. Which means I'll have to spend the next couple of hours tuning out Magpie Black.

"Why anyone would choose Satan's spawn as the Society's new ruler is a mystery to me," I hiss.

Kay chuckles darkly. "I thought Kemsley had it in the bag after that Brutus performance. Boy got snubbed."

"Word is he's the Secretary now," a girl behind us whispers excitedly. It's Nina Petrov, a third-year student who writes reviews and trend pieces for *The Covie Chronicle*.[15] I wonder how much of our conversation she heard. "Frankie Lin was voted Vice President, Rue Sandhu's the Treasurer of Secrets, whatever that means . . ."

I nod at Nina as thanks for the unsolicited intel and lean in closer to Kay, lowering my voice to just a breath. "Secretary? Do you believe that? Not even VP."

---

13 Initially of ill repute among faculty, the club was believed to have corrupted its top students. The story goes that the Society hosted late-night showings of licentious plays in secret locations across the island. Students, reckless and desperate to be a part of the club's growing legacy, became aggressive in their mission to join. A violent and degrading initiation was allegedly required of prospective members. Parental complaints amassed. Later, in the twenties, the Society had become such a campus nuisance—a symbol of moral indecency—that the faculty seized control of the heathen run club once and for all. After this institutional absorption, Society members exerted independence by partying. This tradition continues, and the club's prestige remains.

14 This the students do have a say in. Society Members vote in lower-level council members before school breaks for summer.

15 Dark Cove's student-run paper, known for its no-mercy reporting and always-there photographers.

"It would explain why he's keeping his distance." Kay juts their chin at Kemsley, who stands at the opposite end of the dock from the rest of the Society.

I look over my shoulder to check that Nina isn't listening. She's moved on to flirting with a buzz-cut guy who appears to be more interested in his Canon 400X1D920000, or whatever that long-lensed contraption on his neck is.

"I wonder if Mommy's new Board position has anything to do with it," I say to Kay.

"Are you suggesting political corruption among the Society's sacred council?" they joke.

Nina butts in again, Canon boy forgotten. "VP is *always* a popularity vote. No one ever stood a chance against Frankie Lin. She's super nice."

If Nina weren't looking right at me, I'd roll my eyes.

"Are you in the Society?" Kay asks politely, resigning themself to Nina's participation in this conversation.

"God, I wish! No. But when you get to your third year, you just know these things, LOL"—yes, she actually said LOL out loud—"and, real talk, if anyone's parents gave them a leg up, it's Magpie's. I know she's a good actress and everything and the faculty has favorites, but seriously, who wants to listen to *her* for the rest of the year."

As Magpie continues her very long, ultra-amplified speech, I consider what Nina just said. The newly minted President may be first in command, but she ranks third in popularity among her trio.

Mag's father is a technocrat or CEO, one of those old cornucopian guys who rule and ruin the world, but millionaire (billionaire?) parents are a dime a dozen in these parts. Tuition ain't cheap, and only a small percentage of us are lucky enough to get scholarships by existing at the sweet-spot intersection between "working-class born" and "promising young thing." The rest of the students have been plucked fresh from various McMansions, penthouses, chateaus, and estates with names like "Brackeninney Castle." As if she didn't already have enough, Mag has a tendency to steal stuff, which is where the name Magpie[16] came from. Her birth-certificate name is just Megan, but for reasons best known to herself, she hates when people call her that and insists on the nickname. My guess is she feels a diabolical pride in her reputation as a small-time thief. She shamelessly flaunts and adorns her stolen items all around campus—library books, props, enough silver jewelry to sink a ship—because she knows she's untouchable or at least unpunishable. It's mere coincidence that she also has a beak-like nose and, today, talon-sharp nails wrapped around a megaphone.

I only half-listen to her, instead taking in the imposing beauty of Dark Cove. Rock bluffs stab the sky, insects buzz over clumps of eelgrass, and low shrubs amass into the dense woodland ahead. It looks impenetrable, steeply rising to campus and the summit of Mount Caliban[17] beyond.

"Thank you. Now. Covie girls! Follow me to the dorms. Chop, chop!" Magpie tucks the megaphone into her armpit and claps sharply twice (once per "chop") before she is joined by Mr. Blake, Head of the Theatre Department. He shakes Magpie's talon with his meaty hand.

"Young men, you will be coming with me." His thunderous voice needs no megaphone. It comes from deep inside his portly belly, amplified somehow by the squareness of his head.[18] Renowned in the world of Western theatre as a master in every respect, he is the teacher whose opinion of me matters more than any other. Unfortunately, he also happens to be my former acting teacher. The one who, last year, witnessed me crumble under the pressures of this island. My stomach lurches as he flashes a faraway grin. I catch a glint of gold from his fake incisor. "Leave your luggage and other personal items on the dock."

---

16 In honor of the white-tailed bird that collects small, shiny things.

17 Mount Caliban was named by Dark Cove's second headmaster after Shakespeare's half-human, half-monster. At the mountain's summit, you can find a stone plaque embedded in the ground, engraved with a quote from *The Tempest*: "Be not afeard; the isle is full of noises, Sounds, and sweet airs, that give delight, and hurt not."

18 He teaches his own eponymous vocal technique to students.

"Our professors here have kindly offered to bring those up for us," Magpie explains, cueing the thunk of a hundred or so bags.

The professors in question: Mr. Hendrix (uncomfortably handsome; subject of many student crushes; Head of the Music Department, go figure); Mr. Mitchell (teaches Lit and Latin; probably old enough to have been around when people actually spoke Latin); Mr. Norman (teaches Stagecraft and Theatre History; cold and unfeeling); Mme. Camry (Head of the Dance Department and the school librarian; walks with an epic brass cane; stereotypically Parisian, and by that I mean sharp, chic, and rude), Mrs. Lincoln (Head of the Vis[19] Department; always wears various spotless white smocks; no notes on personality as I've never spoken to her). There are younger teaching assistants who help these guys run their respective departments, but they aren't in attendance. However, there is a fresh-faced woman I've never seen before. She can't be older than thirty, her face smoother and brighter than anyone else up there. She's dressed in an expensive-looking trench coat that billows in the wind, exposing a tulle skirt that reminds me of Carrie Bradshaw's iconic opening-credit look. A Marmaduke-esque dog stands beside her, tail wagging à la helicopter rotor, its pointy head reaching her waist.

"Who's she?" I ask Kay, slinging my satchel and backpack into a pathetic heap on the dock.

"One of the *unfamiliar faces* Henley mentioned?"

"That's not til October."

Kay scrunches their nose. "New TA?"

"None of the other TAs are here."

"I'm out of guesses."

A mystery woman. She beams at us, waving with one hand and using the other to control her curly flyaway hairs. She ducks into the driver's seat of a golf cart, and Mr. Hendrix places his hand on the hood.

Nina Petrov again butts her head between us. "Maybe the music teach moved his girlfriend onto the island," she says, "to send a message to his admirers."

---

19 Shorthand for Visual Arts.

Kay makes goggles with their hands. "Hard to get a chemistry read from here."

"Keep up," Mr. Blake demands, charging up the path to the boys' school with surprising speed. He may be short, but his legs work quickly.

Over innumerable Louis Vuitton duffle bags and steamer trunks, we travel-worn teens maneuver our way up the pier onto a beaten-down path. Two crows sit atop a sign pointing in the general direction of campus, cawing to welcome us back—or, more likely, to caution us against invading their home. Of course, we ignore the warning and wade into the shadowy woods ahead.

Chapter 2

Filtered through a canopy of pine, bluish daylight illuminates the steep path forward. The forest is very *Sleepy Hollow.* A setting that begs for bloodshed and magic in equal measure. Spotted mushrooms sprout from under the roots of twisted hemlocks. Vines and bougainvillaea adorn oaks whose branches reach up in a vault above like the archway of a cathedral. I walk enraptured along the serpentine path west until it reaches a fork where the boys split off from the girls. We lost Nina somewhere along the way, and I can't say I'm complaining.

Kay hooks their arm through mine. "Let's see if the girls give a better tour, shall we?"

As the school's first and only Two-Spirit student, Kay didn't know which side of the island they belonged on. They started with the boys' but recently decided it was "too boys' clubby," so they put in a transfer request this summer. We expected it to go smoothly—Dark Cove admin wanted Kay to enroll in the girls' school in the first place—but it was a drawn-out process in which the Board made Kay jump through a series of ridiculous bureaucratic hoops. Luckily, Kay is a successful hoop jumper, and they've always been better than me at shrugging off the irritating politics and pomposity of the school. Long story short, they're my roommate now.

"It's a pleasure to have you on this gendered voyage with me," I quip and Magpie barks at us to hurry up. The trail levels out to a smooth slope of cobblestone as we approach campus. The wind gasps.

"This is Accolade South, where most of the girls' classes are held,"[20] Magpie explains to the first years gaping at the gargantuan building.

It's a fortified castle. Accolade South stands tall, adorned with stained glass, hatched windows, gargoyles, rose bushes, and stone steps polished from over a century of pedestrian traffic. Cared for by a discreet team of groundskeepers (I've seen them at work in the soil only a few times myself) and planted long ago by some uppity British botanists, the gardens of Accolade South are disciplined in contrast to the unruly brush of the island. Here, the smooth lines of a sculpted topiary. There, a tidy row of chrysanthemums. The first years' mouths form small, stupefied Os. That feeling is one I remember well: total awe, which later transmutes into a lingering sensation of smallness. Seeing that expression on their face makes me realize how jaded I've become in just one year.

"Three stories of the messiest floor plans ever, and nobody's gonna hold your hand if you get lost, so map it out before Wednesday. If you're late to class, you'll get your ass handed to you," Magpie continues, all decorum dropped now that the teachers aren't watching. "There are bathrooms on every level. Faculty lounge, reception, and offices at the top. The girls' infirmary is in the basement. You can figure out the rest."

Fallen needles rustle as we stumble onward past a Tartan Track field[21] with pristine markings, a wide patch of clover at its center, and two cerulean-blue tennis courts[22] encircled by a thick partition of sleepy firs.

---

20 Like the dormitories, class cohorts are gender segregated, but teachers instruct in both schoolhouses. On the Dark Cove Arts Academy website under the Careers tab, the twenty-minute walk between Accolade South and Accolade North is presented as "a brilliant opportunity to maintain cardiovascular health during the workweek."

21 The four-hundred-meter ovular track is rarely used for physical education (athletic Covies opt for trail runs). Instead, it serves as the site of co-ed socializing. Sometimes, desperate students will repurpose the field into a rehearsal space.

22 Tennis is another dying pastime. The closest thing to a sports team at Dark Cove Arts Academy is Improv Club, and participation is low even there. The courts are most frequently used for site-specific mountings of *Rosencrantz and Guildenstern Are Dead*.

Already short of breath, I'm grateful when Magpie halts the group at a signpost pointing north. She continues the guided tour in a bored voice: "This path goes to Raven Lake and our co-ed facilities: Frederick Stine Dining Hall, the library, and Wincroft Theatre. A little farther that way and you're at the boys' school, or Accolade North." What she doesn't mention is the old campsite that lies beyond the boys' school on the island's northern shore—it figures Magpie would want to keep their party venue a secret from the have-nots. The off-limits camp purportedly comprises a cluster of fifteen modest log cabins that once housed students at Dark Cove's infamous summer school,[23] but these days it's a party locale for the campus elite. I've never been to one of these invitation-only events, obviously.

"Do we get to see the boys' school?" asks a first year.

Through gritted teeth, Magpie says, "That would be pointless. It's identical to Accolade South."

"How will we know if we're at the right school, then?"

"The testosterone levels are much higher on that side of Raven Lake. You'll know."

We march on. I struggle to keep pace with the tour as we make our way up the frost-heaved path—a twisted ankle in waiting—that winds up to a thicket of flowered shrubs. A sweet aroma is eddied by the breeze. Covered in vines, there stands the charming—if slightly dilapidated—girls' dormitory.

"Still cannot believe this glorified hobbit hole fits every girl on campus, but okay," says Kay.

The dorm has the Edwardian design of a grand manor, but it's smaller than it looks in the school pamphlet. God, before receiving our admission letters, Kay and I used to obsess over that thing. We each had a copy taken from a school fair in the city when we were maybe ten years old.

---

23 The camp shut down in 1995 following the disappearance of a few campers. The school's official statement didn't give away much at the time of the tragedy, but local legend has it that there was a slasher-type killer involved. Despite the lack of evidence to support this theory, the kids here refer to the incident as the Camp Covie Massacre.

Since then, we'd dreamed about coming here—I as an aspiring Hollywood actor and Kay a film composer. This school, to us, represented everything we wanted to be. We had the Academy website memorized by heart, and we spent more than one sleepover poring over the thick, sacred paper of that brochure. At its centerfold, there was a photo of the girls' dorm that now stands before us.

"My new digs," Kay declares.

I pat their back. "Welcome home."

We file into the stone dwelling, overstuffed with hand-carved tables, high-backed chairs, brass candelabras, old woven tapestries,[24] and other antiques. Though the house is perennially chilly (shoddy insulation), a mantled fireplace burning at the heart of the common room gives the pretense of coziness. No one stands on formality before rushing up to their new rooms. Everyone's already received their boarding assignments via e-mail. Last year, I had a room on the second story that was comparable in size to a broom closet, and my old roommate's tuba took up most of that space. Kay, bless them, rallied for us and we've scored the largest top-level accommodations in the building. There are six floors total, with one bathroom and ten dorm rooms per floor—two girls per room—except for the main level, which instead spans a foyer, the common area, and five upgraded faculty suites.

"All right. Tour's over." Magpie's voice echoes up the spiral staircase. "Welcome to Dark Cove."

By the time we arrive at the top floor, I'm out of breath. Our room is at the far end of the hall. It smells like topsoil and expired lotion, but the bay window overlooking campus makes up for the room's shortcomings. Inside, there are two four-poster twin beds dressed in starchy cotton, and at the foot of each one is a wooden trunk. There's a single wardrobe to be shared, two classroom desks with comically tiny chairs, and one nightstand with a nineties landline phone on it. The phone is a clunky thing

---

24 My favorite one was a gift from the National Ballet of Ukraine, depicting a scene from act 2 in *Swan Lake*: Prince Siegfried and his fellow hunters watching the swans glide across the glittering water.

with a spiral cord and enormous buttons, kind of like the one Drew Barrymore answered in *Scream* (not the iconic cordless one, the other one). I'll use it to call Mom later, but I can't afford to be homesick already. At this point, I'd rather hear Ghostface ask me what my favorite scary movie is than hear my mother's voice.

At least I'll have a live-in piece of home with me—Kay's basically family. Even the sound of them snoring brings me comfort (and, hey, it beats getting woken up by five a.m. tuba practice). We've been best friends for nine years almost exactly. They were the first person I met after Mom and I moved out of my dad's town to live with Nonna. It was September somethingth. I walked into the elementary school shaking like a leaf; Kay was dressed in about a dozen bright Crayola colors, stuffing a lunchbox into their already messy cubby. I instantly knew we were destined to be best friends—though to the naked eye we appeared to be opposites. I was short and quiet and hadn't lost my "baby fat," as my mother liked to say at the time. (I never lost it.) Kay was tall and commanded attention, like a lightning rod. But beneath our night-and-day appearances, we were so similar it was freaky (according to my seven-year-old brain): we both lived with our grandmothers, we both loved *Kim Possible*, and we were both in Mrs. Meyer's second-grade class. We've been inseparable ever since. Of course, Kay and I applied to Dark Cove together. I don't know what we would have done if one of us didn't get in.

Thankfully, that didn't happen. We deposit our now-useless mobile devices into the drawer of the nightstand, kick off our shoes, and collapse onto our respective beds (claimed without discussion). The springs of the mattress creak under my weight; it feels so good to be lying down and through with all the ghastly formalities of the day. It's been something like a twelve-hour journey from our hometown, and delirium has set in. I giggle for no reason. Kay giggles back.

"I was iffy at first," they say, "but, man, this place is so much classier than the boys' dorm."

"Oh yeah?"

"That north-side man cave? It's practically a taxidermy menagerie. Phallic graffiti everywhere."

"Well in these parts, there's nary a reproductive diagram in sight. Just a few scandalous comments etched into the bathroom stalls." I wriggle out of my low-rise jeans and toss them onto the floor. "You can have those."

"Sweet. You can have my *Mario Party* tee. Packed it special for you."

A sleepy smile spreads across my face. It's a men's XXL shirt that reads I'D RATHER BE PLAYING MARIO PARTY. We found it two summers ago in a bargain bin and I've coveted it ever since. "The roomie perks are endless."

"I get majority use of the dresser, though."

"Deal."

Kay has outfits for every imaginable occasion. While they contemplate possible wardrobe opportunities, my brain turns to thinking up potential disaster scenarios: from maulings and earthquakes to failed exams and everything else that could go wrong on this island. Thoughts race as I ogle at the great wood beams of the lofted ceiling—such a grand setting for such small anxieties.

"Are there bears here?" I ask.

"You've lived on the island as long as I have. Ever seen a grizzly?" Kay sighs. "Chill, Vi. No bears . . . although, they can swim. Come to think of it, maybe some polar bears have paddled their way onto the—"

I smack them with a pillow, laughing, but not even the best medicine can ease the tension accumulating at the base of my neck. A billion worries jog around my brain like a fissured Tartan Track with no finish line.

Kay turns on their side to look at me. They reach out into the gap between our beds, wiggling their fingers excitedly. "Roomie, this is our year."

"This is our year," I repeat. My voice comes out all shaky and apprehensive, so I say it again, more to myself than to Kay. "This is our year."

Appendix B

End-of-Year Report, V. Costantino, Acting I

Student Name: Costantino, Violet
Class Participation (25%): B
Written Assignments (40%): A+
Performance Presentation (35%): F
Final Grade: C+

Notes: Violet is punctual. She completes all assignments on time and has a strong grasp on the theories studied in class; however, she struggles to apply these theories to her performance practice. Early in the first semester, Violet expressed that her goal is "to be a leading lady," but that she was unsure of how to get there. *"Then you called me into council. What shall I do?, you asked me."* I would be remiss not to remind Violet that an actor must be a fully realized person in the reality they inhabit before they can become a principal character in worlds imagined. I understand Violet has emotional difficulties and lacks the robustness required of theatre performers, as demonstrated in her final performance presentation at the Spring Showcase, in which she had a fit of emotion and was unable to finish her scene. While I wish her all the best in her future endeavors, I advise Violet to re-evaluate these aspirations prior to enrolling in Acting II.

Supervising Teacher: Blake, Gunther

Supervising Teacher Signature: *G. B.*

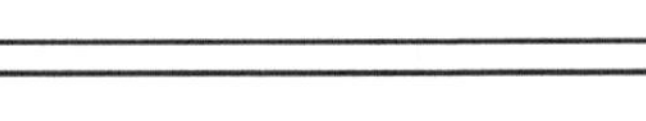

Appendix C

Clipping, Dark Cove Arts Academy's Student-Run Newspaper (Property of DCAAAF)

The Covie Chronicle

Monday, September 9, 1995 (pg. 1)

After loss of two students, Headmaster Henley urges students to "embody courage"

The SS *Spectre* docked last Monday, September 2, 1991, 9:43 a.m., carrying a passenger load dressed in all black. In the wake of the mysterious and sudden loss of several beloved students and Camp Covie counselors at the Academy's summer school, Dark Cove is in mourning. None of the survivors have returned to the island for the fall semester and were therefore unavailable for comment. Though the Academy is at capacity—receiving a full two-hundred-student cohort—there lingers a pervasive emptiness.

A candlelit vigil honoring the departed will be held at Wincroft Theatre this Saturday at 7 p.m. (details on pg. 8), but instead of dwelling in the (albeit obscure) facts of the tragedy, Headmaster Henley urges students to transform their grief into art that will live on.

"'*In tenebris lucem creamus*,'" Henley wrote in a statement to incoming students, "translated, 'In darkness, we create light.' Though these are dreadful times indeed, this is an opportunity to rise to the Academy's values; specifically, we must embody courage." (Cont'd pg. 6). —*Jacobie Mack*

Chapter 3

The floor quivers with the heavy sound of church bells. They ring on the hour, every hour. Island time, at Dark Cove Arts Academy, isn't a thing of fancy and leisure. Instead, the minutes are measured, the seconds are brittle, and the tryst of the big hand and little hand is a guaranteed jump scare. The jittery engine of my heart revs up as I make my way down the corridor to Room 13A.

Thump-thump. Thump-thump. Thump-thump-thump-thump. Thumpthumpthumptumpthumpthumpthumpthump.

This hall, located on the first story of Accolade South, is the narrowest on campus, made narrower by a row of clunky metal lockers, which are painted green but worn silver at the corners. The stone walls, lined with sepia-toned portraits of Dark Cove Theatre Society members, are slanted inward. In some spots, you can see straight through to the basement level between the cracks of the floorboards. I hold tightly to my backpack straps like I'm buckled into a roller coaster. One that threatens cardiac arrest. First period of the semester. *Please keep your hands and feet in the ride at all times, thank you.*

Playwriting, taught by Mr. Blake.

Mr. Blake's approach to teaching is no-nonsense. He's all about digging deep, dredging up personal histories and trauma for the art, and his pupils oblige with the goal of becoming a *serious* artist. I guess I dug too deep during the Spring Showcase. It was a monologue I had cobbled together from different passages from *The Lovely Bones* by Alice Sebold. I watched the movie adaptation when I was way too young—it was scarring but resonated with me in a strange and unsettling sort of way. I never could bring myself to read the book until the day Mr. Blake gave the assignment: to perform any passage of text, classical or modern, so long as it was meaningful to us personally. *The Lovely Bones* was the first thing that came to mind; I checked out the library's only copy of the book and devoured it that same evening, highlighting quotes here and there to weave together. When Mr. Blake learned of my unorthodox selection, he said I should consider a pre-existing monologue, one that I could use my own experiences to draw from in its performance, and, more importantly, a role that I could actually be cast in.

"Why wouldn't I be cast as Salmon?"

He looked at me plainly. "You'll see."

I couldn't understand it. The monologue was about dying, and of course I'd never died before, but who has? And I had had that feeling . . . of leaving yourself, leaving the world you belonged to once and not really knowing where or when or who you even are. So, I stuck to my guns—a decision I wrongly thought my professor would respect—and drew up from that emotion. In the process, I got scared, disoriented, forgot a line, forgot every line, forgot every word but "sorry." I was completely lost. Using memories and pain to guide the character, one of Blake's techniques that worked for all the other students who sat there, watching . . . well, it didn't work for me. Instead, it left me feeling utterly helpless and ended in my total mortification. Mr. Blake's cryptic "you'll see" prophecy was realized. Maybe it was the self-fulfilling kind, I don't know. The case has been closed and it's already cold. I'm a writer now. I *know* I'm good at writing. So, I just need to do a little damage control is all. I'll follow instruction extra carefully, earn a top-of-the-class status and, if all goes according to plan, I should be in my professor's good books within a month.

I arrive twenty-six minutes before the scheduled start of class.[25] Stepping through the threshold into his classroom, I find Mr. Blake wiping down rain-washed glasses at the head of a long table lined with wooden chairs. He makes it all look like doll furniture. Though short in stature, his posture is perfect, his shoulders broad. An open window welcomes in a draft. I tug at the cuff of my cardigan.

Without looking up at me, my professor says, "Nervous?"

"Huh?"

"Your sleeves." He points his gaze at the now-damp fabric in my sweaty grip.

I extend my fingers. "Maybe a bit."

"Welcome to your second year at Dark Cove, Miss Costantino."

After a semester of him referring to me simply as "you there," it's hard to say whether Blake knowing my name is a good sign or a bad omen. "Nice to see you again, sir."

I keep my distance, slide into a seat about halfway down the table, and hold my breath until a few other students trickle in. A couple third years (Nina Petrov, Salma Knight), mostly second.[26] As if entering a dramatic scene, in walk the Gaykeepers, who all specialize in acting but likely chose Playwriting as an elective to keep rapport with the department head. According to the clock, they're one minute late. I wait for Mr. Blake to chastise them. He doesn't—probably reluctant to chew out the daughter of the hand that feeds.[27] Then again, triple-threat, girl-of-your-dreams Frankie Lin has always had everyone, professors included, wrapped around her pink-polished finger.[28]

---

25 Blake's number-one rule: ten minutes early is on time, on time is late.

26 The Academy adopts a collegiate class structure; so long as a Covie has the necessary prerequisites, they can enroll in a course regardless of their year. Enrollment is granted in order of seniority.

27 Dark Cove Arts Academy's Board of Governors comprises educators, artists, and financiers from across the globe. Mrs. Lin falls into the financier category; she is the second woman and first Asian member of the Board.

28 Her OPI shade of choice: Coney Island Cotton Candy.

Frankie Lin spins words like sugar at the circus. Tragically, only I seem to see through her fake-as-Splenda facade, and I think it's because, around here, girls never stop performing; they are tortured artists in front of teachers, shrinking violets for boys across the lake, and, above all, whatever Frankie Lin wants them to be. They play up their industry connections, listen to her favorite bands, and worship the ground her miles-long legs tread. The adulation is sickening.

"Sorry, Sal, would you mind moving up a seat?" Frankie asks Salma, who's a lower-tier member of the Society and one of Frankie's supposed friends/devotees. "Just so we can sit together, yeah?" The "we" is implied and unquestioned: the inseparable trio.

Salma jumps up speedily, apologizing as if she had done something wrong. "Oh, no worries, sorry, of course, girl," she says, giving an eager smile. Frankie smiles back angelically, placing her Coach pencil case on the now-vacant desk.

They chatter, Frankie pretending to be interested in whatever Salma's saying about Lena Dunham's oeuvre. Salma keeps saying that, "oeuvre," a word that is to Rue as the Bat-Signal is to Batman—she chimes in with a commentary on dilettantism and something about the Künstlerroman. Salma only gets a few more words in about Dunham's "propensity for satire" before class begins.

"Close the door behind you," Mr. Blake commands a straggler. "You're the last to arrive, so you'll be in charge of closing it for the rest of the term. Thank you for volunteering." The student, a girl with auburn-dyed hair, winces and gently clicks the door shut.[29] I know her by sight but we've never really spoken. Her name is Margaret. She's in my year, a theatre major, specializing in playwriting—she sat next to me in one of Mr. Mitchell's classes last semester.

"I see a number of familiar faces here. You are all returning students?" Everyone nods. "Well then, I will not waste precious time outlining the rules of my class. You know them well already, or else you

---

29 Though it is not in the official Dark Cove Arts Academy student handbook, it is tacitly understood that Blake does not tolerate door slamming of any kind.

will quickly come to learn them, like young Margaret here." Her ears go pink. Mr. Blake continues, speaking with the pleasure of a man who likes to explain things. "'Reverence, I say, is wisdom.' That's Euripides. Right, then. Rather than wasting time with redundancies, let me instead emphasize that I expect exceptional performance from each and every one of you. You are not here to copy what has been done before. You are not here to whine and moan and write mopey monologues. You are sitting at this table because you have something to say, or at least I hope to every god on Olympus[30] that you do, and that it is something worth saying at all. If it isn't, I will not humor you with As and Bs. I refuse to bend to the handout culture to which your generation has grown accustomed. Mediocrity is like a wart. It must be cut out. If I inform Headmaster Henley of mediocrity in the student body, he will see to its removal."

It's fascinating how he can deliver this tirade and still manage to sound bored. By the time he's finished, he has circled the full perimeter of the table. He pauses at Magpie's seat. "Miss Black, please rise."

Magpie stands up from her chair politely, like royalty at a coronation but without all the fanfare. The only sound in this classroom is the hissing wind and the *clunk-clunk* of Accolade South's internal organs groaning dully.

"As Miss Black is this year's President of the Dark Cove Theatre Society, she will not only set the standard for this class, she will also be assisting me in the running of the Theatre Department at large. As a part of her duties, she will be taking attendance. Moving forward, you are to report in to Miss Black at the top of the period."

Magpie, who has been basking in every syllable of this praise, gives a smarmy, obsequious smile. Blake pats her shoulder, granting her permission to sit back down, and resumes his monologue: "We will begin with character study. In playwriting, as in acting, we study the mechanics of human nature so we can truly know a character. We have to, or what we write will not stick the landing. Once we understand the human

30 The highest mountain in mainland Greece, Mount Olympus was believed to be the home of the gods.

condition, *that* is when we can start to experiment, get our hands dirty, so to speak. *That* is when we can begin to consider what makes an *interesting* character, a character who can captivate. A character who, forgive the turn of phrase, jumps off the page. Right. Who are your favorite characters?"

This is the kind of question that shouldn't have a wrong answer, but in Mr. Blake's eyes, it most certainly does. Hands dart up without hesitation, and I'm grateful; I'd rather sit this one out.

Just as her ears had cooled down from the blush, Margaret is chosen to answer our professor's question first. "Kathy Bates in *Misery*?" she offers.

"Is that a question?"

She shakes her head, auburn hair swishing over the padded shoulders of her school blazer.

"Then, say it like an answer," Mr. Blake demands.

"Kathy Bates. In *Misery*." There's an audible period at the end of her sentence, though her eyes still sparkle with uncertainty. Our professor peers over his half-rimmed spectacles down at her for a long moment. Then, she adds, as if she can't help it, "I think?"

"Can anyone tell me what's wrong about this answer?"

Arms launch into the air, as is custom for the girls of Dark Cove Arts Academy whenever there is an opportunity to assert one's superiority.

Blake picks Magpie to speak first. "Kathy Bates is an actress, not a character."

Rue doesn't wait for our professor's permission to get her two cents in. "Although I haven't seen *Misery*, I *am* keen to point out that it is a shamelessly derivative film. A Hollywood adaptation of a piece of genre fiction."

Ouch—I feel this as both a Stephen King devotee and out of empathy for Margaret, who deflates in her seat.

"Hands down," Mr. Blake barks. The class obeys. "I am certain many of you would have made the same mistake as Margaret if she hadn't been the sorry soul to make it first. So! Your first assignment of this semester will be to write a one-thousand-word reflective essay about a character from any work of fiction—not a celebrity, a *character*—who has earned their spot in the ranks of your favorites. Why do you love them? What has kept them alive in your heart and memory?" Mr. Blake shifts to address the poor Kathy Bates fan. He leans over Margaret's shoulder. "You may want to take note of these instructions."

When I hear the heavy toll of the bell mark first period's end, I actually feel relieved. One class down, one semester to go …

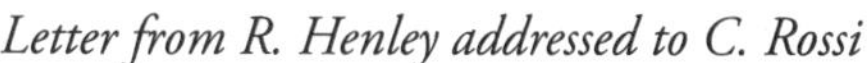

Appendix D

Letter from R. Henley addressed to C. Rossi

DARK COVE ARTS ACADEMY

R. Henley

ATTN: Guardian of Violet Costantino

Dear Ms. Rossi,

I am writing to you with regard to the academic performance of your daughter, Violet Costantino. As indicated in the report card enclosed in this envelope, Violet achieved a B+ average for her first year at Dark Cove Arts Academy. Based on the scholarship contingencies as outlined by the Academy, Violet's progress as a Dark Cove student will be closely monitored in the coming academic year. Violet's full scholarship is contingent upon the maintenance of a 3.8 GPA at minimum, and your daughter is currently sitting just below that threshold (3.6). As a result, the Academy is adjusting its financial support from a full scholarship ($80,000 per annum) to a partial scholarship ($65,000 per annum).

The Academy acknowledges that this average was hampered by only one course (Acting I). Furthermore, the Board is willing to accommodate Violet's unique set of needs by permitting her to change specialization and select courses that more closely align with her strengths in literature, creative writing, and theatre criticism. If Violet would prefer to continue her studies in acting, we would strongly advise she does so elsewhere.

The faculty at Dark Cove Arts Academy hope to see continuous growth in Violet's performance. The administrative team will be in touch with information about work-study opportunities at the school. If Violet's performance is deemed insufficient by the semester's end, her scholarship will be revoked and other financing options will need to be considered.

Best Regards,

R. Henley

R. Henley
Headmaster, Dark Cove Arts Academy

Chapter 4

The library is the prettiest building on campus. Located on the far side of the courtyard behind the dining hall, its stone facade is carved with an archway of book spines.[31] Through that threshold is an antechamber decorated with meticulously trimmed topiaries of assorted shapes. The interior doors, made of brass and glass in the art deco style,[32] open into the library's circular common area, complete with an information desk and musty furniture pointed at a gaping stone fireplace. Beyond, shelves and desks cascade out in a maze. I could spend hours getting lost in the stacks of early-edition prints, but my first shift starts in ten minutes. I follow the hum of old, crappy computers until I reach the Canadian history section at the far back of the 900s. Here, there are five relic-grade PCs and a wrought-iron spiral staircase that descends ominously into blackness. Each step down makes a dramatic metallic clang.

The Dark Cove Arts Academy Archival Facility (or the DCAAAF) is attached to but separate from the library. There is no activity here, no poetry, no organic signs of life. It's at least one degree colder. My eyes

---

31 It chiefly features the tragedians, with the exception of Molière's *Tartuffe*.

32 According to the plaque fixed onto the doorframe, these doors were designed and generously donated by alumnus George Beedle, 1902–1976.

struggle to adjust to the cobwebbed dark. I feel at the wall at the bottom of the stairs and flip the first switch my fingers encounter. Dim fluorescent lights flicker overhead, illuminating a filing cabinet–lined space. The room is no larger than a couple hundred square feet, with only one tiny rectangular window on the far wall. The floor is tiled gray, stained in areas by something that looks like blood but is more likely spilled printer ink. There are six long rows of cabinet shelving, a microfiche reader at the back, and a small workspace with an L-shaped metal desk, a chair, a printer, and a shredder. Though it's far less romantic than the library above, the archives still have a charm of their own—Nordic noir in persuasion. It reminds me of a detective's office. But where's the boss? I assumed Mme. Camry would be waiting for me. Instead, there is only a DCAA-stamped manila folder with my name written on it in a neat cursive. It's stuffed with a thick wad of papers—an employment contract, some sort of confidentiality agreement—and a sadly unsticky Post-it. I hear Mme. Camry's French accent in my head as I read her note: "Violet, sign these and give them to Headmaster Henley at your check-in meeting on Monday morning. Your first shift will be next Saturday. —Mme. C."

"That's it? Do you still get paid for the day?" Kay, who insisted we "get outside" this weekend, stretches out on their stomach at the far end of the Tartan Track, soaking up the cloud-filtered sunshine. It's just over ten degrees Celsius here but they're dressed like we're in Cancun.

I squint down at the contract, barely reading it as I initial the corners. "Hopefully. Every dollar counts at this point."

Over their cat-eye sunglasses, Kay appraises me like I'm an orphan puppy at the local shelter.

"Don't look at me like that. I'll be fine. Just gotta stick to the plan."

"Babe, you keep talking about this plan, but what plan?" they ask.

"Keeping my head down! Writing stuff! Getting good grades! Working! The scholarship! *The plan!*" I gesture obliquely at the overcast sky.

"Right. Writing stuff." My roommate rolls onto their elbows. "How has the transition been?"

"Pretty smooth so far. All things considered."

A Covie changing their specialization is uncommon to the point of taboo. It's like changing your identity. And it probably isn't helping the "crazy" reputation I've accrued.

Kay nods. Something catches their eye over my shoulder. "Shaggy haircut incoming. Three o'clock."

"Violet!" I hear his voice running along a lane on the Tartan Track before I see him. Hunter, decked out in his usual gorpcore[33] weekend getup, with a nondescript film bro at his side, ambles across the red turf toward Kay and me. "Didn't see your name on the tryout list. You not gonna audition for the Halloween show? Isn't it, like, mandatory for theatre kids?"

By "tryout list," he means the audition sign-up sheet for Dark Cove Theatre Society's annual general auditions. Every September, all second- and third-year theatre students must participate in the Society's selection process for its theatrical season.[34] Here's how it works:

1. Acting, playwriting, and directing students are required to audition (non-theatre students are permitted to do so, but it is rare).
2. A handful of third-year production students are selected by Mr. Blake to be designers or crew heads on the basis of academic performance.
3. Crew heads each independently choose a second-year student to be their assistant.
4. All other production students and anyone who hasn't been cast is required to help backstage on an assigned crew.

---

33 Gorp is a West Coast acronym for "good old raisins and peanuts," also known as trail mix. Gorpcore, a derivation of gorp, translates to hike-appropriate fashion.

34 A theatrical season is the set calendar for a particular company. The Dark Cove Theatre Society's season runs during the school year, and it has two shows per annum: the Halloween Play and the Easter pantomime.

"No, I'm not auditioning," I say curtly. "Gonna sign up as a stagehand or something."

Kay's head rotates like an owl's, eyes wide with shock. "Don't playwriting students still have to—"

"I'm not acting this year, you know that."

"I knew you weren't taking acting *classes,*" they say, "I did *not* know that you were gonna give up on acting completely. You've been talking about being in the Halloween Play since before we even started going here!"

"Things change," I snap. "Things *changed.*"

"What changed?"

I discover a new mosquito bite on my elbow and scratch at it. "You know what, we don't need to talk about it in front of"—I glance at Hunter, who shuffles awkwardly on his feet like the friend at a sleepover caught in the middle of a fight between parent and child—"everyone." I pull my arms and legs into the massive openings of my recently acquired *Mario Party* T-shirt, tucking myself into a ball, trying not to scratch the bite.

"But—"

"Kay, please, just . . . I'm not an actor anymore, I'm a writer."

They give a stilted nod. "I didn't know *you* were an actor, Hunter Kinsey." Kay exaggerates the "or" in "actor" to mocking effect, changing the subject for my benefit. I give them a look of gratitude, but they squint at me as if to say *this conversation is not over* before looking back up at Hunter. "I'm surprised a bona fide film bro such as yourself is interested in the theatre."

"We prefer to be called the celluloid boys. 'Film bros' is so . . . crude," Nondescript Bro, who I forgot was even here, corrects Kay. "Sue me, I'm a purist."

"He's an up-his-own-ass documentarian, but we love him anyway." Hunter ruffles his buddy's buzz cut. His voice is deeper when his boys are around.

"Sorry to break it to you, my guy, but fact's more gripping than fiction. And if we're getting into semantics, I'm a documentary photographer," Nondescript Bro says to Hunter, then tilts his head to Kay and me. "Photojournalist for *The Covie Chronicle*. In case you were wondering."

"I promise you, we weren't, *my guy*," says Kay.

Hunter straightens his Arc'teryx shell jacket like it's got a lapel on it. "Like Violet, I'm no hotshot actor. *I'm* a director—or DP,[35] not sure yet—so you know I gotta get in on the action with the great Sophia Spry."

"Sophia Spry?" I ask. The name rings a very distant bell.

"The guest director for the Halloween show. They brought her in from the Big Apple for the gig," he explains. *How does he know this before I do?* "No shade, but Mrs. Lincoln kind of doesn't know shit about the film industry—"

"*Nothing*," Nondescript Bro stresses. "Zilch."

"So this is a huge opportunity," Hunter finishes.

"A guest director?" I say. "But Mr. Blake directs the Halloween Play." As the Academy's oldest club, the Dark Cove Theatre Society isn't known to change how things have historically been done, nor is it wont to invite new blood into its small pool of talented elite.

"I heard from inside sources that it's gonna be a co-directing *sitchyation*," Hunter replies. "They probably just made an exception for the clout."

"I've never heard of her," I mutter.

"Sophia Spry's a feminist legend," exclaims Nondescript Bro, apparently a steadfast ally in the fight for gender equality. "And she's a babe."

"Nice," Kay says dryly. "Pretty sure that's what they put on bell hooks's tombstone: feminist legend comma babe."

By the look on his face, it's obvious Hunter doesn't know who bell hooks is. "Spry was a huge deal at Cannes. Got a standing O and everything."

"Everyone gets a standing ovation at Cannes," Kay retorts. "It's like the spirit of the festival possesses the audience to clap for a random number of minutes and critics assign meaning to it because that's what they do."

"Like the Ouija board of praise," I add.

Kay wags a chiding finger. "Ouija boards are no laughing matter." When I laugh, they add, "Don't come crawling to me when a spirit comes after you with unfinished business, that's all I'm saying."

---

35 Director of Photography, or cinematographer.

Hunter, feeling left out, runs a hand through his tousled, Disney-prince hair. "So ... I'll see you at tryouts, Vi, or?"

"You'll see her," Kay replies dismissively.

I dig my nails into my mosquito bite. "No, you won't."

"Maybe I won't, maybe I will." And with that, he tramps on across the field like the boy scout I'm certain he once was, his buzz-cut goon following just behind.

"And there go the greatest feminists on this island." Kay raises their eyebrows. "You see now? What I had to deal with on the boys' side of the lake? You've got no right to complain, honestly."

"Repugnant," I remark distantly.

"Not that the girls' school is so much better. Everyone keeps messing up my pronouns." Kay sweeps the track with their black lenses. "I got deadnamed yesterday"

"Seriously?"

"Yup. Mr. Mitchell. He was taking attendance, which he hasn't done since, and he was like, 'Kaia?' And I didn't respond. To make a point, right? But he kept saying it ..."

"None of the girls said anything?"

"As if. I had to correct him."

Arms still tucked into Kay's old tee, I roll onto my back next to them like an armadillo. "Everybody on this island but us sucks."

"What about lover boy over there?"

"Shut up. I don't like Hunter Kinsey."

I don't like Hunter Kinsey, I don't like Hunter Kinsey, I don't like Hunter Kinsey. I say it in my head like a mantra.

"You used to," Kay points out, "and it looks like you're on his radar now."

"He's probably just wondering why I'm not fawning over him. I told you, he's repugnant," I repeat, watching Hunter merge into his siloed group of Tarantino fanboys on the opposite side of the track.

Kay looks unconvinced. "Okay, so can we talk about why you're not auditioning?"

"You weren't there last semester. It was humiliating."

"You had a panic attack, babe. It happens."

"Not in the middle of a performance, it doesn't. Not to most people. Not to good actors, at least." I eject my limbs from their cocoon and sit up.

"It was a shitty day for you even before all that went down, and—"

"I lost control. Nearly lost my scholarship. That can't happen again. With writing, I can control the outcome," I explain, pressing the heels of my hands to my eyes, willing away a surge of memories. "I need to focus on that, on my grades."

"This performance wouldn't be graded, though. It's for fun! So you wouldn't have to stress about—"

"Stop. Please. I just want to get through this year in one piece."

"Okay, okay." They lie their head back on the ground but continue to watch me carefully through their stylish sunglasses with lingering concern.

I glance back down at the contract and scrawl my initials into the last few blank spaces, not really reading the clauses too carefully but getting the gist (*private documents, blah blah blah, privileged access, blah blah blah, do not disclose, blah blah blah*). There's a distraction across the field: Hunter and his crew of northern islanders, most of them shirtless now for some reason, are a spectacle. I'm not the only one watching. Other girls openly gape at the bare-chested young men, some with a slight brush of hair between pecs, each slinging their garments aloft in a performance of machismo. It almost looks like a sacrificial ritual from here—but who am I kidding? These guys don't need to give up a thing to gain the favor of the Dark Cove gods. The universe bestows its greatest treasures upon its boys, no payment needed.

Kay follows my eyeline. "Repugnant."

Chapter 5

They flicker their eyes over me, assessing my body in split seconds. I can't say anything about it. I am on their territory: the north side of Raven Lake. The guys' end of the island seems to have its own microclimate. The wind is icier, the soil less fertile.

I dart along the path and up the steps to Accolade North. It's a near-perfect mirror image of the girls' school, just as stately, with some subtle but key differences. Outside, ivy climbs up the trellises instead of roses; the stained-glass windows depict triumphant scenes (the southern windows are distinctly Mother Mary–centric); the bricks are tarnished with graffiti here and there, just as Kay described. Inside, there are a few stuffed bears (brown, black, grizzly, spirit) and even a wolverine, doomed to stalk the halls forever. The same suits of armor that stand sentry in the girls' chamber hall are here cordoned off with velvet rope, forming a silent do-not-touch barricade. Impelled by the primal urge to mark territory, the boys cannot be trusted.

The monumental front door thuds behind me. I ignore the probing remarks ("You're new here," "You lost, bro?") and distant snickers of guys passing by—a few of whom I recognize as members of Hunter's crew—crossing my arms in a fortified stance. The mosquito bite on my elbow flares with a red-hot itch. For every step I take, I allow myself one scratch of the bump. A spiral stairwell winds up for a total of forty-five step-scratches. By the time I reach the top, there's a pinprick of blood sprouting at the site of injury.

It takes me a moment to get my bearings—and my head straight. Whether it's a symptom of the spiral route I took, the mirror effect of the boys' campus, or the minor blood loss, I feel dizzy. My eyes fix on the double doors of the headmaster's office.

At the start of each term, every second and third year is allotted a fifteen-minute time slot with Henley himself. In it, we discuss our academic progress and goals for the year. It's all just a formality, I've heard, but that doesn't stop my hands from trembling as I remove the signed employment contract from my satchel. I do so carefully, trying not to crinkle the papers or get any blood on it.

I knock gently on the closed door.

"Yes?"

Smoothing out the pleats of my skirt, I enter swiftly. *Don't give yourself time to second-guess,* I think. *You must feign confidence. You must make a good impression.*

"Good morning, Headmaster."

His office reminds me of a chessboard, all hard lines and polished stone. On the desktop, there's a paperweight shaped like a horse's head, a neat stack of documents, and an onyx inkwell, its placement calculated. Nothing here is happenstance. A square window behind the headmaster lets in a straight, symmetrical beam of white sunlight. He throws a long shadow onto the checkered floor that reaches all the way to the scuffed leather toes of my shoes. I take a few steps closer. Reluctantly, Mr. Henley peels his eyes from the stack of correspondences before him. He slides a fountain pen into its marble holder and gestures for me to take a seat on the stout stool across from him. His snow-white mustache twitches. I smile back.

"Thanks for seeing me."

"Indeed. I trust you had a productive summer?"

"Yes, I caught up on my readings, spent some time with my grandmother ..." I close my eyes, trying not to think too hard about the world I left back home. That's an unspoken rule at Dark Cove: don't look back. "I got a job. Oh, speaking of, while I'm here . . ." When the headmaster espies the contract in my quivering grasp, he invites me to hand it over, bending his long fingers in a "gimme" motion. I place the stack of papers neatly at the edge of his desk, next to an engraved nameplate: R. HENLEY. *What does the R. stand for?*

He licks a fingertip turns over one of the papers. "You will be working in the archives this semester, yes?"

I nod, though he isn't looking at me. Once satisfied that I've crossed my *T*'s and dotted my *I*'s, he files the papers away and leans back into his high-back office chair, black tufted leather. The sunlight he'd been blocking now attacks my eyeballs. I place my hand like a visor up to my forehead.

"I also understand you have formally switched your specialization to playwriting."

"Yes, sir."

He refolds his wrinkles into a leer that I think is supposed to look kind. "I see. And how has the semester been going thus far? Are your studies proving to be too much for you?"

My spine stiffens, the vertebrae fusing together with the memory of what happened last semester. "Oh no, not at all."

"Mind you, we are not yet seven days into the semester. Things will ramp up next week, once production for the Dark Cove Theatre Society's Halloween Play begins. Your Theatre Practicum will turn from a period of independent study to one of—" He's cut off by a knock on the door. The headmaster's gray-eyed gaze levitates over my shoulder as he invites the disembodied caller to enter. Heavy footsteps, creaking floorboards, squeaky leather . . . "Gunther, thank you for joining us."

"Good morning, Headmaster," says Mr. Blake. "Lovely day, isn't it?"

There's a fluttering in my chest, my pulse quickening. "Would you like me to leave so you two can—"

Entering into view, Blake holds up a conciliatory hand. "Please. I've come to listen in, Miss Costantino. As you know, Headmaster Henley and I will be closely monitoring your performance this year."

The walls of the office close in on me. "Yes."

"Violet and I had just been discussing the Halloween Play," says Henley.

"Ah, my arrival was well-timed, then. Auditions will be held on Wednesday." Mr. Blake looks not at me but at the deer head affixed to one of the walls. "I take it you've read the play."

"*A Midsummer Night's Dream*, yes, sir. I look forward to seeing what you and the new co-director do with this text," I say, my voice five octaves higher than its usual pitch.

He sneers. "I will merely moderate the October production this year. On behalf of the Society, I have invited Sophia in as a guest director."

So it's not just a rumor. It's hard to believe Blake would really relinquish creative control—the Halloween Play has been his baby for decades—and he doesn't seem happy about it either. I wonder if someone's forced his hand. "Is this for the whole season or just the first show?" I probe.

The two men answer at the same time. Blake states "No," while the headmaster gives a less definite "We'll see." At my puzzled look, Henley elaborates, "Times are changing. There are bright innovators of different . . . *backgrounds*"—this word he says like it's the name of a new and contagious disease—"and the Board feels it's time to welcome these perspectives to Dark Cove."

"Tradition is not as valued as it once was, it seems," Blake adds coolly.

Abruptly, the headmaster clears his throat, either signaling to Mr. Blake that he should zip it or working at a stubborn bit of phlegm. Hard to tell, but Blake recomposes himself.

"As I was saying, it is Sophia who will be making all creative decisions," Blake continues, "while I superintend the strategic developments of our department. I trust you have booked your audition slot?"

Completely taken aback now, I reply only in fragments of sentences. "No. Mr. Blake. Well. You don't want me to act. So I figured I would . . . I don't know. Support the production on the other side of the curtain. As a stagehand. Or something."

"Or *something*? Wasn't it you who dreamed of being a leading lady?" Blake's jowls jiggle with every over-enunciated word.

Yes, I think, *and it's you who encouraged me to change that dream. Why is everyone so obsessed with* my *dreams, anyway?*

Headmaster Henley dabs his mustache with a crisp white kerchief. "Miss Costantino, if I am not mistaken, and mind you I very rarely am, you have heretofore expressed no interest in theatre production."

"No, sir, you aren't mistaken," I say hoarsely. With effort, I adjust my tone according to my audience: two people who will determine my fate at this school and beyond. "My specialization is playwriting now, but obviously I can't write for the play; Shakespeare already did that." I laugh, hoping they'll join in. They don't even crack a smile. "And since you both advised I stop acting, I thought I would fulfil the Theatre Practicum requirement by "

"Do you conceive of your education here as a mere set of requirements?" Mr. Blake interrupts, appalled.

"No, Mr. Blake. Of course not, I—"

"If it is *requirements* we're speaking of, only students who specialize in production are permitted to stay *on the other side of the curtain* without first auditioning. For those specializing in acting, directing, and playwriting, auditions for the Society's theatrical season are mandated." Mr. Blake takes a beat to analyze my painstakingly neutral expression. "Does this come as news to you?"

The dizziness returns, no spiral staircase necessary. Trying to figure out what my professors want is enough to make my head spin like an off-kilter globe. "No, sir. I just assumed that since you encouraged me to step back from acting, you'd—"

"Give you more special treatment? No, I think we've been generous enough."

"Miss Costantino," Headmaster Henley begins gravely, "it is not a common occurrence that we allow a student to change their specialization. *The Board* reckoned it was prudent that we accommodate your unique set of needs; that is, as it pertains to your academic trajectory. Thence, we made an exception for you. One exception. We will not be making any others."

Judging by their stony demeanors, Headmaster Henley and Mr. Blake only begrudgingly granted the Board's suggestion. My professors don't actually care about my success here; they're merely pacifying the school's stakeholders. It dawns on me that there must be some new inclusion efforts or diversity quota in place. *That's* why Mr. Blake invited Sophia Spry to guest direct. *That* must be why Frankie's mom joined the Board. And ... that's why they didn't just kick me out of the Academy.

I'm on even thinner ice than I thought.

"We expect our students to challenge themselves beyond the classroom," Henley continues, "to be active participants in campus culture. This is the foremost institution for arts education in North America—in the world, arguably."

"Most certainly," says Mr. Blake. "We've scored top ranking for more than twenty years."

"The point is, Miss Costantino, you cannot merely subsist, rest on your laurels. You must rise to the expectations and reputation of Dark Cove. Do you need to be reminded of the Academy's values?"

I try to gulp down the quickly forming stone in my throat. It doesn't budge. Blake interprets my dumbfounded silence as an invitation to pontificate.

"Persistence, courage, and excellence," he recites, puffing his chest with pride. "Recall the foundation Frederick Stine built for us. Choose a path and stick to it, come what may, hm? Giving into fear shows us only infirmity. Weak students, students satisfied with mediocrity, students who favor ease, do not belong at the Academy. There is no shame in that, of course, but these values are ours for good reason. The creative industries favor the strong-willed. Do you understand?"

I nod. "Yes. You want me to audition for the Halloween Play despite my ... troubles with anxiety."

Blake flashes his gold tooth, eyes gleaming amber. He rubs his knuckles methodically, like one cog sliding into the grooves of another. "Not despite, rather *because of*. This is what we are getting at, Miss Costantino. We have obligingly made curricular arrangements to support you, but your circumstances aren't a free pass to skate by on your own terms. This is a golden opportunity to demonstrate to the faculty that your emotional problems are under control, *if* you are able to perform the monologue from start to finish. Of course, the Dark Cove Theatre

Society doesn't hand out roles on the basis of progress. And I will have no say in casting. I'll merely advise our new director, nudge her in the right direction."

The headmaster clears his throat again. "If it calms your nerves, Miss Costantino, conceive of this audition merely as a practice in resilience. *Persistence.* It might even provide some insight into your individual competencies; that is to say, if you feel capable of continuing your academic career here at Dark Cove."

"Oh, I absolutely feel capable—"

"You aren't at your *little hometown high school anymore*," Mr. Blake says in a playful (though convincing) Southern accent, like I'm from Texas rather than northern Ontario. He gives a hearty laugh at his own joke, one hand on his belly. Then, back to his normal voice: "You must quash this quote-unquote anxiety of yours if you wish to be an artist. Or at least leverage it to create something worthwhile. Let me put it plainly: Do you wish to walk amongst the greats or do you want to go home?"

My face burns fever-hot with embarrassment. This goes against everything I mentally prepared for all summer. I had a plan: focus on writing and stay under the radar. I blink at the time-etched faces of my professors. Mr. Blake looks down on me, a tinge of pity in the eyes hidden beneath his bushy gray brows. It's as if I am sitting in an already dug grave, as if I have already failed. Without being dismissed, I stand and force an acquiescent grimace.

Change of plan: I am auditioning for the Dark Cove Theatre Society's Halloween Play. With a half-curtsy, I thank the headmaster and Mr. Blake before absconding from the room into the hall. It is an endless tomb.

Appendix E

Clipping, Dark Cove Arts Academy's Student-Run Newspaper (Property of DCAAAF)

The Covie Chronicle

Monday, September 6, 1997 (pg. 1)

Meet Professor Gunther Blake, Dark Cove's newest faculty member

When the 1997 International Art School Association (IASA) rankings were announced this April and Dark Cove Arts Academy failed to qualify as a top-ten arts school for the fifth consecutive year, Headmaster Henley knew something had to change. In an effort to restore the Academy to its former glory, the headmaster has called on an old friend and colleague to head up the Department of Theatre. Joining our midst is esteemed Professor Gunther Blake.

"Grades [have been] low, far lower than we tolerate at the Academy," a somewhat flustered Headmaster Henley told *The Chronicle* after his opening remarks to the incoming SS *Spectre* cohort last Monday. "And while we could make excuses for a period—that of mourning [for Covies lost at the infamous DCAA Summer Camp of '95]—this performance dip has gone on far too long, far too long, indeed. Something needed to be done, and I knew immediately that Gunther was the man for the job."

Even Vis kids have likely heard of the Blake Vocal Technique, and yes, it is named after none other than our new professor. Blake brings with him over two decades of professional experience at the top level. "He accepts nothing short of excellence," the headmaster explained.

Needless to say, Blake's reputation precedes him. "Rumor has it," an anonymous Covie told *The Chronicle*, "he rules with an iron fist." (Cont'd pg. 4). —*Belinda Norris*

Appendix F

Graffiti, Dark Cove Arts Academy Girls' Dormitory, Fourth-Floor WC

flush the damn toilet!!! NAH EAT SHIT

ghost wuz here

DARK COVE THEATRE SOCIETY = CULT

SKINNY DANCER CLUB

IS MICHAEL K HOT?

~~frankie>mag~~

YES

YES

stop being mean?

NO IM GAY

I WANT TO HAVE HENDRICK'S BABEEZ

P, spring fling w me? - M

FRANKIE UR MY MAIN BITCH

Chapter 6

You can tell a lot about a person by their handwriting. I stare at the curlicue signatures on the audition sign-up sheet; next to those neat, cursive names, my penmanship looks equivocal to a child's.

Kay places a supportive hand on my back. "I'm proud of you for doing this."

"Not like I have a choice," I mutter. "I won't get a role, anyway."

"Says who?"

Everyone. It was clear in that meeting that I'm only here by the grace of the Board. My professors asked me to audition to make a point, not because they plan on casting me. Why would they? All of my shortcomings as an actor are the unchangeable facts of me: I am five-foot-three, anxious, stubby, and I wear C-cups but they look bigger somehow, so the best roles I can expect are matrons and maids. When I asked for more leading parts in acting class last year, Mr. Blake said I needed to prove myself, though I never received explicit instructions on how to do that. My voice is too high-pitched, he said, so no one will ever take me seriously. Students in the class agreed. Peer review sessions were no less brutal than the professor's. Then, my "emotional outburst" happened in front of all of them.

Yeah, there's no way I'll get a role. "I'm keeping my expectations low."

"I prefer cautious optimism," Kay says.

"It's fine. I'll audition, show them I'm *persistent*—or whatever the value du jour is—then it's over. Back to writing."

"You know, you can be an actor *and* a writer. You contain multitudes, Violet Costantino."

All of my multitudes and I are fixed in place, gawking at the sheet. It's almost completely full. The crew sign-up list is bare in comparison—those slots usually fill up after the auditions are through. My eyes carefully trace the name right before mine: Frankie Lin.

That timing won't bode well for me. The only thing no one covets in relation to Frankie Lin is the audition slot following hers. I'm about to cross out my name and move to the only other open cell in the sign-up sheet when a blonde girl clears her throat from behind. "Excuse me," she says, and I sidestep. She fills out the last remaining time slot with a purple gel pen then she strides away as if she didn't just sign my death certificate.

Kay squints at the latest entry on the sign-up sheet. "I know her, she's a bassoonist. Why's *she* auditioning?"

"I suspect Hunter and his goon aren't the only ones who googled Sophia Spry."

"Guilty. I waited forever for a computer in the library this morning just to look her up. Apparently she was a Broadway performer as a kid and then went to NYU for directing, and her short films were screened at South by Southwest and shit."

"Wow." I'm impressed, both by Sophia Spry's resumé and by my friend's ability to memorize a Wikipedia page.

Kay bites their lip, chews on it for a moment—this is their plotting face. "If Spry has an in with some real-world movie music guys, that connection could be a game changer for me," they muse. "I'm down to be the next John Williams or Michael Giacchino or one of those big boys. Or composing for indie movies. You know I'd rock that."

"Thought composing for Nintendo was the dream?"

"Gotta start somewhere, babe."

"You should talk to her. Ask to do the a score for the show."

"That's not a thing, is it?"

"I dunno. Wouldn't hurt to ask."

Kay adjusts a side-saddle bag over their shoulder, a determined look on their face. "Let's go find her, shall we?"

"Now?"

"Yes, now."

Meeting the famous guest director before I audition sounds like a bad idea—I don't make a good first impression—but Kay's eyes are wide with a rare kind of excitement. After all the support they've shown me, this is the least I can do. I follow them out of the dining hall and trot down the path leading to Accolade South.

"So, if you compose the score, would that make you a part of the Dark Cove Theatre Society?" I ask. "Or is it something you need to be sort of initiated into?"

"Michael's old roommate was the set designer last year, and he said there was just, like, a form to sign and a couple events to go to," they say. Michael Flores is Kay's bandmate. I'm not close with him at all, but he was one of the few guys at the school who didn't act weird about Kay's gender identity, so I like him. "If you're in, you're in. At least til the end of the school year."

"Even if you're just crew?"

"*Just* crew?" A deep groove zigzags across the freckled skin of their forehead. "The crew is the backbone of any production."

"You know what I'm getting at. The Society's so . . . closed off. From what I can tell, most of the Society cool kids are actors."

"Let me impart some wisdom on you, my dear friend. Within every clique, there are sub-cliques, and even those sub-cliques have their own respective hierarchical structures. Designers are like . . . the actors of crew." Kay uses their hands to illustrate an imaginary diagram. "But, yeah, whichever way you cut it crew kids are probably at the bottom of that pyramid."

"And where'd you get all this wisdom and insight?"

They shake their bob. "Look at me, I'm coolness incarnate. It's only natural that many a popular kid has tried to recruit me," they say sarcastically. Kay may be more outgoing than I am, but that hasn't exactly granted them immunity from bullying. They haven't told me so, but I suspect that was a motivating factor in their transfer to the girls' school. "Just trust. It's High School 101."

We press into the entrance of Accolade South. In a far-off room, someone plays a melancholic tune on the piano. The notes tickle me in the gut. "I hate high school."

"I, on the other hand, *adore* all the teenage drama. And if we both work on *Midsummer*, we're gonna get early access to every dirty scrap of Dark Cove Theatre Society gossip," Kay says delightedly, taking two steps at a time up the grand staircase.

"You sure the new director will be in the teachers' lounge? She's not technically a teacher."

Kay leads the way through the twisted corridors with inexplicable expertise. They've attended classes in this oversized manor for a mere week and know their way around better than I do. "All the campus adults basically live in the faculty lounges. Nurses, cafeteria ladies and all. It's the only place where they can bitch about students. And flirt."

I never really considered what the adults do after hours. The image of them socializing is uncomfortable. "Ew."

"I ship Hendrix with the newbie."

"Double ew."

"Come on, they'd be the hottest couple ever."

"Please stop. Let's just get this over with."

I've never been behind the doors of any faculty lounge before. Students typically don't gain passage unless they've received some sort of invitation. Nonetheless, an uninvited Kay enters without hesitation. I skulk in their shadow, trying to attract as little attention as possible. The room smells lightly of toffee, but that's the only welcoming aspect of the space. Thick-cut drapery blots out all traces of daylight. An espresso machine screeches unpleasantly as Mr. Norman hovers nearby, a few TAs in line behind him. Mr. Blake dwells in a corner by the dim light of a banker's lamp, sipping thick coffee out of a tiny porcelain cup and skimming *The New York Times*. I make out half of a front-page headline before he folds it over and I realize I've no sense of current affairs, no idea what's going on in the world beyond this island.

At the back of the room on a cognac leather couch is that curly-haired fashionista I saw down by the docks—Sophia Spry, apparently—this time wearing an oversized blazer and sparkly rouge on the apples of her cheeks. She's chatting with Mr. Hendrix, to Kay's transparent delight.

"Excuse me, Ms. Spry?" Kay waves casually. "Sorry to interrupt."

"Ms. Spry, I like the sound of that," she says in an unexpected cool-girl vocal fry, leaping up from the couch like a popcorn kernel. "Most people just call me Sophe. But you girls are onto something."

"Glad you like it. My pronouns, by the way . . ." Kay flashes a *they/them* pin on their bag.

"My apologies! She/her," she says, not making a big deal of anything, pointing at herself.

Mr. Blake erupts into a spontaneous coughing fit.

Kay turns to him. "I'd get a throat lozenge from the nurse if I were you," they say tartly before introducing themself to Ms. Spry.

She surveys me with wide amber eyes, looking even younger up close. "And what's your name, hon?"

"Violet. Costantino," I reply robotically, doing my best to maintain an inoffensive air of neutrality.

"*She's* going to be auditioning for the play on Wednesday," Kay interjects. I wish there were a shrinking potion or an invisibility cloak around here.

Ms. Spry's retro red lips spread into a wide smile. "That's rad"—did she just say *rad*? —"I'm so excited to see you all perform. This is my first time working with teens." Her voice lowers to a schoolgirl whisper, "But I can already tell you guys are more fun than all the old fogies I'm used to."

Kay snorts. "We're just getting started! I won't be auditioning, mind you . . ." and so the two of them engage in a conversation that I participate in as little as possible. Ms. Spry prattles at *Gilmore Girls* speed and Kay smooth-talks their way into the composer position for the Halloween Play in two minutes flat.

"It'll be a first. I don't think there's ever been live accompaniment for the show," Mr. Hendrix points out from his post on the couch.

"I'm all about firsts," Kay says boastfully. "Got first place in the talent show last year ... I was the first out of me and Violet to kiss anybody—"

"It was a game of spin the bottle," I mutter.

They put a finger to their mouth, thinking. A little cartoon lightbulb goes on above their head. "Oh! And I'm pretty sure I'm the first Two-Spirit student in the school."

"Wow," Mr. Hendrix utters in the uncomfortable cadence of a white man confronted with his privilege. "I didn't know ... that."

"It's not that surprising, considering Indigenous students have only been admitted to the Academy for—what?—a decade?"

"That's awful," Ms. Spry says, "but I'm so glad to have you here. And that we get to make history with your music! Pretty cool!"

Kay, a social chameleon, matches the director's energy. "Very cool."

"Super cool! And this means maybe you and Violet will be working together."

"If I get a role," I mumble, all too aware of Mr. Blake's presence.

"I'd love to see what you can bring to the stage. You have such an expressive face." She laughs, and I wonder what my face has been doing all this time.

Kay darts their *watch-this* eyes at me before leaning to look over at the idle music teacher. "And that must also mean you and Mr. Hendrix will be working together. Mr. Hendrix, I take it you'd like to supervise my compositions?"

He rises from a patinaed couch cushion, draws himself up to his fullest height.[36] "Ah, yes. Good thinking, Kay. Come by my office sometime, we'll set you up with everything you need. I talked the Headmaster into buying the Music Department a few laptops. Think I can spare one for this."

"Awesome! It's a family affair now," Ms. Spry coos, and Kay and I exchange a knowing look: Mr. Hendrix has been friend-zoned, despite Kay's best efforts. I personally love to see it. "You ready for your audition, Violet?"

---

36 Five foot seven.

"Sure, sure. Gonna get my lines down tonight."

Mr. Blake coughs again. "I'd hope that from my class last year you learned that audition preparation involves a great deal more than memorization."

"Violet and I were just on our way to do some deep character work," Kay lies. "Come on, Vi. Thanks, Ms. Spry! Mr. Hendrix." They grab my hand, exiting with their chin high despite the cis-male crappiness they just endured. Kay takes it all in stride.

"Nice one back there," I say once we're a safe distance from the closed door. "Deep character work?"

"You're welcome."

Our chuckles travel with us down the polished stairs. "Let's just hope I make it more than one line into the monologue." I'm only half-joking. Actually, I'm not really joking at all.

"Don't worry your pretty little head about that. This is our year, remember?" They push open the grand doors of Accolade South with full force, hurtling out onto campus. "Fresh start. For both of us."

A crow swoops past with a loud croak, landing on a nearby branch that's spangled with golden leaves. The summer trees are turning already.

Chapter 7

It's audition day, and despite my better judgment, the sight of his golden head four rows in front of me makes my heart flutter. Hunter Kinsey. Every time I see him, it's just like the first time I saw him. I hate it.

It was early December by Raven Lake, the misty purgatory between the girls' school and boys' school. The sky was a pale, pre-sunrise shade of lavender. There was a thin layer of frost on everything, and that looked purple, too. A morning test in Theatre History had rendered my sleep fitful and the effort to get back to it futile, so I decided to go for a stroll and clear my mind a little. Quiet, cold mornings are one of the few things in this world with the power to cut through my anxious thoughts.[37] It was a handful of minutes after I arrived at the lakefront that I spotted Hunter jogging on the opposite shore in a blue hoodie and compression shorts. It was so early, the only sounds were the soft ruffle of water and his heavy footfalls crushing gravel. Our paths were set to cross. I had been intent on ignoring him when he passed me, staring down at the dusted earth, but as he approached our point of intersection, he did not yield to my unsociable demeanor. His lean, tan

---

37 Perhaps eighteenth-century doctors were onto something when they prescribed fresh air for the nerves.

legs slowed their pace. His voice came soft and sweet, breath smoldering against the morning.

"Hey!" His voice was crisp, like biting into the perfect apple. He pulled his hood down to reveal a copse of curly, golden locks. "Did you hear that loon?"

I just tee-heed stupidly as a non-answer before walking away. Even made it a couple of yards thinking I'd successfully avoided conversation, but Hunter wasn't done yet.

"Oooooooh!"

I looked over my shoulder to see him beaming like a kid behind me, proud of his (strikingly accurate) imitation of a loon call.

"It sounds like that. Only . . . more haunting. Very epic. Keep an ear out for it!"

An unattractive sort of chortle came out of me. "Sure, I'll do that."

"I'm Hunter," he shouted, beginning a reverse jog away from me. I could've sworn he was checking me out.

"Violet," I said, probably too quiet to reach him, but he smiled as though he heard me, then turned and sprinted toward the boys' school.

I watched after him thinking, *This was our meet-cute.* We were Harry and Sally on our way to NYC. We were Bella and Edward in the cafeteria. We were Jack and Rose on the *Titanic*, sans shipwreck.

My crush intensified over the holiday break, and the subsequent winter term was spent secretly pining after Hunter Kinsey. Puppeteered by that devil desire, my every action had strings attached. I set an earlier alarm, lingered at the pancake line, memorized his schedule, and returned to Raven Lake before sunrise in the hope of seeing him. "We have to stop meeting like this," I would say, or some other hackneyed phrase. Something about Hunter Kinsey makes me speak in clichés. I never saw him at the lake again, but I did hear the loon. It really was haunting.

It was on the morning of the Spring Showcase, caught in the act of ogling in the middle of the dining hall, that I was persuaded by Kay to ask Hunter out.

"Are you just going to keep on yearning in the background? It's been months," they said, stabbing their fork in my direction. "I did a sound editing workshop with him, Vi. Trust me: Hunter Kinsey's harmless. A himbo, honestly. A puppy dog. There's nothing to be intimidated by. Just ask him to be your date for the Spring Fling! Then you can go back to not waking up at ungodly hours, and you get a new pet golden retriever. Seriously, Vi, you look tired."

One of the few co-ed events at Dark Cove, the Spring Fling is a very hyped-up, very clichéd end-of-year dance that happens after every department's through with Showcase Week. The school goes all out with a late-night DJ set (the DJ is always a first-year student; last year it was Kay), kitschy decor, punch bowls, and confetti. It was the last opportunity to put myself out there before we broke for summer. See, it's extremely difficult to grab a moment of Hunter Kinsey's time. Boys orbit around him like he's the sun; girls steal glances at him likewise. It hurts to look too long at something so bright and distant. And that morning at breakfast, a rare moment presented itself to me: he was alone, walking away from the buffet with a heaping tray of pancakes (that last part is less of a rarity). The room was mostly empty. Emboldened by desire (and a little desperation), I ran up to him. Of course, my run turned into a stumble and I collided with Dark Cove's golden boy like the hopelessly geeky character in an after-school special.

An apology was mumbled. He said something like, "No worries, all the pancakes made it and that's what matters." I giggled, pleasantries were frantically exchanged, and then I ripped off the Band-Aid.

"Would you like to go to the dance with me?" These words fell to the ground like petals. *He loves me, he loves me not, he loves me ...*

"Sorry, um, do I know you?"

He loves me not.

At this point, I melted onto the floor, replying with something like, "Violet, from the lake, I go to the girls' school," which is a very embarrassing thing to say, because obviously I go to the girls' school. Dark Cove is a speck of rock with a boys' school, a girls' school, a forest, a lake, a handful of beaches, and nothing else. There's nowhere else I could possibly *go*.

After that, he said, "Nice to meet you, Violet," before looking down at his syrupy stack of flapjacks and explaining that this was awkward but he was going to the dance with someone else. "Let's get to know each other sometime, though!"

I think I said, "For sure. See you around!" and then pretended to be fine the rest of the day. That was, until the unfortunate events of the Spring Showcase. You fly too close to the sun, you get burned. Call me Icarus.[38]

A week later, the caf was cleared out for the Spring Fling, decked out in streamers, helium balloons, and pastel crepe paper. Pop music played too quietly. No one else had arrived except for two teachers and a a few other unfashionably early students kicking around balloons under an oversized disco ball. Apparently the first to go in on the punch bowl, I ladled out ragged pieces of grapefruit and red Kool-Aid into a Solo Cup for something to do. I'd been lurking in the corner sipping on the sickly sweet drink when Hunter came up to me wearing flip-flops and a Hawaiian button-up. I nearly did a spit take—this was a definitively black-tie event and here he was looking fresh off the beach volleyball circuit.

"Hey, Vi!" he said, as if we went way back. "You look great!"

I entered *how to accept compliment* in my brain's search bar. Zero results. Instead, I choked on a piece of grapefruit rind.

"Woah, you okay?"

Hunter patted me on the back. A pleasant warmth bloomed from his touch.

"Mm-hm. Wrong pipe. You look . . ." I trail off, evaluating his outfit and trying to find a kind word to describe it.

"Stupid as fuck? Yeah. Bet you're glad you didn't take me to the dance now, huh? Didn't pack a suit. My date was totally humiliated. She went to go find me a tux before anyone else gets here . . . You know Rupinder, right? Rue? Big glasses?"

Gaykeeper Rue? Lesbian Rue? Brilliant Rue? "Sure, I know Rue."

---

38 The legend of Icarus sees a giddy young man don a pair of waxen wings made by his father, the inventor Daedalus. Daedalus warned Icarus not to fly too close to the sun, but Icarus ignored these instructions. The beeswax in the wings melted, and Icarus fell to his death.

I couldn't even imagine Hunter in the same context as Rupinder Sandhu. I guess it makes sense—the it-girls and the golden boys of any given school will always befriend one another to form the ultimate popular group, no matter how little they have in common—but still. Rue is a wellspring of facts and quotes, every round of conversation with her a challenge of wit and intellect packed with academic references and name drops. Banter with Hunter, on the other hand, feels more like an episode of a smooth-brained dating show.

"Rue's awesome, right? She's my best friend. Well, my best girl friend. Girl-space-friend. Girl who is a friend," he rambled. "Anyway, Rue's chill but my boys are always gonna be numero uno."

Was I desperate for taking that clarification as, I don't know, maybe a hint that he was interested in me romantically? Or at least definitely not interested in Rue, and he wanted me to know that? Ergo, he liked me? Perhaps. Regardless, I brushed right past the cringe-worthy *my boys are always gonna be numero uno* bit and we chatted a while. About summer, school, the weather, the gross fruit punch. Nothing special, but also so goddamn special. I was all fireworks inside. It felt like we were talking forever, but it must have only been thirty minutes before his tux arrived, delivered by one of Hunter's numero unos (who, by the way, didn't even glance in my direction). "Thanks, bro," Hunter said. Then, before leaving, he put his hand on my shoulder and uttered these words exactly: "I'll find you later. We can finish this chat! Maybe you'll let me steal a dance?"

That he-really-really-likes-me moment has branded itself in my memory. I said, "I'm not sure you'd want to do that with me; I have two left feet."

"I'll teach you," he replied warmly.

Despite my better (feminist) judgment, I said, "Sure!"

Teach me, teach me. Pathetic.

"Sweet, I'll see you soon." He sauntered off into a torpid sea of streamers, tuxedos, and bedazzled ball gowns. For the rest of the night, I held onto this promise like a precious stone. Sure, I hung out with Kay in the DJ booth for a while, but my mind never left Hunter Kinsey. He was particularly elusive that evening, drifting in and out of the caf like there was some secret second party somewhere else on campus. It was when I went to touch up my makeup that I discovered said subsidiary gathering in the boys' bathroom, door ajar. In the adjacent girls' room, I over-powdered my nose at the sink closest to the exit and eavesdropped on Hunter and his boys. They were engaged in some classic (repulsive) locker-room talk. About five disembodied voices echoed into the hall, not even trying to be quiet as they discussed how hot Rue was, how they were envious of Hunter, how Hunter should "bag" her tonight. He laughed. He didn't do anything but laugh, even though he knew she was gay, they all must have, and he couldn't "bag" her and he never would. I felt sick. Like, physically nauseous. Too much punch, maybe.

"What about that other chick you were talking to?" I heard a voice ask.

"Who?" Hunter replied.

"I don't know, the fat-ish one?"

Hunter chuckled. "Violet? I don't know … she's into me."

"Isn't she that crazy chick Mag was talking about? The one who lost her shit last week?" A running tap turns off. Hunter doesn't reply to his friend. *Did he nod?* "Why the hell were you talking to *her*?" his friend probed. That's when my nausea threatened to manifest into actual vomit, forcing me to run to a toilet and miss the rest of the boys' conversation. Something tells me I wouldn't have wanted to hear it anyway. Once I recovered from a brief and uncontrollable bout of sorrow—what is it about school dances that brings peoples' emotions to a peak?—I made my way to the refreshment table and munched on finger sandwiches. Each one tasted of shame. And too much mayo.

Later that night, Hunter did find me, right at the center of the dance floor. In the whimsical, fractured light of the planetary disco ball, he asked me to dance. Stared directly at me with those sour-grape eyes and said, "Can I have this dance?" It was a film snippet cut from a John Hughes movie. And even though it was all my fantasies actualized, I somehow found it in me to turn him down. I wasn't about to give him and his friends more material with which they could make fun of me in bathrooms across campus. I'm sure his numero unos were waiting in the wings, watching my dance moves, my stupid dress, my desperation.

"Sorry," I said. "All danced out."

Just for a fraction of a second, I think I saw his smile falter, but I felt no satisfaction.

My head was full of his words from the bathroom, how he said it so confidently. "She's into me." And of course *he* wasn't into *me.* It was just an amusement to him. In one night, he shattered all my illusions (or delusions) about who he was. About what we could be. All I am to him is "the fat-ish one," "that crazy chick," and that's all I ever will be to anyone on Dark Cove Island.

We watch in anxious silence as Frankie performs her monologue. She's auditioning for Titania (the queen, of course). My bet had been on her getting the role of Hermia, but she makes a convincing matriarch. She looks even taller than usual, her black hair billowing around the small moon of her face. Her clear, clean timbre cuts powerfully through the auditorium. It's met with applause like artillery practice.

Ms. Spry consults her clipboard. "Very good, Francesca, thanks so much." Frankie Lin descends, leaving motes of dust to drift in and out of the spotlight. "Next we'll have . . . Violet!"

It takes me the stretch of a long moment to realize (with a substantial pang of terror) *Oh, that's me.* I clamber up to the stage, passing Frankie on the way. She doesn't even look at me, eyes set somewhere beyond in fairyland, supposedly still in character. The wooden steps creak under my weight. I situate myself on the mark[39] taped front-center. X marks the spot where I last embarrassed myself in front of everyone.

Don't think about that, I tell myself.

To get fully grounded, I take in the scenery. The theatre is over a century old but shows few signs of age, all glittering gold, polished oak, tassels, green velvet, and red damask. Hundreds of seats sprawl out and up from the stage like a tidal wave frozen in time; it threatens to crash

39 A mark, or marker, is an indicator for where an actor should stand on set.

but never does. Above, the frescoed ceiling depicts a religious tableau, meticulously painted in the Neoclassical style: a blue sky, angels with horns, saints with halos, hands bloody with nails, and so on. I think of the crosses in the kitchen back home. I ward off the mental image with the real-life vignette before me. A thick clump of rosy-cheeked students occupy the first fifteen rows. Somewhere in the middle of that mass, Ms. Spry sits behind her clipboard of notes. Mr. Blake, far back in the shadows of the theatre, is unreadable. Hunter is visible only by a flying thumbs-up. The one face that's crystal clear to me is Kay's. My best friend sits at the piano in the pit wearing an exaggerated smile.

Breathe. Focus. My mind grasps for the first lines of my chosen monologue ... Helena's famous one. Out of everyone in the play, I'm most like Helena, so that's the role I'm going for. She's more verbose than I am, but she's relatable—often feeling like the odd one out, the butt of the joke. She can act a little desperate. She compares herself to Hermia a lot, and as much as I know it's very internalized-misogyny of me, I compare myself to other girls all the time. I catch Frankie's twinkling eye in the audience and quickly look away. *Not now.*

My pupils fix on a light sconce at the far back wall. For a second, it glints like the disco ball at the Spring Fling—actually, like Mr. Blake's gold tooth. I rub at my temples to stop my head from spinning out. Take a breath. Too shallow. Another attempt, into the trenches of my stomach.

"Whenever you're ready," Ms. Spry says softly.

I think of how it feels to want someone to like you back, to want you there, to see you in a different light for the first time. Close my eyes, concentrate on the air filling my chest, and then: "How happy some o'er other some can be ..."

Applause. Weak and slow at first, then louder. The golden light sconce winks at me, flickering my brain back to the real world.

I did it.

The room, which had been dissolved by the cocktail of Shakespeare and adrenaline, now reassembles itself for me. Steadily, I find Ms. Spry's doll face in the audience.

"Thank you, Violet, that was wonderful!"

Another thumbs-up from Hunter. Kay, the only one still clapping, smiles even wider now.

"Now," says Ms. Spry, "let's see Phaedra!"

I move clumsily offstage, my legs wobbly with relief. I wish the bassoonist girl good luck on my dismount.

A whisper comes from somewhere in the audience: "Wait, did we know she was good?"

Appendix G

Clipping, Dark Cove Arts Academy's Student-Run Newspaper
(Property of DCAAAF)

The Covie Chronicle

FEATURE STORY

Monday, October 29, 1973 (pg. 6)

The Dark Cove Theatre Society: Fact vs. Fiction

Every Covie knows at least one outlandish story about the Dark Cove Theatre Society (DCTS). Perhaps you have heard of a secret cave on the island's southern coast where pornographic plays were once presented, or of the blood ritual the President performs at his or her induction, or perhaps of the bootleg operation they ran out of the cellars beneath Accolade North. These stories have been in circulation for decades, and still we know very little of the self-mythologizing club.

Here is what we know of the Society's history: The Academy had been open for just half a decade when a second-year student named Edith Arnett formed the DCTS with a few close friends in 1897. Though the group was considered exceedingly talented, they were expelled from the Academy in their third year upon being discovered by Headmaster Frederick Stine. Still today, the names of DCTS's first cohort (Arnett, Dietrich, and Vanderbilt, among others) are synonymous with theatre of the early twentieth century. It was believed by faculty that the Society had been disbanded, but DCTS operations continued for two more decades under strict secrecy until the faculty crackdown in 1920, which marked the Society's official absorption by Dark Cove's Department of Theatre. All extracurricular functions of DCTS were prohibited, but aboveboard, in-class productions had been sanctioned by Headmaster Lewis Keaton.

Fast-forward to 1930: famed Hollywood director and known prohibition oppositionist Richard Rourke self-published a memoir in which he identified himself as a former DCTS President and shared his dismay for the Academy's restriction of student creativity. Supposedly in response to Rourke, Headmaster Keaton redistributed DCTS power by anointing one second-year student as President. The President would serve four semesters representing the club's members in departmental meetings. Henry Walker, the first DCTS President by Keaton's approval, was the one to pitch the annual DCTS Halloween Play, which would be a production of the highest caliber.

In the years to follow, DCTS re-established its prestige—only the Academy's best and brightest are welcomed, and only then after a rigorous audition process—and the tradition of the Halloween Play is indeed Dark Cove's most highly anticipated event of the year.

Enter 1973 President Jade Boucher, the first female faculty-selected leader in DCTS history, who is, according to her Orientation Day address, "dead set on resurrecting the old traditions of the Society's past." Though she (and all other members) remain tight-lipped on the traditions to which she referred (Boucher declined to provide a comment to *The Chronicle*) she has reinstated a democratic voting system whereby a DCTS sub-council is elected. Earlier this year, Gerald Moseley was elected as Vice President, self-proclaimed anarchist Jackie Poulter as the Society's Treasurer of Secrets, and Wendy Arnold as Secretary.

Perhaps relatedly, this past Saturday, October 27, the boys' dormitory toilets were backed up with vomit. Many are speculating that this marks a return of DCTS's rumored liquor outfit. Could it merely be the sign of a bug going around? Is the Society tempting fate by repeating history? And will Boucher's *traditional* tactics bolster or hinder the performance of her castmates on Wednesday night?

Find out what your peers think in this issue's Letters to the Editor.
—Jack Leland

Chapter 8

At seven-ish in the morning, the sun decides to make its first full appearance of the school year. Foolishly golden light filters through the lace curtains of our room. For a second, it's nice. A songbird warbles pleasantly by the window. Then a crow scares off the smaller creature, and the reality of the day catches up to me. I shield my eyes with a sleep-lined hand, which Kay apparently takes as an invitation for a high-five. They're already dressed in the Dark Cove tennis skirt and cardigan, oversized. A folded white collar perfectly lines up with the blunt cut of their bob.

"Good morning, roomie," they sing. "Do you know what today is?"

Ugh. I roll over onto my belly, hiding my head under a pillow that leaks feathers like water.

"It's the day my *best friend* Violet is getting a callback for *the* Dark Cove Theatre Society Halloween Play," they declare, tugging at my pillow in a successful attempt at extraction.

"We don't know that."

"Oh, come on, grump. I know you had fun up there. You can't deny it. Saw it myself. Plain as day. You were, I dunno, lighter."

I did feel . . . different. For the moments spent delivering that monologue, sure, I was scared, but I was fully in the moment. I wasn't thinking about anything else, not once I got into it. And that's rare for me—my mind typically hops from one concern to the next with amphibian deftness. Some sort of primordial brain function kicked in when I made it through those first few lines and my nerves switched off for a while. But I don't want to say all that out loud. Kay has had a VIP ticket to some of my most embarrassing moments ever, but that doesn't mean they get access to my cringey inner monologue.

"It's done now. Finito. The powers that be have been appeased and I will be perfectly content if that's where it ends, thank you very much." I don't sound convincing.

"Keep telling that to yourself, you star of *A Midsummer Night's Dream.*"

"A midsummer nightmare, more like." *Badum-tss.*

"'The lady doth protest too much, methinks.'"[40] Kay tenderly removes goose feathers from my gnarl of morning hair. "We're leaving in five to get there before all the good spots are taken."

Callback postings are to Dark Cove what organized fist fights are to the stereotypical high school: a juicy spectacle. The list goes up on the community bulletin at the entrance hall of Accolade South, and every girls' school Covie—even the ones who didn't audition—shows up with their glossiest lips ripe for gossip. Because who doesn't want to know who's worth knowing? It's nauseating. Seriously. My intestines are in knots. Or maybe it's the thought of my name being on that list that's making me queasy . . . the idea of everybody judging me, talking about me, questioning how the panic-attack writer girl could have gotten a callback.

Not that I will, I remind myself. I drag my body of mediocrity out of bed and throw on a plaid ensemble. "And we're off," I say, conveying as much contempt as possible to my roommate, who's having way too much fun teasing me. "I'm ready."

They hum a tune from *The Legend of Zelda*, a flourish of horns that, in the game, happens when you do something right or get something good. For Kay and me, this little ascending chime translates to satisfaction with one's work.

---

40 An often misquoted line from Shakespeare's *Hamlet,* deployed to accuse another of insincerity.

"Shut up," I say.

"You might want to run a brush through that frizz. All eyes are gonna be on you."

"I'll do it on the way," I grumble, grabbing a backpack and a comb.

Kay gestures for me to lead the way out the door. Not even the thick carpets in the dorm hall can soak up all the anticipation. Girls are buzzing from room to room like bees in a hive. And there is their queen: Frankie Lin, standing at the end of the long corridor expectantly, arms open to her subjects in a High Renaissance tableau. Her uniform hugs her swimmer's body,[41] dark mane swept back by a padded, crushed-velvet headband, lips tinted with NARS's best. Today will be, no doubt, one of many highlights in Frankie Lin's year, and she's done up for the occasion.

"Hey," she chirps. "How're you two feeling?"

"Ready for the bloodbath," Kay deadpans.

Frankie giggles, then tilts her head. "How about you, Violet?"

It's strange, her addressing me directly. We've only ever spoken once before, really, and that was enough for me. I mentally map a way past her and this vapid conversation, but she's blocking the stairwell too perfectly. "I just want to rip off the Band-Aid that is this morning."

"It'll all work out. Hopefully we'll both be at callbacks this afternoon," Frankie says, straightening herself into a tall tower. She flashes an ersatz, tight-lipped grin before shifting away from me to Kay. "And I'm really excited to hear what you compose for the show."

"Oh, thanks." Kay's obviously surprised by this sudden interest. "I've been working on some stuff with my band and I'm pretty psyched. It's kind of *Over the Garden Wall* vibes."

"Love that," Frankie says in a way that confirms she's never seen the show. "Your band is you and Michael F., yeah?"

Kay brightens with a look that only comes when they talk about their music. "Us and another guy, Paul, but he graduated. We need a new bassist."

---

41 The term "diver's body" might be more appropriate; Frankie Lin holds a gold medal from the Youth Artistic Swimming Championship in the Female Solo category.

"Didn't Michael audition for the play, though?" Frankie asks.

Kay shrugs, unconcerned. "He did, which is hilarious." Michael's a musician by trade, not an actor. "If he gets in, I'll just recruit the marching band kids. They're always desperate for something to do."

"Yeah, it won't take you long to find a replacement. Is that the kind of music you make? Marching band stuff?"

"They're more alt-rock," I say, trying to fast-forward to the resolution of this conversation. I tug at a knot in my hair with the comb.

"The music for the play is gonna be different than our usual alt stuff for sure," Kay explains.

"Cool. What's the band name?" Frankie asks with the rising inflection of polite curiosity. I guess now that they're a part of the Dark Cove Theatre Society, Kay is worth Frankie Lin's attention.

"Last year we were Elemental Dust but now that we're a two-piece, we changed our name to Shin Pads for Ghostie."

"Love it, kind of like Death Cab for Cutie?"

I tuck the comb into my bag and zip. "Not really."

Kay gives me a *woah-easy-there-girl* look.

"What?" I say defensively. "The band isn't at all like Death Cab for Cutie."[42]

Frankie's face falls, apparently wounded.

"I see where you get that connection," Kay says kindly.

Frankie sidesteps so we can bypass her. "Yeah, well, I guess I'll hear it at the show." She's *so sure* she's going to be in the show.

"See ya!" I yell, already bolting down the stairs and out the door seconds later. A swell of brisk autumn air fills my lungs.

It takes Kay almost a minute to catch up with me. "Um, what was all that about?"

"Excuse me?" I bristle.

---

42 Sonically, Shin Pads is closer to Keane or *Parachutes*-era Coldplay. Ethereal, atmospheric, gut-wrenching, with the whimsical storytelling sensibilities of Kate Bush. Opposite to Bush, Kay's vocal range is deep and sultry.

"You were—how do I put this nicely?—mega bitchy. She was just being friendly, you know, making conversation," Kay says as we speed along the battered flagstone walk to campus. The earliest of the season's fallen leaves crunch lightly underfoot.

"You seriously think that was an earnest effort by Frankie Lin? She's only talking to you because you're a part of the Society now. Either that or you're a new collector's item for her queer clique."

"Okay, harsh." Kay's brown eyes glint with injury. Before I can apologize, they say, "Maybe you're just uncomfortable with her confidence. Ever think of that?"

"*You're* confident, and I'm comfortable with *you*."

Kay inhales to speak, but no words follow. We're both quiet for a few seconds, just the scuff of our shoes on the cobblestone. Finally, after a few unlike-us awkward paces, they say, "Frankie can't help that she's a Gemini. Social climbers by nature."

Although I am more skeptical of astrology than my roommate, I agree with them on this one. "You can say that again."

"Seriously, though. What's your issue with her?"

"Nothing." I fold my arms across my chest against the wind. "I'm surprised she even remembered my name."

The first and last time I ever had a real conversation with Frankie Lin was roughly twelve months ago, when I was less privy to her shallowness and the Dark Cove Theatre Society's caginess. Uninformed as I was, I made the mistake of trying to befriend the Gaykeepers. Since I didn't have any friends at the Academy other than Kay—who had been spending most of their time at the boys' school—I wanted to lock in some allies on the south side of the island. My efforts to fit in were highly calculated. I am nothing if not a girl with a plan. I would approach Frankie's group where I knew they could be found on Saturday mornings:[43] in the library, typically in an intimate formation by the oversized fire. Here, I'd find an open seat where I could do homework very casually, as

43 The library is closed on Sundays but is open from seven a.m. until seven p.m. all other days of the week.

though I belonged there. Then I'd weave myself into the tapestry of their epicurean conversation by talking about everything I knew the Dark Cove Lipstick Lesbians liked: Shakespeare, Starbucks (which the dining hall proudly serves), and Sofia Coppola. Oh, and gossip, extra hot. The campus library houses historical tomes, leather-bound plays, and literary anthologies inasmuch as it does hearsay.

As anticipated, I found the Society cool girls in their usual places. A few of them lounged elegantly on the sumptuous old furniture, others on the floor. There were seven of them in total, their bodies leaning steeply forward. I can recognize the gravitational pull of scandalous conversation when I see it. They sipped at lattes in to-go cups, mouths hovering over plastic lids, speaking in urgent whispers. Frankie's pink-petal lips moved quickly and I allowed myself to imagine what it would be like to fit into her world. She sat with crossed legs, elbows on the low cedar coffee table. The thick textbook spread out before her had long been forgotten, now merely an accessory.

Acutely aware of what I must have looked like, an ugly duckling approaching these swanlike girls, I waddled over to them, stumbling over the edge of a thick carpet and nearly knocking over a Tiffany lamp on the way. Heads turned, brows knitted, Magpie glared at me. I had interrupted something.

"Hey–hello–hi. Yes. Um, can I sit here?" I stammered.

"Of course." This was Frankie, ever the sanguine angel. She scooched a few inches to create some room by the hearth (though not nearly enough for all my bulky limbs to fit, I appreciated the gesture). "I'm Frankie," she continued, like I didn't already know that, which I found charming at the time.

"Violet, or Vi, if you want." Nicknames, I figured, are like small keys to friendship.

"Nice to meet you, Vi," she said, and I felt like I'd really unlocked it. A connection, for a fleeting moment. Once the moment died, her rosy cheek turned away, re-engaging in the gossip session.

The library is a quiet space, so if you talk in anything above a whisper, you're out. Furthermore, I couldn't hear a goddamn word these girls were saying. My ears were unable to register their dulcet, confidential tones. My body was too round and sweaty to fit into their compact, clandestine huddle. The enormous fire at my side wasn't helping. I dabbed my wet brow with my sleeve. The soldier must march on. Time to initiate phase two of my plan: casual studying. I went to pull a notebook out from my backpack, and the zipper, impossibly loud, re-alerted Frankie to to my existence. She glanced first at me and then down at my Moleskine, which was covered in stickers: a *Twilight* quote[44] in bubble font, a Keanu Reeves x Sandra Bullock cartoon, a still from *Lost*, the lighthouse from *Harper's Island*, that meme of Ina Garten summoning flames directly from hell, and so on. Amidst this spread of pop-culture clutter on the vegan leather cover, the Pride flag pasted on the top-left corner caught Frankie's eye.

"You're queer?" she asked, an edge of intrigue to her voice.

Though I'd contemplated the question before, I still hadn't formed an official, satisfying, press-release answer. I'd never kissed anyone before—still haven't. At the time, I thought Hunter was cute, but all my big celebrity crushes were women. Did that give me a right to call myself queer? "Um, yeah, I'm queer," I said, sounding as uncertain as I felt.

This caught Magpie's attention. She had been lying back on an old velvet chaise on the other side of the coffee table. Swinging her legs onto Rue's lap, she shifted her focus from the primary conversation to me.

"So, what's your sexuality?" This question was posed like a challenge—like someone might have said, "Oh, you like the Cure? Name five of their songs."

I repeated myself, shakier this time: "I'm queer."

"Okay. But, like, what does that mean though? Are you bi?" Mag asked, rolling her eyes, tossing her legs back up onto the arm of her chair; I had lost her attention. "Everyone's bi now."

"Oh," I said, blood boiling, tongue like a useless paperweight in my mouth.

---

44 "Where the hell have you been, loca?"

I looked to Frankie—surely, she would call her friend out—but all Miss Popular did was shrug. That was the moment I understood that Frankie Lin isn't actually a nice person, she's a person who's nice only in moments of self-interest. "Magpie didn't mean that in a biphobic way or anything. We love bi girls. Salma is bi—"

"A non-practicing bisexual," Magpie muttered, throwing a pointed glance at another member of their beautiful circle.

"—and we love Salma," Frankie continued as I wondered what on god's green earth a non-practicing bisexual was. "But these days a lot of girls are using other girls just to seem more attractive to guys."

"Or to be *different*." Magpie's eyes pointed back at me. "It's problematic."

"Even just last semester, Magpie had this—"

"Frankie, love," Rue, prompted by Magpie's grimace, piped in, "I'm sure we can illustrate the issue of queerbaiting to our new friend without the aid of anecdotal evidence." Rue fixed her hoity-toity, bespectacled gaze on me. "Performative bisexuality perpetuates the sexualization of lesbian relationships and weaponizes—"

That's when Mme. Camry thumped her cane on the wooden floor, letting out a terse "Silence!" (in French), to immediate effect. The girls leaned forward once more into their angular flock. I, at the outskirts, made my quiet departure from the library, and as I did, I overheard Magpie whisper, "It's so gross when the scholarship kids try to ally themselves with real money.[45] For what?"

Rue gave some wordy answer that I tuned out. I'd heard everything I needed to know—I didn't want to *ally myself* with *them*. And yet, I was the one who felt rejected. I hated it and I still feel the reverberations of that hatred to this day. Of course, Magpie was the rudest of the bunch. But it's just as bad—worse, I'd argue—to be complicit, to pretend you're nice when really, you're just another mean girl. Since then, I've overheard countless Frankie Lin niceties fall hollow onto the ground. Here's the truth: there's only one thing Frankie Lin cares about and that's

---

45 In the glimmery bubble of Dark Cove Arts Academy, scholarship students are unwelcome reminders of the lower-middle class.

popularity . . . which, consequently, miserably, renders her inescapable. Wherever I turn, there she is—in every class, every social club, every Dark Cove Theatre Society production, every promotional poster—with her killer bone structure, skin like starlight, and endless fount of talent.

That's the other reason why I hate her, the one I'll only ever admit to myself: she's so damn good at acting. I'm in constant flux between wanting to be her and wanting to eradicate her from my life (more often than not, I settle on the latter). She's going to be famous. I know it . . . this girl's going to haunt me forever. And, no duh, she'll be at the top of this callback list.

Gargoyle sentries stare me down as we approach Accolade South. The building's heavy doors are propped open to let in a stream of impatient students. Inside the foyer, strange orange light pours from the stained-glass windows onto cool marble floors, overlaying the scene with a hellish filter. What could ostensibly be a witch's circle forms at the heart of the hall. The musty air is scented heavily with floor wax and wool. The whispers of blood-thirsty thespians. The scuffle of leather shoes. Kay leads me through the ring of bodies to the battered corkboard, still bare. It's guarded by two empty suits of armor. Mounted on the wall above are several oil paintings of previous headmasters looking down on us. *Silly girls,* I imagine them saying. A clock between two of the sideburned faces tells me it is 8:56 a.m. Kay's the first to break our graveyard silence. "So, since we have four minutes to burn, do you wanna talk about why you're so sassy today?"

I try to apologize, but it comes out all breathy and weird.

"What's going on?"

"I'm terrified," I admit. "I'll be a wreck if my name is up there, I'll be a wreck if it isn't. It's a lose-lose situation."

"You keep saying you don't want it but, babe, are you sure about that?"

"I don't know."

They thread their fingers through mine. "Whatever happens, I'm proud of you, and I'll be by your side."

"Thanks. Sorry I called you a collectors' item."

"I kind of took it as a compliment. But I'm not the only one you might want to apologize to."

"I'll talk to Frankie later," I say through gritted teeth. "It's just—"

"It's all right," Frankie chimes in from behind me. Jump scare. I spin around and notice the vulturine crowd closing in. The throng shoves forward and Frankie jostles into me.

My breath gets shallow as I edge further into the electric plane of my anxiety. "Oh, yeah, sorry. I'm just—"

"Forget about it." Quick smile, her eyes black and frozen like sewn-on buttons.

"See? That wasn't so hard," Kay says under their breath. They make an *I-told-you-so* expression that coaxes a laugh out of me. Kay always keeps me in check.

If I could have it my way, I'd be left to indulge in social isolation, melancholic literature, and catty remarks in peace. Most people find this attitude off-putting, but it's not that I'm a total misanthrope. I just have my reservations—I'm a good judge of character! And my judgment is that most people are selfish, or rude, or even, on occasion, evil. A behavioral scientist might deduce that this critical tendency of mine is rooted in insecurity, that my bookishness is my own suit of armor, that I am less a good judge of character than a treacherously cynical person, blah blah blah. I may not be a behavioral scientist, but I *am* a writer, which is close enough. I get it: I'm not perfect.

"It's okay to want this," Kay assures me, "and it's okay to be scared. It's just not okay to be mean to people for no reason."

Sure, if I step back, it's plausible that Frankie Lin isn't the narcissistic fraud I suspect her to be. But I have to listen to my gut, right? Or whatever it is inside me that tells me Frankie Lin is my mortal enemy.

En garde.

The soft, rhythmic click of stilettos on marble alerts me to Ms. Spry. She parts the crowd with ease in a stylish pinafore dress and white button-up blouse. She bestows me with a half-conniving look before brandishing the list, pinning the dreaded A4 sheet to the board, and *click-click-click*ing her way out of the hall, bound for the boys' school, where she'll post another copy. The crowd transforms instantly into a beast with many limbs advancing toward the list. My hands start to tingle. I squint at the paper but fail to make out any meaning from the twelve-point serif font. Behind, I hear gasps, murmurs, squeals of "Frankie!" "Mag!" and then, from my roommate, "Violet!" and the triumphant tune from *The Legend of Zelda.*

The text reveals itself, and everything else falls away. I read it twice, thrice, to make sure my eyes aren't tricking me. Something inside me twinges with a feeling that could be excitement or terror.

Megan Black, Violet Costantino, Frankie Lin, Rupinder Sandhu, and about fifteen others. These names are now grist to Dark Cove's hungry mill.

Appendix H

Student File, V. Costantino
(Property of DCAAAF)

Student Name: Costantino, Violet
Student E-mail: vcostantino@darkcovearts.edu
Sex: F
Pronouns: she/her/hers
Year: First
Specialization: Theatre
Scholarship Status (and Conditions, if Applicable): Full scholarship; renewal contingent upon maintenance of 3.8 GPA or higher
Current GPA: 3.6
Allergies: N/A
Medical Conditions: Generalized anxiety disorder (GAD), moderate
Guardian: Rossi, Carmen; mother.
Guardian E-mail: carmen.rossi@mackenzienorthhealth.ca
Guardian Address: 305 Grace St., Mapleton, ON. Canada

Notes: Numerous members of the faculty remark that Violet demonstrates above-average skills in literary criticism and the analysis of contemporary texts. Communication and social skills need developing. Violet visited the infirmary after a severe panic attack (see medical record). Violet has demonstrated intense criticism of herself and peers (likely related to GAD, further assessment needed).

Chapter 9

Dancers stretch in black spandex along the narrow hall outside the callback room. They work at their pointe shoes, chatting about remedies and preventative potions for torn ligaments, sprains, and the common cold. Actors engage in irritating vocal exercises. Kemsley belts the word "hey" repeatedly, though he greets no one. A few doors down, someone practices piano scales. There is an atmosphere of controlled chaos as groups of twos and threes are called into the studio for chemistry reads.

"Laila, Freja, Jayden," the disembodied voice of Ms. Spry beckons from down the corridor. One of the girls does a little pas de chat down the hall.

The door to the studio is heavy and clunks shut so loudly it gives me a start every time, no matter how much I brace myself for the sound. I'm clenching my fists into small, fleshy stones. All the energy inside of me has to go somewhere, and I'm not about to start doing over-the-top body rolls like the actress clique. Frankie moves up and down like a wave. It's astonishing how fluid she can make herself. Rue and Magpie have taken to massaging their jaws. I wrench my own open from its default clamped position.

When the dancers burst out from their audition after just a few minutes, they're in a fit of giggles.

"So?" asks Nina Petrov, who'd been hovering outside the door, listening for clues. "Tell us everything."

"Oh, it's chill. You get sides[46] to read, and Ms. Spry's cool," the dancer named Freja replies calmly, tying her white-blonde hair into a high ponytail.

"Is Mr. Blake there?" Nina asks.

"He wouldn't be," Magpie interjects. "He's in meetings all afternoon."

Nina's shoulders slump a little, relaxing.

"Don't worry," says Laila, "there's a dog in there for emotional support."

"Romeo," Freja whines affectionately. "He's so cutie-cutie."

"*Cutie-cutie*," Magpie mutters in condescension as the dancers tiptoe down the hall.

"Suppose ballerinas aren't assigned much reading," Rue replies, mid-stretch. Her voguish glasses slide down the arch of her nose as she moves into a forward fold. "Limited vocabulary."

Ms. Spry pops her head out of the door, eyes scanning a clipboard. "Can I have Violet and . . . Francesca?"

You've got to be kidding me, I think. *Frankie Lin is my scene partner?* My anxiety increases by several orders of magnitude. I leap up from my spot on the floor and scurry down the hall, keeping pace with my racing heart, not even looking at Frankie as she holds the door open for me.

Seated with one leg delicately crossed over the other, Ms. Spry waits for us inside. The studio has a long, mirrored wall with a wooden ballet barre running across it. Light lands in rectangular patches on the rubber floor. Occupying one of the blocks of slanted sunshine, Ms. Spry's Great Dane is splayed out in an unguarded napping position.

"Don't mind Romeo," the director says, relaxing into her chair. She slips one of her stockinged feet out of a high heel and reaches her toes to pet her dog, who doesn't appear to be comforted nor disturbed by the touch. "He's my sleepy boy."

---

46 Sides are sections of a script that actors are given to either memorize or cold read for an audition.

"Do you mind if I pet him?" Frankie asks coyly, cheeks blushed, chin tucked. I wonder if Ms. Spry will see through this little performance of bashfulness.

"Oh my gosh, of course you can," Ms. Spry exclaims, extinguishing my hopes for an ally against Frankie Lin. "Romeo-Womeo, look alive, you've got a new friend here."

The dog raises his oversized head, and Frankie extends her hand for him to sniff. He licks her pink-polished fingers. I stand uncomfortably on the criss-cross mark taped at the heart of the room, waiting for Frankie to finish her little display. She squats down next to the dog as Ms. Spry rambles on about Romeo's breed and temperament and diet. "But I guess we'd better get down to business—unless you want to come and give him a pet, Violet? He's very friendly."

Frankie sprouts up from the ground and Romeo does the same, shaking himself and creating a cloud of dander that catches the sunlight. I sneeze.

"Wait, are you allergic to dogs?" Ms. Spry asks, throwing her arms around Romeo in a panic. He wriggles free and moves to a far corner of the room. "I'm so sorry, I'll get him out of here."

I shake my head. "No, don't worry. Must just be the dust in here."

"That's one thing I've noticed about this school," Ms. Spry sighs, "it's so dang dusty!"

"It might sound weird, but I love the dustiness." Frankie smiles. Cool girls love finding weirdness in their most mundane opinions and actions. Frankie Lin isn't weird. Frankie Lin will never be weird. Frankie Lin is too perfect to be weird. "Dark Cove is so old, just being here, you feel like a part of history!"

Ms. Spry claps her hands together lightly. "Let's make history then, right, girls?" She re-crosses one leg over the other, shifting into a more business-like demeanor. From a briefcase next to her, she pulls out two sheets of paper. "Here's your scene. Violet, I want to see you read for Hermia. Francesca, you'll be Lysander. Sound good?"

Frankie squints at the script in her hands and purses her rose-petal lips around the words she won't say—she's disappointed in her role assignment.

I scoff and then try to pass it off as a cough. "Sounds good."

"I know you auditioned for different roles," Ms. Spry explains, "but it's just a chemistry read, and this is one of the most intimate scenes of the play." I scan the page, a section of act 2, scene 2 in which Hermia and Lysander are going to sleep in the forest and she insists they take up two separate makeshift beds, basically because they're too horny and it would be too tempting, too improper to sleep next to each other. "Now, whenever you're ready . . ."

The accordion lines around Frankie's pout smooth. I study her face: her pearlescent skin, ski-slope nose, and exaggerated cupid's bow—all the details of Frankie Lin's perfection that usually spark an honest rage in me—and I allow myself to admire them. Her eyes dart up to meet mine, glistening with a dark glamor, an invitation, a silent question: *Are you ready?* I take a measured breath and give a curt nod.

"Fair love, you faint with wand'ring in the wood," Frankie says, her voice breathy from a long journey already traveled, her eyes still locked on mine. She has become Lysander. "And, to speak troth, I have forgot our way. We'll rest us, Hermia, if you think it good, And tarry for the comfort of the day."

I glance down at my script as I move to the floor. "Be it so Lysander. Find you out a bed, For I upon this bank will rest my head."

Frankie descends swiftly after me. "One turf shall serve as pillow for us both; One heart, one bed, two bosoms, and one troth."

My breath catches. "Nay, good Lysander. For my sake, my dear, Lie further off yet. Do not lie so near." I press a hand to her chest and push her gently away so our bodies are a safe distance apart, my arm like a metal barricade between us. She traces the length of it delicately with a long, pink nail.

"O, take the sense, sweet, of my innocence! Love takes the meaning in love's conference. I mean that my heart unto yours is knit, So that but one heart we can make of it," she says boldly, taking my hand on her upper breastbone and moving it up to her neck. My skin responds with a real shiver. "Two bosoms interchained with an oath—So then two bosoms and a single troth. Then by your side no bed-room me deny, For lying so, Hermia, I do not lie."

I look down at my paper, face hot from the intimacy of the moment. "Lysander riddles very prettily. Now much beshrew my manners and my pride If Hermia meant to say Lysander lied." I slide away to further the distance between our bodies. "But, gentle friend, for love and courtesy, Lie further off in human modesty. Such separation, as may well be said, Becomes a virtuous bachelor and a maid. So far be distant; and good night, sweet friend."

Now laying on my side, I face the mirror. In its reflection, there's Frankie behind me, her brows angled up to a soft point on her forehead. I wonder, fleetingly, how she can control her face so precisely, how she is able to master an expression conveying both disappointment and adoration perfectly—I'd believe the feelings behind it were pure if we weren't in an audition (and if she weren't Frankie Lin). "Thy love ne'er alter till thy sweet life end!"

We close our eyes, only opening them when Romeo's paws drum an erratic beat that jostles us out of our faux slumber. The dog congratulates me on surviving my callback with a sloppy kiss across the cheek. I giggle as Ms. Spry rushes to tug him off, relief washing over me once again. Legs like Jell-O. Frankie appears above me, offering a hand to help me back onto my feet.

"You girls set this room on fire," Ms. Spry squeals. "I'm not just saying that, either. Are you close in real life?"

I reserve the "hell no" for my inner monologue and decide to let Frankie take this one.

"Not exactly," she says in her sweet sing-song cadence.

Ms. Spry flashes a knowing grin, though I don't know what it is that she knows. "All the more impressive. You two belong up there together! Keep an eye out for the cast list. It'll be up in Accolade South tomorrow morning."

"Will do. Bye-bye, Romeo-Womeo," Frankie baby-talks to the dog, and I hope for her sake that her friends outside can't hear her. Appearing to have the same thought, her twinkling midnight eyes go to the door, then to me. She holds my gaze. I hold hers. It's like we're gripping at two ends of a tightrope and there's a secret suspended in the space between us. "See you around, Violet."

When she brushes past me, a staticky shiver raises the hairs on my body.

I don't need anyone to tell me that was a good callback. I felt it. The ambiguous *it* every actor talks about: Chemistry. Fire. Hope.

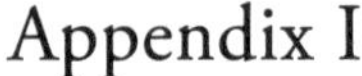

Appendix I

Cast list, Dark Cove Theatre Society's 90th Annual Halloween Production

A MIDSUMMER NIGHT'S DREAM
(in order of appearance)

MEGAN BLACK as Hermia
XANDER PRINCE as Egeus/Quince
HUNTER KINSEY as Lysander
FRANCESCA LIN as Demetrius
VIOLET COSTANTINO as Helena
KEMSLEY DRAKE as Bottom
MARGARET SONG as Oberon/Theseus
SALMA KNIGHT as Titania/Hippolyta
RUPINDER SANDHU as Puck/Philostrate
FREJA ANDERSSON, JAYDEN BINGHAM,
and LAILA FISCHER as Fairies/Mechanicals
(see Ms. Spry at lunch today)

Appendix J

Invitation to the Dark Cove Theatre Society Welcome Ceremony, Addressed to V. Costantino

THE DARK COVE THEATRE SOCIETY WELCOMES YOU

Dear Violet,

On behalf of the Dark Cove Theatre Society, I invite you to the annual Welcome Ceremony this *Monday, September 19 in room 13A* after the first lunch bell. This will be an opportunity for you to meet and mingle with your fellow Society members. We will also take a portrait of this year's cohort, so be sure to look your best!

To accept this invitation, please fill out the attached form and have it signed by your Department Head and submitted to Secretary Drake before the ceremony begins.

In the words of our founder, Edith Arnett, "To shirk this duty is to bring about bad fortune for yourself and the Society. History is history, dust, paper, stone, a bloody gash in the back. Will you hold the rusted dagger?"

Regards,

Magpie Black

Magpie Black
President, the Dark Cove Theatre Society

I ______________________________ formally accept this invitation to join the Dark Cove Theatre Society. I attest that I am devoted to the preservation of the Society, its traditions and secrets. I will strive for excellence and discretion in all I do as a living representative of the Society. I understand that members are expected to give themselves fully to the work, no matter the cost.

I will attend the Welcome Ceremony, rehearsals, and all other official Society events. I hereby commit to the entire show run of THE HALLOWEEN PLAY, *A MIDSUMMER NIGHT'S DREAM* and the season to be determined thereafter. I understand that this invitation is valid only until *MONDAY, SEPT. 19* and that membership is guaranteed only until the end of the current school year.

If any of these vows are broken, an inquest will be conducted by the President, and membership will be determined by the Theatre Department Head.

Member signature: ______________________________

Date: ______________________________

Department Head signature: ______________________________

Chapter 10

You know that trope in apocalypse movies or video game cutscenes where the protagonist is gunning it in one direction, but then they reach a herd of people or deer or something running in the opposite direction, away from some supposed threat (zombies, aliens, pick your poison)? Right now, I'm the protagonist in that situation, moving against the cafeteria-bound crowd, heading instead toward the final boss: Mr. Blake. I have to ask him to sign off on my participation in the Halloween Play, after which I will be an official member of the Dark Cove Theatre Society.

The people I pass look at me with some puzzlement, and it isn't because I'm going in the opposite direction. I'm on their radar now that I've been cast in the Halloween Play. The attention is more invasive than gratifying. There is only one person whose reaction to my new Society status is of particular interest to me. Fortunately, that's the person whose class I'm bound for. The crowd has dwindled to nothing by the time I turn the corner into the narrow hall leading to 13A. The sepia-toned portraits stare me down. Every frame is dated, beginning with the year 1931,[47] on a small gold plate. The years ascend as I approach the classroom. Each photo contains a cohort of students, most of whom went

47 Eleven years after the Society was formally absorbed by the Academy.

on to achieve greatness not long after the camera flashed. There are no listed names, so it's hard to say who's who, but there are a few actors I recognize here and there, standing in the front rows of what appears to be the classroom I'm bound for. Once I've caught up to nearly present day, Frankie materializes in the doorway of 13A. We almost collide in the narrow passage, but she takes a nimble sidestep.

"Sorry," she says. Her hair is parted in the middle today, running like a stream down the smooth sides of her heart-shaped face. "Here for the Welcome Ceremony?"

"I guess so."

"It's just a picture." She bobs her head. It reminds me of an apple in water. "There's no need to be so nervous."

"What's that supposed to mean?"

Frankie tosses her hand in the air like she's shooing away an insect. "You're going to be fine, that's all. I can tell you're anxious about today and the play." That's definitely a reference to my infamous panic attack. There's a twinkle of pity in her eyes. She looks at me like I'm a ticking time bomb. Or a toddler.

"No loitering in the hall,"[48] Mr. Blake bellows from beyond the door, startling me backwards into a row of lockers. I never understood why the schoolhouses have lockers in the first place—I mean, we live *right here*. Mine is somewhere in the basement, unused, full of cobwebs and spiders and whatnot, just like this one: the one my funny bone hits. The clang of it echoes in the emptiness. A padlock rattles against the metal. The overall effect is very loud, which makes Blake holler, "What's going on out there?"

I rub my tender elbow. The nearly healed scab from my mosquito bite has opened up again. Magpie rushes out of the room, feathers already rustled. "Violet. You're late. Are you guys coming in or what?"

"Slow down, Madame President," Frankie teases. "We have five minutes. I'm running to the washroom and coming right back. Violet, try not to break any limbs before then."

---

48 Rule 22 in the Dark Cove Arts Academy student handbook.

Is she being cheeky or bitchy? I wonder.

"Wouldn't be surprised if she did," Magpie snarls. There's no question about her bitchiness. "It'll only prove she's this year's Cursed Girl."

"I don't follow," I reply stonily.

"You don't get out much, do you."

At my blank stare, Frankie gives an explanation. "It's just a silly Society legend. Sometimes a cast member drops out before the Halloween Play goes up. It's, like, a thing, but it's not a curse. And I don't think anyone's ever broken a limb."

"The Dark Cove curse is not just a *silly Society legend.* First of all, Sarah Lynch, 2004 dropout. Fractured wrist," Magpie recites. "Secondly, it's not *sometimes*, it's *always.* Without fail. Every year for like . . . ever, a weak link breaks before October's end, leaving the island for one pathetic reason or another."

I have an inkling that this conversation is a trap, but I can't help it, my curiosity has been piqued. "Weak link?"

"The ones who just aren't Society material. Whether they're not talented enough, not equipped to do the emotional work, or just too poor to afford tuition. *My* money's on you for this year's victim, Violet. You're a triple threat." Magpie snatches the paper from my hand and darts back into Mr. Blake's classroom before I can get a word in. Anger starts to simmer in my belly.

"Ignore her. She's on a power trip," Frankie whispers, tucking a stray strand of hair behind her ear. A diamond daisy stud sits on her lobe. "Magpie's all bark and no bite. You'll see."

When I don't say anything, Frankie struts away like a runway model. She makes the crooked hall look straighter. It's as if her mere presence can alter the architecture of a room. "Be back soon," she coos.

Inside 13A, an old-fashioned camera stands on a tripod facing the blackboard. Mr. Blake sits at the table, signing the sheets he's already collected with an expensive-looking pen that you just know feels significant and heavy to hold. Kay's already here, standing in the middle of a group of twenty bustling Society members.

"Lead cast first row, supporting cast second row, crew heads and assistants third row, and the rest of you in the back," Magpie hollers, ushering students into position. "Usually we have a bench for the short people to stand on but it didn't work out so we're going to have to make do."

"Excuse me," a meek, five-foot-nothing third year says, hand raised, "I'm in stage carp, but—"

"Are you a crew head?" Mag asks.

"No, but—"

"Back row!"

I awkwardly step two rows' worth of space in front of Kay, feeling remarkably out of place. We exchange looks amidst the chaos.

Frankie enters the room and rushes to my side. "Did I miss anything?"

"We're supposed to be in the front," I say, even though she probably knows that—not her first rodeo. She smiles and thanks me anyway, ever polite, never not pretending.

Hunter is the last to arrive, slapping his signed letter onto the small stack at the end of the table.

"Is that everyone, Miss Black?" Blake asks impatiently.

She takes attendance. A chorus of names and "here"s ensue. I look around at my new teammates: my best friend, my ex-crush, my arch-nemesis, and a bunch of other people who only know me as the anxiety attack chick.

When "Violet" is called, it takes me a moment to register the name as my own.

"Sorry, would you prefer to be called Cursed Girl?" Magpie asks.

"No. Violet will do," I say flatly, determined not to let her get the best of me. Not in front of Mr. Blake. I need to show him, show everyone, that I've got what it takes to do this: new nerves of steel. "Present."

Blake doesn't even look my way, and Magpie, unimpressed, continues down the list. "Kemsley." No answer. "Kemsley Drake?"

"Mr. Drake has elected not to accept his role as Bottom," Mr. Blake explains. "I believe Mr. Flores has stepped in."

Scandalized whispers ripple through the room. Michael (Mr. Flores), close behind me, waves.

"The role wasn't good enough for Kemsley?" Magpie remarks with grim satisfaction. Mr. Blake doesn't answer the President. Her face blots with red. "Well, I'll make note of that." She crosses Kemsley off with a heavy-handed stroke.

Once all the names have been called, and the whispers have died down, and collars have been straightened, and four orderly lines have been formed, Magpie grabs the end of a trigger cable attached to the old camera. She counts down. A crow swoops by the window on "one." The shutter fires with a click and there's an overwhelming flash of white. I wince.

Magpie gives a single clap and everyone drops their poses.

"Actors," she announces. "I'll see you at the table read on Wednesday. Be sure to check in with me on the way in. All of you, welcome. Welcome to the Dark Cove Theatre Society."

The nostalgic buzz of dial tone sounds in my ear. I punch my home number into the phone and roll onto my bed as I wait for the answer. It comes before the second ring even finishes.

"Hello?" The soft sound of her voice elicits a small burst of homesickness in the pit of my stomach.

"Nonna, it's me."

"Violetta, I've been waiting for your call," she says sternly. "It's been a whole two weeks!"

I hear my mom in the background. She's shouting over clanging pans and the muffled voice of Alex Trebek on the TV, which places Nonna at her usual spot on the slouchy chair in the family room and Mom in the kitchen on the opposite side of the bungalow. Mom asks who's on the phone. In my imagination, she wipes her brow with the end of her favorite apron, one I got her as a Mother's Day gift years ago, which has since been stained by countless pots of sugo. I can almost hear the sauce bubbling on our stove a million miles away. I can see the house, its pink carpet, stained in the one spot next to the couch, crosses hung on the walls here and there, every door open except for the bathroom door because that door must always be closed, house rule. Nonna tells Mom it's me on the phone. "My daughter's too busy and talented to call us!"

"Tell my mother, with love, to shut up."

"Statte zitta,"[49] Nonna commands, her voice faint so I know she's saying it directly to Mom.

"I miss you too, darling daughter," Mom calls.

I twirl the phone cord in my finger like a strand of hair. Just talking to them, I feel like a little girl again, gone away for a sleepover. "I do miss you guys, you know."

"Oh, you're not missing anything," Nonna assures me. "Just the usual bickering. We're watching *Jeopardy* tonight. 'Shakespeare's Characters' is one of the categories. I was just thinking of you."

"Well, that's as good a segue as any. I have some news." I allow a grin to spread across my face just imagining the reaction I'm about to get. "I got a lead part in *A Midsummer Night's Dream*."

"Brava bravissima! Oh, Violetta," Nonna yells.

"What is it, Ma?" Mom asks from the kitchen.

"Violet got a lead role!"

"Put her on speaker!"

"How do I do that?"

"I just showed you how to do it, Ma."

"I'm an old lady, I forget."

A staticky kerfuffle sounds, then a series of beeps as my mother and grandmother fight over the phone. It's the kind of interaction that would irritate me endlessly if I were back home, but I wish more than anything I could be there to see it. A pressure accumulates behind my brow. It's only been fourteen days, but the homesickness is setting in already. I brush away a renegade tear and focus my stare on the slivered moon out my window. "Hello?"

---

49 Statte zitta translates to "keep quiet" in English.

"We're both here, honey. You're on speaker. We're so proud," my mom coos.

"Thanks, guys."

A pause. "Will this interfere with your studies?" Mom asks, concern turning her formerly warm tone cold and shrill. She sounded like this all summer, starting from the moment she peeled the wax seal off that dreaded letter from the headmaster. "Violet? Will it interfere with your studies?"

The question feels like a full-frontal belly flop, a reminder that if I don't keep my scholarship, there's no way she can afford my tuition.

"Classes are going well," I assure her (and myself). "Already got an A+ on my first Lit quiz."

Mom doesn't even try to contain the sigh of relief that crackles in the phone receiver. I can't blame her—I did the same thing when Mr. Mitchell handed me the paper, the circled letter like a smiley face beaming at me.

"I'm well on track," I say, "don't worry—"

The aggressive beeps of Nonna accidentally dialing numbers on the phone interrupt me.

"Ma! Stop touching it! Great, now you made me lose my train of—sorry, Vi. Where were we? Oh, the perfect grade! I'm so happy to hear—it's all excellent news. And about the play, what role did you get?"

"Helena."

"Wow! That's the best part! Helen of Troy!"

"How do you know that?" I ask. My mom is a nurse, not a thespian. My interests were not inherited.

"Helena was just an answer in *Jeopardy*," Nonna answers. "One-thousand dollars! The lady contestant got it wrong. Stupida."

"Well that's amazing," says Mom, punctuated by more beeps, more confusion.

"Who is going to be Helena's love interest? Is it that boy?" Nonna asks. "The handsome one you talk about?"

I cringe openly in the privacy of my dorm. "No. Hunter is playing another character, but Demetrius is actually going to be played by a girl."

Mom clears her throat uncomfortably. I came out to her last year. Not formally, but I told her I had a celebrity crush on Kristen Stewart. I know she got the message because her voice went all shrill—it's not an irregular occurrence—and then she randomly asked me if I wanted to watch *Glee*. She's mostly supportive, just not great at talking about it. "Well that's very ... modern. Sounds neat."

"Her name is Frankie," I say, though I'm not sure why.

"That's a boy's name," Nonna replies bluntly.

"It's short for Francesca."

"She's Italian!" Nonna exclaims. "How wonderful!"

"No, she's Taiwanese."

"Oh. Your school is so international! But too bad you won't be in a couple with that California boy you like so much." Nonna's laughter blasts across thousands of miles of telephone wire into my ear. "What was his name? The mangiacake[50] from California?"

"Now it's your turn to statte zitta," I groan, and she laughs even more. "I don't like him."

"Ignore your Nonna. Ma, that was back at Christmastime she liked Hunter. Last Christmas," Mom explains, doing her best to demonstrate her allyship. I appreciate it. "So, Vi, tell us, are you so thrilled?"

A twinge of joy cuts through the homesickness. "Sure, I am a little, I guess."

"Are grandmothers allowed to come see?" Nonna asks.

I chuckle. "No, Nonna. Sorry. The play is just for students and faculty. And the Board, I guess. And then there's the Art School Alliance people." My breath quickens with every utterance of "and."

"And have you started your new job yet?" my mother probes casually.

"Had my first shift on Saturday, but Mme. Camry just showed me around the archives."

"How was it?"

---

50 Roughly translated to "cake eaters," mangiacake is Italo-Canadian slang for Anglo-Canadians. Its origins are contested, but it is believed to stem from Italian immigrants' distaste for Canadian Wonder Bread, which is sweet (like cake).

"Fine."

"That's not an answer."

"There's not much to tell. We looked at shelves for thirty minutes and then I was dismissed." That really *was* all that happened. "Next week I'll get trained."

"But *how was it*? Do you get paid for the full hour?"

"Mother, please—" I'm interrupted (or saved) from my mother's work-related interrogation by Kay, who bursts into the bedroom belting out "Love on Top." I shush them. They mouth "who is it?"

"My mom," I answer at full volume, "and Nonna. Wanna say hi?"

"Is that Kay?" Nonna asks excitedly. "Is that their beautiful singing voice I heard?"

I sit up and put the phone on speaker, laying the receiver it in its cradle. "Mm-hm, it's Kay."

"How is they?" It's not that Nonna's transphobic, she's just confounded beyond reason about how to use they/them pronouns.

Kay laughs, not bothering to correct my grandmother. "I'm right here, Nonna, and I'm good!"

"They're actually composing the music for the play," I announce.

Kay rolls their eyes at me, knowing they're about to receive a barrage of questions and compliments not dissimilar to what I just got.

"Kay!" my mother yelps. "We're so proud of you! Will you be singing? Or playing an instrument?" I let my roommate answer a billion follow-up queries. The moon hovers above their shoulder outside. It's curved into a grin.

Chapter 11

In the dining hall the next day, I am greeted by the usual morning spread: snowy cloth napkins, decaf coffee, sugar cubes, and cornflakes, accompanied by the pleasant aroma of Earl Grey and clink of fine china. I run a hand through my wind-mussed hair and scan the room for Kay, instead accidentally locking eyes with Hunter in the pancake line. He waves. I blink him out of vision.

When I had a crush on Hunter Kinsey, I developed a sensor to detect where he was in any given room. Infatuation granted me a sixth sense, and I guess it's not the sort of thing you can just switch off. My brain understands that I don't like Hunter Kinsey anymore, but my body (much to my chagrin) doesn't run on logic. Even a glimpse of his golden locks in my periphery sparks an intense physical reaction. My stomach bursts with butterflies—and not in a cute way. These butterflies are like evil killer insects of doom and fire and mayhem.[51]

The dining hall is a repurposed church with a lofty exposed-beam ceiling and wide windows overlooking Raven Lake, which is today a cool cobalt under the September sky.

Once upon a time, I imagined Hunter and I getting married right here. A sugar-cube-scented ceremony to celebrate our unlikely love. Kay mocked me relentlessly for that, but, come on . . . this place is wedding-fantasy

51 Clinicians call this "anxiety."

fodder. To add to the gothic romance vibes, there's a small, sequestered graveyard in the courtyard behind the dining hall with only two tombstones, one each for the founder and his wife. At this point, the death markers are merely set dressing for the path that connects the dining hall to the library. Students walk by the bones of the lovers without thinking a morbid thought—the nearby buffet is a natural distraction.

Where teens once came to pray every Sunday, we now gorge ourselves on exceedingly okay food. Actually, that isn't entirely fair of me to say—lunch and dinner aren't anything special, but the breakfast banquet is reliably delicious. There's a pancake and waffle station with fresh whipped cream, cardamom-maple syrup, berries foraged on the island, and butter curved into careful swirls. Other hot tables gleam with silver trays of creamed spinach, plates of toast, bacon, and sausages (turkey, pork, beef), soft scrambled eggs, and boiled ones of varying doneness, still in their shells and hot from the stovetop. The cereal buffet is lined at the back with glass cases containing an assortment of General Mills's finest, plus tureens of porridge, dishes teeming with all the fixings—B.C. honey, dried currants, candied orange peels, raisins, a variety of nuts—a few carafes of hot water for tea, and four sizable canisters of coffee (light roast, medium, dark, and decaf). For obvious reasons (i.e., Hunter churning up my guts like butter), I decide against pancakes this morning, loading my tray with porridge, berries, and a single hard-boiled egg. It is already cracked on top, a web spreading along the shell.

Finding Kay in this sea of cedar tables and Covie-green button-ups is like locating Waldo. After some searching, I espy them sipping from a Victor mug[52] at the far back corner. I lock my eyes onto Kay, my North Star, looking very private-school chic in their DCAA rugby sweatshirt. They wear the same pleated skort as mine, only they've got knee-high socks where my hairy legs remain visible—I can't be bothered to shave, so I've appropriated my laziness into a feminist statement.

---

52 Insulated, dual-walled, and curved at the sides, these drinking vessels were originally made for the Navy to prevent coffee spills but are today used in diners across the Pacific Northwest.

Everyone clings onto any possible semblance of individuality by making the uniform their own. There are popped collars, undone buttons, trinity-knot neckties, and other passable dress code remixes.[53] Unfortunately, Dark Cove garb is unflattering on me no matter what I do.

After fighting my way through the entire student body—getting jostled and elbowed more than a few times on the way—I dramatically slam my breakfast tray onto the table. Kay has managed to find the only quiet spot in the caf, shaded by a thicket of pine trees encroaching the windows, away from the bustle of the hot-lunch counters. The patter of a just-starting rain outside.

"The guys in the Admissions Department need to accept fewer people. Too many limbs in this building," I complain uselessly, sliding onto the trestle bench opposite Kay. "I just narrowly dodged a goblet of grape juice."

Kay doesn't acknowledge my presence.

"Earth to Kay."

They place their mug down and palm a tangerine, rolling it lightly between their tan hands. "Sorry, what did you say?"

"Nothing important. You were up early this morning!"

They nod, eyes glazed over. "We've started six o'clock band practice. Mondays and Tuesdays."

"Jesus."

"It's the only times our schedules all line up." They begin peeling the tangerine in one long orange strand. A mist of citrus sprinkles the air. They separate a wedge from the fruit, plop it into their tea—another Kayism—and take a sip.

"Are you just tired or is something on your mind?" I ask, mirroring their motions as I peel the shell off my egg.

---

53 Dark Cove dress code is intended to obscure class divides among students, though the student body primarily comprises international imports hailing from high-income families. Hometowns include Manhattan, Rome, Stockholm, Seoul, London, Dubai, and Hong Kong.

Steam rises from their mug like a sigh. "I'm thinking about . . ." Kay says slowly, eyes brightening now, "what I want to be for Halloween." They begin eating the tangerine, not by the segment but by taking a bite right out of it.

I do the same to my egg, which burns my tongue. I place it back onto the plate. "And? What are the contenders?"

"Swamp Thing, a sheet ghost, the little climber girl from *Celeste*, or Buttercup."

"The flower or the Powerpuff Girl?"

"The toughest fighter, though I appreciate your unassuming nature."

"I appreciate how far ahead you plan for Halloween."

"Are you kidding? We've got like one month left—I'm running behind! There's nothing in this life I take more seriously than Samhain, my friend."

Of course, I already knew that. The first fall after I met Kay, Nonna was in the hospital[54] and Mom couldn't leave her bedside, so Kay's kokum invited me to go trick-or-treating with them. Kay and I haven't spent October 31st apart since. These days, we eat our weight in candy and watch horror flicks instead of going door to door, but we'll never age out of dressing up. It's our favorite holiday; we live for the camp, the aesthetics, the candy . . . it's kind of the glue that's kept us together (even when we were separated by the school's archaic gender divide).

Kay pushes their still-steaming mug across the table. I drink from it with caution. Peppermint. Undercurrents of tangerine. Like my egg, way too hot to be consumed any time soon. "What do *you* want to be for Halloween?" they ask.

"I'll be onstage, I guess." I blow on the tea, sending a pirouette of steam across the table. "Which works out, because I forgot to bring any costumes."

"Just pull a Magpie and steal one from the Theatre Department."

"I'm not rich enough to get away with stealing." Over at the Gaykeeper table a few benches away, Rue braids Frankie's hair into two twin plaits down her back. Frankie smiles serenely. Magpie catches me

---

54 Lung cancer.

goggling and returns my stare over her keto-friendly breakfast platter. She pushes herself off the table and makes her way toward Kay and me. "Speak of the—"

"Hey, Cursed Girl," Magpie says as she approaches our table. "Did you see the Society portrait yet?"

"Good morning to you too, Magpie," Kay mutters.

I brace myself for whichever trick the President has up her sleeve. "No, I haven't."

"Well, you blinked. Sorry. It's film. No do-overs." She looks at me expectantly. She wants a reaction. I don't give her one. "Just ... thought you'd like to know. I'd *die* if I knew I blinked. Those photos are basically historical documents."

"Well ... thanks for the heads-up."

"See you at the table read ... break a leg." Magpie gives a caustic look as she turns to leave. I lower my face into my porridge, but my appetite is quickly diminishing.

"Who shit in her smoothie bowl this morning?" Kay asks once Magpie is out of earshot.

"Have *you* heard of this Society curse before?"

"Duh."

I confess that it was news to me before recounting Magpie's prophetic threat yesterday.

"'October's end'? Well double, double, toil and trouble,"[55] Kay pauses to spit out a seed. "Violet, please. You're not going anywhere."

"How are you so sure?"

"Because you're my best friend. You're not allowed to leave me on this island alone."

"Sure." I give a tired smile. "That and curses aren't real."

---

55 From the famous rhyming couplets in Shakespeare's *Macbeth*, delivered by the prophetic Three Witches (a.k.a., "the weird sisters"): "Double, double toil and trouble; Fire burn and caldron bubble. Fillet of a fenny snake, In the caldron boil and bake; Eye of newt and toe of frog, Wool of bat and tongue of dog, Adder's fork and blind-worm's sting, Lizard's leg and howlet's wing, For a charm of powerful trouble, Like a hell-broth boil and bubble."

"You never believe in anything fun."

I point out that Ms. Spry must not believe in it, either. "She didn't cast any understudies."

"*Or* she didn't get the memo. Someone oughta tell her that the theatre's haunted. *And* that she unknowingly joined a freaky cult," they say, licking their fingers clean of tangerine juice.

"You joined the Society, too," I remind them.

"Yes, I *knowingly* joined the freaky cult." They shove me playfully from across the table. "And so did you."

"How long has this curse even been a thing for?"

"Probably as long as the Halloween Play has been a thing. The first case I can think of is that one girl, what's-her-face, the one who flew the coop in the nineties."

"What's-her-face?"

"Third-year student, she had one of those last names that sounds like a first name, let me think ..." Kay snaps their fingers a few times in quick succession to summon the name. It works. "Nora Ingrid! She was doing some special stunt from up in the rafters of Wincroft on the night before opening, the story goes. She was afraid of heights and begged to be roped down, and then beelined out of the theatre and into the forest. It was just a couple of years after the camp massacre, so everybody freaked, but it turned out she just left the island on a late-night ferry, never to be heard from again."

Though colorful, Kay's story does nothing to abate my slow-growing worry. "Is there a pattern?"

Kay shrugs. "Let's place bets. Hunter as the cursed one. What say you?"

"No way. Nothing bad ever happens to Hunter Kinsey." I tilt my head toward the boy in question. He sits at the center of his table in the middle of the caf like Jesus in *The Last Supper*. "You said it best, he's Dark Cove's pet golden retriever."

"It wasn't even that long ago that you were gushing about his biceps!"

"My *point* is, even if the curse *is* real—which it isn't—if anyone had to worry about it, it would be me." I stare down at my slightly congealed porridge. "Of *course* I would blink in the portrait."

"Stop right there, buster. I know the beginning of a spiral when I see it." They check their watch. "Let's go see the picture. We have time."

"What, fifteen minutes?"

"We can make it if we leave now."

"I'm not in the mood to get told off for being late just to see myself blinking in a picture."

"We *need* to see it to get this out of your head. Maybe it isn't so bad. That camera is *ancient*; there's no way you'll be able to tell. Magpie's just trying to mess with you."

"Fine. But I have first period with Mr. Mitchell on the other side of the building, so we have to run."

Kay slings their bag over their shoulder and reaches across the table. "Leave the gun, take the hand."[56]

We ditch our trays, darting past the Gaykeeper table (I think I hear Frankie saying "hi"), and the bro table, and a blur of others. Once clear of the dining hall, we make a mad dash through the rain to Accolade South, up to the crooked hallway that ends with room 13A. The portraits of Society's past flash by in a strange time warp that ends with our cohort. Crow at the window. Me: front row, blinking.

"I'm the only one who doesn't look perfect in this," I say, scanning every pair of eyeballs. "The *only* one."

"Okay, fine, we *can* see your eyes are shut, but look" —Kay points to the adjacent frame—"someone blinked last year, too."

I squint at the portrait, noting a half-lidded girl in the second row. "Who is that?"

"Never seen her in my life. But that's not the point. Other people blink too. Valuable life lesson here. I'm glad we made the tri—"

"You know everyone on campus, Kay. Maybe you've never seen her because she doesn't go here anymore."

"In the words of the great Shania Twain, 'don't be stupid.' There are a couple hundred kids on this island. I don't know *one,* sue me."

---

56 A remixed reference to *The Godfather* (1972).

I sidestep to the preceding portrait and then the one before that, poring over every sepia-toned face, every corner of the room. "Are you seeing this? In the window, every year, again and again, there's this crow . . ."

The bell rings.

My friend waves a hand in the space between my face and the 2002 Society portrait. "Okay, Inspector Violet, we need to run. Now."

"You go on without me," I say.

"What about Mr. Mitchell—"

"Seriously, just go."

Reluctantly, Kay leaves me alone in the crooked hallway, where I continue to examine every face within each frame.

2015, first-row blink, girl, crow in the window.

2014, second-row blink, girl, crow in the window.

2013, first-row blink, girl, crow in the window.

I make my way all the way back to the seventies before the second bell rings. For the last fifty years, there has been a crow in the window. For the last fifty years, there has been a single student—almost always a girl—blinking.

Appendix K

Excerpt, Dark Cove Arts Academy Code of Conduct

Rule #21

No running in the halls of any building on campus.

Chapter 12

I'm back in Wincroft Theatre. A crow flies by me, up to the rafters, and I think of how unusual that is, and then I feel worried for the poor thing for a moment before I have to feel worried for myself. Poor thing. The seats are mostly filled, more flesh than velvet in sight. My peers are whispering at a speed faster than light as I take my place on the marker center stage. The tape is in the shape of an X, and I think about treasure hunts and how treasure hunts seemed so relevant for a time of my life until suddenly they weren't. Like the fear of quicksand, which has since been traded for the fear of something more immediate, like rejection. The room looks black from here because the spotlight is right on me.

"Miss Costantino," comes the gruff voice of my acting teacher. "Whenever you're ready."

Right. My monologue. *The Lovely Bones.*

I press my eyelids together. Beneath them, a swirl of orange reminds me of Creamsicles, like the ones they sell at the cafeteria back home. I used to have one every day as a treat after lunch because they were just a dollar and tasted like summer. The kids started commenting about that, though, how I ate the ice cream every day, so the Creamsicles stopped tasting as good.

I open my eyes to the light and forget to breathe. I'm running out of time. I have to say something. Get in the right mindset. For the character.

My name is Salmon.

That isn't the line I start with, that's just a reminder to myself—Mr. Blake encourages us to tap into the reality and emotional life of the character.

The first line in my monologue is this:

Hope is what I had traded on in heaven and on Earth.

I don't say the words out loud, though.

Look what happens when you dream.

My eyes adjust to the light. I wish they hadn't.

The end came anyway.

Now I can see them: my professor, Frankie Lin, Magpie Black. Rupinder Sandhu, and the rest.

I began to see things in a way that let me hold the world without me in it.

"Miss Costantino? Whenever you're ready," I hear Mr. Blake say in the memory.

My ears were like oceans in which what I had known, voices, faces, facts, began to drown.

My breath catches in my throat like a wriggling fish. Salmon. Her words don't come, nothing does but the feeling of loneliness, followed by a never-ending streak of terror.

"I'm sorry," I say.

I wish you all a long and happy life.

A rush of laughter comes like wind turning the leaves on an old oak tree.

"I'm sorry," I say again. "Sorry."

The laughter is water now. White-water rapids and I can't breathe. I am crying. As soon as I realize it, I realize all of it: that whomever plays Salmon must be pretty enough to be pitiable, strong enough to root for. I am neither. I tear myself too easily off the stage to the morbid music of the laughter and the water and the snapping wings of that black crow up in the rafters. I am nothing as I flee from the theatre and across the wild grass, through a clump of mating gnats, more grass and gravel and weeds, I half-trip over the flagstone—no a gravestone, two gravestones—rushing like a downpour up to the half-empty dorm, up to the bathroom, the bathroom, if only I can make it to the bathroom.

Hovering over the sink, hands on porcelain, I feel at a crack under my finger. I look to my face, but I can't face myself: a ghost dwindling to nothing. I am in a vacuum. Nowhere. No one.

Raising my head to my reflection, I'm almost sure there won't be an image in the glass. But there I am. In the smoked glass, eyes closed, caught in the forever-hell of a sepia-toned blink.

Look what happens when you dream.

Fresh from the country of sleep, my body tremors in sweat-soaked sheets until I recalibrate myself with reality. My first nightmare of the semester. It's honestly unprecedented that the stress dreams have taken this long to kick in. My REM cycle typically keeps me coffin conscious year-round.

I peer through bleary eyes at the quiet dorm room; I vaguely recollect waking up already but must have fallen back asleep after Kay left. The clock reads 8:17 a.m. Class is in thirteen minutes and my face is a roadmap of sleep lines. Awesome. I throw on a wrinkled polo and a skort, lace up my Docs, stab two silver studs into my earlobes,[57] and make for the exit. A strong wind outside renders the front door heavier, harder to open. The fierce wind tosses up the hem of my skort, but thankfully no one's around to see this Marilyn Monroe moment. The strong current of cold air and that heavy gray sky warn of a storm.

57 The Dark Cove Arts Academy dress code mandates stud earrings only, a rule that is strictly enforced. In their first year, Kay once wore a pair of beaded earrings, which were confiscated by the end of first period. The headmaster only begrudgingly granted that the jewelry be returned to Kay after they explained the sentimental significance of the earrings, which were made by their kokum, and even then the earrings were returned only on the condition that Kay exclusively wear them outside of the classroom and after school hours.

This afternoon, the Dark Cove Theatre Society will have its first read-through of *A Midsummer Night's Dream.* Everything until then is just agonizing foreplay.

Crows circle overhead. Like a field mouse, I skitter across the dewy witchgrass[58] to Accolade South—no time for breakfast—and race down the stairs to the basement level. The rubber soles of my loafers produce an ear-splitting squeak on the freshly polished checkered floors. The vinyl pattern of black and white diamonds blurs together as I gain speed in the final stretch.

At this point, arriving to Mr. Norman's class on time is a pipe dream, but every passing second threatens detention.

"A bit late, are we?" Mr. Blake's voice comes from behind like a hammer in search of a nail. "*And* running in the hall. Has fame made a rule breaker out of you?"

I stop dead in my tracks, my Docs producing a piercing trill, and turn to face the man himself. Mr. Blake emerges from a faculty lounge like a town sheriff from the saloon. He's poised for a showdown, except instead of reeking of ale and gunpowder, he smells like mothballs and chalk dust.

"I'm sorry, sir, I got caught up in a bottleneck at the dining hall," I lie.

"I suppose congratulations are in order. You're officially a *leading lady* in the Dark Cove Theatre Society's Halloween Play. This Spry woman clearly sees something in you!" A gruff chuckle punctuates his joke. I wonder if I'm the punchline.

I stutter the start of a sentence that contains no real words.

"The pressure isn't already getting to you, is it? Buck up, girl. This is just the start of it. Remember what we talked about with the headmaster. Perseverance, yes?"

"Of course." I try on a tone of self-assurance. "Will you be at the table read this afternoon?"

---

58 Also known as panic grass or *Panicum capillare.*

"Not yet. Waste of time, at this stage, and I'm a busy man. Once you are all on your feet, that's when you'll see me in the room," he says brusquely. "I do look forward to sitting in. Our guest director made some . . . *interesting* casting choices." He unmistakably means "interesting" as an insult. Is he talking about the non-actors in the cast? Or is it the gender bending he's referring to? *Or,* I think, my heart racing like a wild rabbit in my chest, *he could be talking about me.*

I try to reply with some sort of witty remark, something to get me in on the joke, but there isn't enough oxygen in this basement to breathe, let alone speak. My lungs are hollowed out.

"If I catch you running in these halls again, Miss Costantino, you'll be given a detention slip. I can't make exceptions, even for starlets such as yourself. Consider this your first and last warning."

Blank, despondent, I nod, turn, and scamper on toward class, prepared to receive yet another reprimand upon arrival. A sense of dread looms over my shoulder like a ghost.

Is this what it feels like? To be cursed?

My eyes are closed, so I can't see anything, but here's the scene: One of the rehearsal studios has been set up for the Halloween Play table read. There is no table, just a vaguely satanic-looking ring of chairs, a candle lit at its center—the Dark Cove Theatre Society will never beat the cult allegations. Romeo the dog lounges by the door like a dragon on guard. The cast and a few of the designers all sit facing one another, but no one is permitted to look. We're supposed to be focusing on every sensation other than sight, but I'm having trouble concentrating on anything other than my extremely loud internal monologue.

I am not thinking about the curse. I am not thinking about my panic attack. I am not thinking about what Mr. Blake said. I am not thinking about—

"I want you to take a deep breath in, all the way into your belly," Ms. Spry says in a soft, yoga-instructor voice. "Feel the air in your lungs, feel your diaphragm expand and contract. Your ribs, your belly. If it helps, place your palms on your stomach."

Bodily awareness has never been my strong suit. Instead of following orders, I clutch tightly to a tattered copy of *A Midsummer Night's Dream*. I borrowed it from the library. It's soft, with a long rip in the center of the cover and a bit of hard plastic on its spine where the Dewey Decimal label is.

"What do you smell?"

Parchment. Wax. Notes of Frankie's floral perfume from two seats away. I flare my nostrils a little. There's the sound of a girlish snicker. Is someone laughing at me? I want to take a peek, but I resist the urge. On high alert now, I instead pull my shoulders back and straighten my slouch.

"One final breath in ... out ... and now I invite you all to come back to the room whenever you feel ready."

I beam my eyes open. A quick scan of the room tells me I'm the first to follow our director's orders. Ms. Spry winks at me (though it's more of a blink). The others slowly reanimate, shaking off their various states of zen. Hunter erupts in an exaggerated yawn. Next to him, Michael follows suit. I barely repress the reptile-brain urge to do the same.

"How do you feel?"

Ms. Spry's question was presented to the whole class, but Rue answers like it was directed solely at her. "Refreshed. Alert. Present."

"I feel the opposite," Hunter remarks. "Nap time!" He leans his golden head on Michael's shoulder and fake snores. All the girls giggle at the boys except for the Gaykeepers and me, then Margaret stops laughing when she sees Frankie isn't. Ms. Spry, oblivious to the teenage politics at play, grins politely.

"Better go splash some water on your face, hon," she says. "It's time for our table read! We're just gonna work our way through the script from top to bottom to get a feel for the text. I'll do stage directions. I want you to write down any thoughts, ideas, questions, memories, or anything else that might come up for you as we go, and we'll set aside some time to share all that good stuff at the end of rehearsal. Sound good?"

A small chorus of "mm-hm"s. I hear myself chime in, though I would say this sounds less "good" than "highly triggering."

"Here we go." Ms. Spry fans the candle with her script from a safe distance. The flame turns into a thin column of smoke, which drifts up in a nervous dance at the center of our circle. "Enter Theseus, Hippolyta, and Philostrate, with others."

Act 1, scene 1 begins, and the actors are already doing the absolute most. The who's-the-best competition has begun, just as Shakespeare intended it. It's primal, like a mating ritual or fencing match. Entertaining to spectate. But that doesn't mean I want a part in it.

"What say you, Hermia?" reads Margaret, the unfortunate girl from Playwriting class. She delivers every one of Theseus's lines with an upward inflection. "Demetrius is a worthy gentleman?"[59]

"So is Lysander," Mag says, dropping her usual Valley-girl lilt for the role of Hermia. This is her first line in the play, and she's already wiping away a tear.

Frankie, as Demetrius, opts for a more subtle performance right off the bat. "Relent, sweet Hermia, and, Lysander, yield Thy crazed title to my certain right." Every word is uttered calmly, naturally, like she isn't even trying at all. I study her out of the corner of my eye, wishing I could figure out how she does it. What it takes to crack the code to confidence.

"You have her father's love, Demetrius," Hunter says, projecting his voice so it bounces off the studio walls. Shakespeare sounds like a foreign language on his slang-happy tongue. "Let me have Hermia's. Do you marry him."

Hunter's slightly overripe Lysander performance somehow irritates me less than Mag's Hermia does.[60] She's still crying. "Belike for want of rain, which I could well Beteem them from the tempest of my eyes."

It's almost time for me to unsheathe my foil and enter the piste. Anticipation builds as the cast progresses swiftly through the text. My eyes are trained on the words now, but they begin to quiver in my grip.

---

59 This is not a question in the script, but for the sake of conveying intonation, a question mark feels more appropriate.

60 Is this thought a result of mankind's vestigial drive toward gendered competition for a mate? Or is it merely a product of institutional misogyny? Discuss.

Adrenaline may be useful in sport, less so in this instance. I hear Hermia agree to meet Lysander to marry, which means . . .

"Look, here comes Helena," says Hunter.

The stiffly starched collar of my uniform chokes me.

"Godspeed, fair Helena. Whither away?" There's an unfamiliar kindness in Magpie's voice.

"Call you me 'fair'? That 'fair' again unsay. Demetrius loves your far—I mean, fair!" Of course I made a mistake in the first line. From there, I keep messing up the rhythm and stumbling over my words even when they're right on the yellowed pages in my hands. "O, teach me how you art and with what art—sorry, um—teach me how you look and with what art you sway the motion of Demetrius' heart!"

The niggling thought of the curse sits at the back of my throat like a choking hazard. I recall how my panic attack felt: uptempo heartbeat, tingling limbs, star-spangled vision. These sensations threaten a full-fledged remanifestation. I swallow them down. I try to conceal my panting the best I can. My chest's rapid rise and fall betray me. Not once do I dare look up from the book in my hands. I focus on the hard, unyielding serif type. My next line looms like the naked blade of a guillotine.

The rest of the scenes go on for an indiscernible length of time, but not a second passes that I'm not wishing this whole thing was over already. I lose myself in a haze of anxiety during most of Helena's scenes. After what seems like forever, Rue reads off Puck's closing monologue and it's done.

Hunter applauds and whoops, joined by Ms. Spry. "Yes, you can clap! You guys deserve this," she says. "Every step in this process is an accomplishment."

Others begin to snicker, cheer, and huzzah, but my wild heartbeat muffles it all out.

"I want you to stew in your initial reactions for a bit and write down every thought you have in your journals." Here, the room fills with the din of notebooks being extracted from rucksacks. "What ideas do you have? What do you know about your character? What do you know about this world? There's no right or wrong here, just pour it all out onto the page and we can discuss after."

Grateful for any excuse to retreat into a book, I pen some basic facts about *A Midsummer Night's Dream.* It's a comedy set in Athens. There is an upcoming wedding. There are six actors in a play within the play. There are four lovers. There is a woodland, inhabited by fairies who meddle with the actors and lovers all.

At the beginning, Helena loves Demetrius, Demetrius and Lysander love Hermia, and Hermia loves Lysander. When Hermia and Lysander run away to the forest to be together, Demetrius follows, and Helena chases after. There's some fairy drama, and the lovers are caught in the middle of it. Lysander and Demetrius, enchanted by a love potion, are now enamored with Helena. More drama ensues. In the end, the spell breaks, a wedding happens, the actors' play happens, and everybody—fairy and human—lives happily ever after. Fin.

Ms. Spry springs up from her cross-legged position and begins pacing outside of the ring of chairs like we're about to play a game of duck, duck, goose. "Okay, guys, who feels ready to share?"

There's a long beat, which isn't a common occurrence at Dark Cove. Usually, one of the girls would pipe up immediately. But today, we're in the company of boys.[61] Their presence looms large. The girls sit uncomfortably, like porcelain dolls on a shelf.

Hunter is the first to speak. "Well, I was kinda thinking that—"

A window on the far wall bursts open with a sudden gust of air. Outside, a nasty storm has been brewing. Startled, Romeo leaps up to bark at the disturbance. "It's all right, you big galoot, calm down." Ms. Spry attempts to soothe her gargantuan companion, whose barks soften into quiet-but-still-protective woofs. Hunter goes to shut the window without waiting to be asked.

As he fusses with the rusty latch, Frankie gives her two cents.

---

61 Classes and dorms are gender segregated; however, extracurricular events (e.g., Society rehearsals, the Spring Fling, mealtimes, etc.) are co-ed.

"I will say I'm really excited to work with all of you," she says, a page of enthusiastic scrawl spread out on her lap. "I know that isn't a real discovery, but that's what I felt during this read. Like, I can't wait to discover *with* you all." She stretches her arms open wide to invite a group hug in. Her fingers graze my shoulder. Gooseflesh covers my body like a cold mist. One final draft blows in before Hunter slams the window shut.

"Anyways, as I was saying, there's a lot of fun wordplay," he finishes, returning to the circle. "Some kind of dirty lines."

"Kissing 'the wall's hole'?" Michael trades back-slaps with Hunter. As far as I know, these two are not friends, but they seem to have established a makeshift brotherhood as two of the only non-theatre (and non-gay) males in the cast. The only two other guys have been excluded from the brotherhood, it seems; they aren't laughing at Michael's crude observation.

Mag sniffs. "Yes, I also made some textual discoveries in this read."

Must. Not. Roll. Eyes.

"I think my biggest obstacle," Rue says, "will be adjusting to the rhythm of iambic pentameter, calculating where the stresses are and what that might tell us about the character."

"I swear, it'll all come naturally the more we do this," Ms. Spry exclaims, her face glowing with enthusiasm (though it could just be some luminizer applied to her high cheekbones). "You'll get to know the intention behind what you're saying, and that'll drive the delivery. Then you'll get a hang of the meter. It's no sweat. You know, Mr. Blake wrote me a letter inviting me to direct this show. In that letter, he said, *The Halloween Play sweetens the exile we have brought upon ourselves.* And since getting here, it's just been—what? a couple weeks?—but in this short time I can already tell how real that is. This island is super isolating, but theatre has the power to connect us. That's all this is about. Connection. Don't think too hard. This is supposed to be fun, guys. Remember that!"

This is supposed to be fun, I tell myself, surveying the elated faces of my peers. They all shoot up from their seats when the church bell rings.

"Fairies and Mechanicals, I'll see you for a rehearsal tomorrow. Lovers, I'll see you Friday. Stack up your chairs before heading out," Ms. Spry shouts over the din of excitement, parting words, and jokes that I'm not in on. I sneeze and hope that it's just Romeo's dander and not that I'm catching a cold. I wrap myself with my school cloak, gather my things, and slot my chair onto the shortest tower.

"Pretty early for a line fumble," Magpie leers at me, placing her chair on top of mine with a loud clang of metal on wood. "But, then again, that's a pretty regular occurrence for you, Cursed Girl."

I don't even acknowledge her. She isn't worth it.

"Violet," Ms. Spry calls, "can you stay here for a couple minutes? Quick chat, I promise."

This can't be good. I don't dare look at Magpie, but I can imagine the told-you-so look on her face. When the door clicks shut with the President's departure, there are two chairs left unstacked. Ms. Spry cuts right to the chase: "How's everything going?" Her eyes are large, unblinking, and notably readable. Almost like a child who hasn't yet learned how to conceal their emotions. She's concerned, but no wrinkles mark her complexion. How old is she? Seriously, has someone carded her? "Is everything okay?"

"Everything is fine."

"But is it awesome sauce?" she asks. No need to card her—her vernacular is definitely from a different generation.

"Yup, awesome sauce," I assure her, but not very convincingly.

"Well that's all good, then. I just wanted to check in. You seemed maybe a little nervous today. Totally normal to feel jittery for the first read, but as I said, I wanted to check in."

"I guess, sure, I feel a bit nervous. Just . . . out of my element." Romeo nudges his wet snout under my hand, begging for attention. I scratch behind his soft ears.

"You seemed in your element in the audition room. What's different now?"

"It's nothing. Probably just because we were on our feet before. I'll be better next time."

"Oh, don't worry about that." She places a French-manicured finger onto her pout. "And what's this curse business all about?"

Ah, she heard Magpie.

"It's stupid. Just a stupid legend."

"That's all?"

I shrug, but Ms. Spry waits for a verbal answer. "People didn't expect me to get the part, and now it's a joke. All in good fun." I don't enjoy defending Magpie, but I don't want this to turn into a thing. "Honestly, I didn't expect to get the part either, so . . ."

"Why not?"

Another shrug.

Ms. Spry closes her eyes, understanding, nodding. "You deserve to be here as much as anyone else."

"Sure. I'll just have to prove that over time."

"That's a lot of pressure. Proving yourself."

"It'll be fine."

A long silence. Ms. Spry taps the chair next to her for me to sit in. I do, but I keep my backpack on, mentally plotting conversational escape routes. "You know, it's okay to make mistakes. That doesn't mean you're cursed, or whatever the kids are saying." She cackles at herself here, as if "cursed" is a bit of newfangled slang.

I intend on joining her with a pity laugh, but words spill out instead. "Every time I think I'm making progress I screw up."

Her smile falters. "That's just part of the process. Learning. Growing. I've been in your shoes, hon. Not even that long ago. Failure is super natural."

"Supernatural?"

"As in *very* natural. And it's easy to get in your head about it. I know that too well. That's why I've got Romeo here." His ears perk up adorably. "He's my emotional support dog. I call him my XD dog, 'cus he keeps me smiling. Looks like he's warmed up to you pretty quick, too!"

I make an effort not to cringe at the emoticon reference. I reframe it from embarrassing to endearing. The Great Dane sighs heavily, lying down at my feet. "He isn't so bad himself."

"He's great at sensing people's emotions. I think that's how he found me. We were in this terrible production of *Annie* together—an ex of mine directed it—and Romeo wouldn't leave my side. It's like he knew

I was having a hard time. Honestly, that experience was a huge part of why I stopped acting and started teaching."

"What happened?"

"Long story short, that ex was really awful to me, but he was a big deal in the New York theatre world. He still is. When I finally told some of the head honchos at the company that this guy shouldn't be in a position of power, they talked in circles. Basically said they needed proof or they couldn't do anything." Ms. Spry blinks away a stray memory like an eyelash, and then her oversized eyeballs fix themselves on me with an unsettling intensity. She gets the conversation back on track: "The nerves I had around that whole situation never left me. I kept trying, but I knew it wasn't good for me. I wasn't enjoying it anymore. So I took myself out of that environment. I left theatre and went to work in film."

"You had to leave and he gets to keep working in the industry?"

"I accepted that it was time for me to stop. People called me a quitter, said I didn't have what it takes, yadda yadda yadda. The thing no one tells you is that giving up is sometimes a really honorable and brave choice," she muses. "It's a choice that takes guts, for sure."

"But it isn't fair," I insist, "that you had to leave. That people are criticizing *you*."

"I can't say it doesn't bother me sometimes. But leaving was what was best for *me*. I know that, and I know who I am, so it doesn't matter what anyone says about me after I've left. And now, I want to empower the next generation of women in the industry to make their own choices about their artistic careers." She leans in an inch closer. "Listen, you can't let your fears get in the way before you even try. Find out if you like it . . . work through the emotions a little. You might surprise yourself. If you make mistakes, you can always course correct, right? And if it's not for you, you need to listen to your heart, your gut. You can always back out down the line."

I know this is supposed to be heartening, but it isn't. The curse sprouts up from my brain stem, a bad seed in bloom. "I have a hard time discerning my gut instincts from my fears, I guess."

"Maybe journal about it?" she suggests. "I probably say the word 'journal' more than any other human being ever, but it's just a suggestion.

Journaling helps me get in touch with my intuition. It's a great creative tool. I've even gotten ideas for the show by free writing."

"What ideas?"

"Casting ideas! Props. Costumes ... me and the designer are thinking pajamas! A little PJ party. But old-timey. Victorian frills and all that. Do you likey?"

"The comfier, the better."

"Now, there's another thing we have in common. Me? Can't wait to get out of these shoes." She casually gestures to what I'm pretty sure are six-inch Jimmy Choos. I chuckle, and she takes the laughter as a sign that I can relate to her struggle. In fact, I've never worn heels higher than two inches for longer than ten seconds—that's the time it took to try them on at my town's Walmart, at my mother's request. Ms. Spry and I have little in common, no matter how hard she tries to convince me otherwise. Still, I can tell she's trying to get on my level, and even though it's very awkward, I appreciate it.

The window blows open again. A crow sits on the sill making a sort of clicking sound. I leap out of my seat.

"Hon, what are you so afraid of?" Ms. Spry asks me.

"Everything."

She says nothing, her expression doubtful.

"I'm serious. You name it, I'm afraid of it. Failure, rejection, drowning, earthquakes, climate change, bears ... even stupid things." I hesitate. "This Dark Cove curse—"

Ms. Spry produces another brief, explosive burst of laughter. That such a small woman can make such a big noise is remarkable. "You weren't kidding when you said 'everything.'" She drapes her arm lightly over my slumped shoulders—this is a joke I'm actually in on. "When it comes to rejection et cetera, I've learned that those fears will kind of always be there. But it's exposure therapy, doing this. Those little nagging thoughts quiet down when you start putting yourself out there. You start to understand yourself. Who is Violet? What's she really afraid of? What does she love, hope for? The answers to these questions will probably change over time. But let's find out who you are today. This afternoon. Once you start figuring that out, you might be able to tell when it's your instincts talking. And selfishly, I want to see more of *her*. Violet. Let's bring *her* to the character and see what happens. Because I bet it'll be magic."

I shuffle uncomfortably at the edge of the seat, my backpack taking up most of the real estate. "Sure, guess I can try figuring it out."

"As for the earthquakes and bears, they say we fear what we don't understand. What's the saying? 'Know thine enemy'? I bet, with a little research, the fears will become less scary. And if you want, you can look up ways to protect yourself. Just in case."

Research. Now *that* is something I know I can do.

Chapter 13

A low thunder rumbles outside. The radiators in the archives are clanking, dripping, and hissing to no avail; I'm cold to the bone. Another sneeze. This is my second shift—third, if you count the first time I went down—in the archives, so I've learned that a sweater is imperative. I flip the collar of my rugby shirt up for extra warmth. Mme. Camry blows down the iron steps like an Arctic wind.

"Violet," she says in her deep Parisian accent. "Last week, I have show you 'ow this files are organized.[62] Today, I show you the process which we discussed. Now is when the real work begins."

"Yes, madame."

"Bon." She places a bony hand on a stack of folders piled higher than the desktop computer screen. "You will digitize these." Mme. Camry turns on the computer. We wait for ten nearly wordless minutes as it boots up. "As you can tell, the 'eadmaster isn't fond of the new technology."

Understatement of the year. There are thousands of files in this room. For some reason, it's been decided that I should start at *H*, probably because that's the shelf nearest to the desk. I scan the tabs of the files at the top of the stack: Bernadette Hanks, Xander Harvey, and so

62 Alphabetically, then by year.

on. I offer Madame the swivel chair to sit on but she blows a dismissive raspberry. She instead hunches over the desk uncomfortably, I assume because she doesn't plan to stay long. On the other hand, it may be that her tweed pencil skirt prevents her from sitting at all. She clicks at the bibliographic data storage program the school has opted to use. She tells me to just focus on grades.

"What do I do with the medical records and all these other notes?"

With the pointed toe of her heel, she nudges a shredder toward me. It takes her fifteen minutes to demonstrate uploading a single student file from the year 1997. I could probably do it in five myself, but the software has its limitations, having been developed around the turn of the century.

Once Mme. Camry is satisfied that I understand the functions of this ancient device well enough, she outlines the strict rules I must abide by when using the computer. "Do not, 'ow you say, surf the internet. Do not click on these images"—she means icons—"they are not required for this work. Donc, ne touche pas. D'accord?"

Stifling my amusement at the technological ineptitude of the people who run this school, I drag the cursor to the envelope *image*. "I can just take these shortcuts off the desktop if—"

She swats my hand off the mouse. "Ne. Touche. Pas."

"Yes, madame."

No sooner than she says "bon" am I left alone in the gray glow of a computer screen and an inundation of *H* names. There are about ten papers of information per student, each one revealing intimate facts about the Covie in question. It's a voyeuristic job, but the best part, I quickly discover, is placing the documents into the shredder after they've been digitized.

On occasion, I recognize a student name, the ones who have gone on to achieve greatness, fame, fortune, etc. It figures that they notably received perfect marks and praise from Mr. Blake. I take particular care with these files, poring over every morsel of information: their grades, their class choices, hell, even their blood type. Primarily, I study the comments they received from professors, entering each letter carefully into the blank pixelated textboxes. “Harcroft exceeds expectations with his ability to tap into breath as an emotional resource”; “Huxley defines his actions and intentions before even arriving to class, they are clear from moment to moment onstage, and he demands the same from his peers”; “Hyde watches his fellow actors closely, at all times, listening always, whether or not the scene at play is directly relevant to his work. This steadfast of patience and vigilance is rarely demonstrated by young actors.”

Instead of shredding these student files, I decide to keep them. For reference. It’s a blatant infraction on my contract, but I need all the help I can get. Besides, who’s going to notice that I saved a few papers from the recycling bin? It’s Warren Manzi’s perfect crime, except I won’t get caught.[63] I slip the files into an empty manilla folder. On the left side, which I have labeled “GOOD,” I’ll keep all the notable student records of those who have succeeded. On the right side, labeled “BAD,” I’ll store the dropouts and failures. (A very advanced system of organization, I know.) Here, in the underbelly of the school and inhaling a vast accumulation of dust, I have found the solution to my problem. It’s a cheat code, a guide for what to do and what *not* to do. I don’t need a rabbit’s foot or protective charm to ward off the Dark Cove curse—I can outsmart it. Embody the traits of the brightest alumni, avoid the pitfalls of the duds, and there’s no chance of failure.

It’s simple: I have to be the best.

“Babe, you’re so missing the point of what she was saying,” Kay says over dinner after I tell them about my good/bad folder. They wipe tomato sauce off their chin with a white cloth napkin, trimmed with Covie green threading.

“She told me to research how to protect myself. *Know thine enemy.* That’s what I’m doing.”

63 In Manzi’s thriller play *Perfect Crime* (1987), detective James Ascher exposes a wife’s elaborate and brilliant cover-up for the death of her husband.

"She didn't tell you to compile this excessive, undoubtedly prohibited and, honestly, kinda creepy folder." Kay waggles their fork at me from across the table. "You're supposed to *understand* your fears."

"This is my way of doing that." I kick my bag with the toe of my boot. "Even grabbed a book about Dark Cove wildlife to address the bear thing."

"Okay, that's a start. But you might wanna think about why you, the mocker of all things supernatural, are suddenly so afraid of this curse."

"I don't *believe* in it. This folder is just my insurance policy." I stab at the kitchen staff's sad attempt at a meatball. "It's only for, like, a month. After Halloween, I'll know I'm safe and shred it all. You can even watch me do it."

"All right." They drop their look of disapproval, leaning in a little closer over our twin mountains of spaghetti. "Well, at least tell me if you've gleaned anything juicy in your sleuthing endeavors."

"Not sleuthing. It's mostly straightforward stuff. Plus, they're all old student files."

"No dirt on current students?"

"Nope. Alumni only. Nothing exciting goes on in the DCAAAF."

Kay snickers to themself. "Figures that *the decaf* wouldn't be exciting."

"Good one." Lowering my voice to a whisper, I say, "But it does seem the teachers have eyes everywhere. They see what we do out of class. They keep our medical records, club memberships, even dorm call logs."

Kay slurps up a long strand of spaghetti, their mountain diminishing by the second. "Like, transcripts of calls?"

"No. They don't listen in or anything, but they keep track of how long you spend on the phone. It's like it's a scale for how homesick you are"—I nudge my pasta bowl across the table—"you can finish that. Now that we're talking about it, maybe I should keep those logs, just in case."

"Okay, I can see your rationale for keeping the report cards. But I will not let you become the Call Log Lady of Dark Cove."

"You're right, you're right. But also, Log Lady is an icon."

"Knew I never should have shown you *Twin Peaks*."

"Kay, you begged me to watch that show."

They snort, mid-noodle-slurp. "Call logs are just a thing billing companies send, babe. Probably just a budgetary consideration. Either that or this whole island is an Orwellian experiment."

"I'm partial to the Orwell theory."

"Better tell Nonna to cut down on the phone calls, then."

"I'll tell her tonight. God, I miss her cooking. And your kokum's."

"Don't remind me," Kay says, polishing off my spaghetti dregs. "This food . . . it leaves something to be desired."

"'That's because it isn't made with love,'" I say, quoting Nonna. I skip over dinner and go straight to dessert: two chocolate éclairs with sugared purple flowers atop. The icing is so smooth you can almost see yourself reflected in it. I pluck one from the porcelain plate and take a small bite. Creamy vanilla custard oozes out. "These are delicious, actually."

Kay grabs one from the plate and chews fastidiously. Their eyes close as they make a sound of appreciation. "We'll always have éclairs."

Appendix L

Excerpt, *Dark Cove: A History* by Marian King

CHAPTER TWENTY-TWO: Flora and Fauna

[. . .] The bear and coyote populations were managed and eliminated prior to the establishment of the school in 1892 by a dedicated team of off-island hunters, resulting in an uptick of rabbits and deer in subsequent years. [. . .] Coyotes were reintroduced to restore ecological balance.

Chapter 14

For the first few rehearsals, we're using the big studio at the top floor of Accolade South, the same one where callbacks were held. The room has black rubber flooring and a long mirror wall, which I am not particularly fond of because I don't like to be reminded of how I look during movement sessions. This is our second rehearsal since the read through last week, and we begin with a warm-up in which Ms. Spry encourages absurd, full-body movements "to loosen up [our] body and spirit." You can tell Mr. Blake thinks it's all hogwash, but he's uncharacteristically quiet in these rehearsals. For the most part, he remains postured in tight-lipped observation.

"Each rehearsal, a different cast member gets to choose the music for our groove sesh," Ms. Spry explained last week. "The idea is that, by opening night, we'll have curated the ultimate pre-show playlist."

For today's "groove sesh," Michael is quick to volunteer as DJ. "Can I play a song with explicit words?"

That gets a laugh from Ms. Spry. She's easy to please, it seems. "Why not? Shakespeare's all about playing with language!" Blake chokes on something, but the noise is drowned out by the music blasting from the studio speakers. Michael tells us it's Baby Keem, an artist I'd heretofore never listened to, though I'm into whatever this song is. While the dancers make a show of their skill, dashing across the studio floor like birds of paradise, I self-consciously wiggle in the corner opposite from Mr. Blake. The files in the archive made no indication of what type of dance moves he approves of. Thankfully, he doesn't seem to be watching.

"Take up the whole space! Don't just stay in one area of the room. Touch every square inch of this floor," Ms. Spry commands, her orders punctuated by the thick drumbeat. "Use every square inch of your body!" The boys laugh at the unintended innuendo. Ms. Spry, oblivious to the boys' crude interpretation of her words, says, "If it's easier, find someone to groove with!"

As I tentatively step into the center of the room, a warm hand meets my elbow. "May I have this dance?" Hunter asks all over again. "And before you warn me, I already know about your two-left-feet sitch-y-ation."

"Um." Before I can get an actual word out, he takes my cold-sweat hand in his warm one and charges across the studio, punching his free arm straight ahead. "Okay, I guess we're doing this. What do you call that move?"

"The Superman," he says simply.

In the mirror, I see myself grinning, swinging my arms wildly in the air.

"And that's . . . the Spider-Man?" Hunter laughs.

"If I'm getting superpowers, I'd rather invisibility. Much more useful." My feet take me in a new direction, away from Hunter and the mirrored wall.

"You're totally missing the point of superheroes, Vi. Luckily, I've seen every DC and Marvel movie ever, so I can explain it to you: superheroes *help* people. Right? You being invisible would be a crime against mankind," he calls over the music, and that's exactly when the track skips and stutters like a scratched CD even though the music is coming from Ms. Spry's MacBook. Baby Keem's voice distorts into a low, slow demonic thing. A discordant growl. Everybody freezes.

The laptop is mercifully slammed shut and the music stops. Ms. Spry tucks it away in her designer saddlebag. "I'll pretend that wasn't super freaky and take it as a sign from the universe to get rehearsal started. Places!"

I wince and wonder if everyone heard what Hunter just said, or if I even heard him correctly myself.

When we finish our last scene, I'm totally spent. My body is heavy and satisfied with its work, my brain is a wrung-out sponge. I gave this rehearsal every bit of my mental and physical attention, making a show of watching my castmates intently at all times. Not for a moment did my focus waver, and Mr. Blake noticed, I think; he gave me what I interpreted to be a small, almost imperceptible nod of approval sometime during Act 3, one that could signal my inauguration into his good books. To be seen.

Once he's gone, I relax onto the studio floor with the other actors, all lolling about. I'm currently using Romeo as a headrest.

"I know we're super sleepy, because you guys threw yourself totally into the work today, and I'm *sososososo. so* proud of you, but I have some homework to assign," Ms. Spry begins, and everybody stifles a collective groan.

"Isn't our homework to be off book for tomorrow?" Hunter asks, rubbing his eyes like a kid at the kitchen table waiting for his mom to pour him cereal.

"All right, two homework assignments," Ms. Spry concedes. "Don't worry, it's fun stuff! We have to start thinking about our individual characters' motivations. What does your character want in each scene? And what is their superobjective—what do they want more than anything? How do they go about getting the thing that they want more than anything? Do your actioning,[64] or just try getting to know your character in whatever way works for you—you have a world of options. Try writing a poem from your character's point of view! Or, if you're more of a visual artist, make a mind map! Get creative with it!"

This time, none of us hold back the groans rumbling in our chests.

Ms. Spry laughs. "Oh, come on guys, it's fun!"

"Take it as a compliment, Miss," Hunter says. "We don't complain in front of any of the other teachers."

---

64 Actioning is a process in which actors allocate an active verb or intention to each line. A strong action verb is one that is "done to" another character (e.g., beg, tease, threaten).

"In that case . . ." she replies softly with a grin before calling us up onto our feet and into a circle. (Ms. Spry evidently loves circles.) Someone more merciful might just let us go and enjoy our evenings. Instead, she invites us to play a game she calls the "I can't wait" game. It's exactly how it sounds: everyone has to say something that they're excited about.

"I'll start," she offers. "I can't wait to see this play come together . . ."

Rue is about to volunteer when there's a soft clatter right behind me, out of sight. Everyone looks over to investigate the source of the mysterious sound. Romeo lopes around to sniff out the room, but it's littered with the usual smattering of folding chairs, backpacks, scripts, shoes, and props. His search yields no clues. It's as if the disturbance happened in a different room in a distant dimension, but its imprint on this room in this dimension brings Ms. Spry's attention to me. How lucky.

"Um, I can't wait to go relax," I say. Sleep is the only future event I can think of right now that doesn't freak me out. At least the answer comes off as a joke; a few people even laugh. Ms. Spry just stares at me, waiting for the serious answer. "There's this spot on campus I really like to go to," I add. "A beautiful, quiet willow tree."

Excerpt, V. Costantino's Acting Journal

September 27

OK, so Ms. Spry told me to write down things I'm afraid of and things I love so, here you go, Ms. Spry . . .

THINGS I'M AFRAID OF

1. Coyotes
2. Deep water
3. Heights
4. Falling off the stage in the middle of a show
5. A variety of other embarrassing scenarios
6. Rejection
7. Ending up alone
8. Ending up like my mom
9. Ending up like any woman in my freaking bloodline
10. Blood
11. Every movie in the Saw franchise
12. Acting in a movie and not being able to cry on command
13. Crying in front of people
14. Losing
15. Dying
16. Everything

Chapter 15

I like to know my escape routes before I enter any place or situation. For this reason, I generally prefer open spaces or corners with an unobstructed view of the door. This willow tree is the best of both worlds. It gives me something sturdy to put my back against while offering exits from every angle. My locus of safety and control on this island, the willow stands tall on a foothill overlooking campus. In the afternoon, its shadow stretches out across the distance between it and Accolade South. Its branches have the bulbous knuckles of a protective hand. The grass at its base is soft and usually dry under the cover of leaves. I position my back to the rising peak of Mount Caliban so I can see if anyone comes my way. (Besides the occasional Vis student looking for a good spot to follow their muse, hardly anyone ever does.)

This is my watchtower. From here, everything is bite-sized yet impeccably rendered. Here, see the sloping hills and twisting paths, count the few prematurely bare trees, follow the branches splitting off into twigs like a map to every possible outcome.

It's with a comforting sense of detachment that I observe my ant-sized peers. I could spend hours just sitting and watching, but there's just too much to do. I'm behind on Mr. Mitchell's readings, and it wouldn't be a bad idea to go over the *Midsummer* script to figure out all of Helena's objectives, fill in the action verbs. What does she really want, beyond all things? Surely "love" is too simple an answer. If the files on the fatter, fortune-favored side of my good/bad folder have taught me anything, it's to listen for what isn't being said out loud.

I scour a patch of grass, brushing my fingers through dried strands in search of clues or distractions. I find one of the latter: a cunningly concealed bird's nest in the shape of a dome. It's vacant, made of bracken, heather, fine roots, and dead leaves. Its residents have left for the season, I guess. This bird left when it knew it had to.

I wonder if that's all the curse is: nothing supernatural, just a student's instinctual understanding of one's time to go. Again, I find myself wishing I was able to tell the difference between my anxiety and my instincts. Surrounding Dark Cove is an invisible archipelago of my imagination, each island another threat composed of razor-sharp rock, floodplains, sinkholes, and mean cliff faces.

A small breath; *I'm safe. I'm here.* I pat my bag, the good/bad folder tucked inside. *I'm prepared.*

Back to my director's non-assignment: write down everything I fear and everything I love. The spine of my notebook cracks loudly. Let's begin with the fears. They come to me easily, sprouting freely from my pen like blood from a wound. Every point on the list stings like a gash, too, but by the time I've reached the bottom of the page, the pain is over.

Like my willow tree here, writing provides a safe distance. That's what's always drawn me to it: you can take a feeling, a memory, a dream, a concept, anything at all, and displace it. The writer is able to label the anything, translate it by assigning words to its components, transmute it into something beautiful or ugly or neutral, even. The writer can contain the anything.

Live performance, on the other hand, is far messier. It blows the anything up and throws the actor in the consequential crater. The actor is left to push every boulder, every rock up and out of the hole. Only once the actor has cleared out all the debris is it time for curtain call.

Fade to black. Then back at it again the next night. It's Sisyphean.[65] And yet, every time, something is different—I'm learning that in rehearsal.

A strong wind turns the page of my notebook.

Onto the love list. This one isn't hard to compile either, though it still makes my chest ache. Of course, I begin with my nonna. Kay. My mom … the rest of the points follow at an accelerated pace, ink flowing breathlessly from my pen. As if the writing has broken down some sort of dam, tears prick at my eyes. But I don't stop until I hear approaching footsteps. Papery leaves on soft earth. I quickly wipe my cheeks dry with my sleeve.

"You must love acting." It's Frankie Lin, emerging from behind the willow and out of nowhere.

Was she reading my journal over my shoulder? Did she see me crying?

"What?"

She wears an unnecessary suede sun hat that shadows her face so I can't make out her expression, but I imagine it's smug. "You must really love acting," she repeats, taking another step forward. Dandelions go to seed at her feet. "You can't be *that* good at acting without loving it."

I snap my notebook shut. *Crack.* "Are you making fun of me?"

"No." She steps forward, a twig snapping like a bullet fired. "No, I'm not."

"Then you're just being obsequious. Well, I'm not going to be one of your devoted followers. I can't give you that! In fact, there is *nothing* I have that you want. So just … back off."

If she feels offended, Frankie Lin doesn't show it. My words have no impact on her. Quickly, I gather my things, hitch up my trousers, and set off down the hill to campus, but I misjudge a foothold in the witchgrass and stumble a few feet, nearly falling over. Why is it that I am clumsy in the company of others and never when I'm alone?

---

65 In Greek mythology, the gods punished Sisyphus, King of Ephyra, for his tyranny and trickery by condemning him to an eternity spent rolling a boulder up a hill. Every time Sisyphus neared the top, the boulder would roll back down.

"Are you okay?" she calls after me. I look back at her, the wind tossing up her tunic like a sail. She, an anchored ship. No force of nature can sway Frankie Lin. She is immovable. Her hair barely ruffles in the torrent of autumn air. Her hat blows off her head, but she doesn't go after it. To her, it's just a hat.

Appendix N

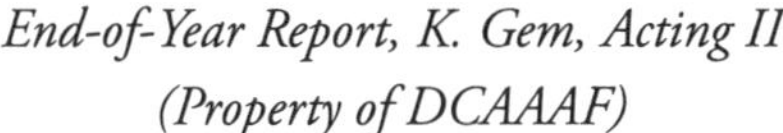

End-of-Year Report, K. Gem, Acting II
(Property of DCAAAF)

Student Name: Gem, Kristen
Class Participation (25%): A+
Written Assignments (40%): A+
Performance Presentation (35%): A+
Final Grade: A+

Notes: Not only is Kristen a pleasure to have in class, but she is also dedicated to developing onstage chemistry with her peers outside of school hours, by extent elevating the performance of her peers. She understands that acting is listening, and the energy between actors is molecular. Kristen spends much of her time strengthening these bonds, and it showed in her beautiful and nuanced final performance. I look forward to developing her talent further in the coming semester, digging a little deeper. I foresee a long and successful career as a performer.

Supervising Teacher: Blake, Gunther

Supervising Teacher Signature: *G. B.*

Chapter 16

We're in the actual theatre today—or "in the space," as Rue keeps saying—for our first off-book rehearsal. Mr. Blake is sitting in to watch. Beside him is Kemsley.

"Why is *he* here?" I overheard Magpie ask when her rival walked in at the top of rehearsal. "He turned down his role."

I strained my ears to make out Rue's whispered response. "He could be having regrets."

Frankie said something too quietly for me to make out. Magpie still looked uneasy. "Well, I don't like it."

Neither do I. I need an extra set of eyes on me about as much as I need an anvil to drop out of the sky onto my head. Every muscle in my body is contracted with the anticipation of something going wrong: corpsing,[66] a line flub, a prop amiss, a technical malfunction. The air is fraught and still, like even the theatre knows that catastrophe is inevitable. Everyone feels it. Tension mounts with every passing moment, especially with the cold war going on between Frankie and me. We haven't exchanged an unscripted word since I told her to buzz off yesterday.

---

66 A theatre colloquialism that describes when an actor laughs out of character while performing.

There is, at least, a friendly face in the crowd today. Kay's sitting in on the run for their spotting session,[67] which means I have an ally to run to when Ms. Spry calls for a break.

"I know we're all nervous about being off book," she says, "but remember to stay loose, guys. Go spend some time with each other. I dare you to sit with someone new today while you eat lunch!"

Kemsley leaves the theatre like a thief in the night. Our director opts to spend her break in the back row with Mr. Blake, though even their conversation seems strained. He looks my way and I almost flinch, knowing how stiff my performance was today. I descend into the orchestra pit with Kay. They're already digging into a brown-bag lunch that they brought us: two sandwiches from the dining hall.

"Are rehearsals always this . . ."

I finish their question: "Tense? Not until recently." I unwrap the foil and tear off a hunk of thick crust with my incisors. Everybody has separated into their respective social groups like oil and vinegar . . . with only one exception: Frankie. Her group is set in the center of the Theatre, but she floats in, out, and around as she pleases, pouring herself into conversational gaps and soaking up smiles from admirers. I'm eating ham on rye like a normal human being who has a limited social battery. Some people can go up there onstage, lay their heart out—or at least pretend to—and then go on networking, performing their archetypal roles well after curtain call. But Kay and me are just Kay and me. We do what we have to; we don't brown nose. And if that places us at the bottom of the Society hierarchy? So be it. We're real, at least. Flesh and bone and ham sandwiches. We eat comfortably, wordlessly as a cacophony of voices intellectualizes the needless. I watch Frankie while I chew. Half-baked jokes prompt insincere laughter. Boring stories elicit a faux-empathetic line of questioning. No human being on the face of this earth could do what Frankie does without extreme effort. It must be exhausting.

---

67 Typically a post-production meeting between a film director and a composer, this spotting session is for Kay to plot the sonic elements of each scene.

"Maybe you should make nice with her," Kay suggests when they catch me staring at Frankie, "if it's affecting the vibe."

That's when Frankie Lin turns to meet my stare. I can't quite read the expression on her dewy face, but it isn't a "make nice" face, let's just say that. If I had to describe it I would call it a glower. And it's directed right at me.

"Hi," she says in a stage voice. Bright, clear, resonant. Cast members stop their chittering to look as she approaches the pit.

I glance over at Kay. *Is she talking to me?* Kay gives an affirmative nod. "Hi?" I reply.

Frankie quickly changes the glower into her trademark smile. "I know you've got some sort of issue with me, but I wanted to invite you to join us tonight. After rehearsal. Society-only outing to Fleck Beach. You, too, Kay."

I narrow my eyes. "Why?"

"Society initiation," Frankie says, still smiling.

"We already signed the contract."

"This is, like, the fun version of that—sorry about the last-minute invite, there's been a little bit of back and forth—but it's tradition. Every year at sunset on the last day of September."

"Friday's the last day of September."

"Scheduling conflicts. Don't bring that up with Magpie, though? She's a little intense about all this . . . so you guys kind of have to come. But, as I said, it'll be fun!"

"I'm in," Kay says, before looking at me, "if Vi is."

If I'd known I was agreeing to field trips with the Gaykeepers when I joined the Society, I might not have signed on that dotted line so quickly. I glance at Mr. Blake, who appears to be watching us from the farthest row. No backing out now. "Sure," I hear myself reply.

Frankie looks surprised. A moment of genuine emotion filters through her plastered-on expression. "Perfect!" she chirps before doing a 180 spin and catwalking right back to Magpie and Rue. She rejoins her ever-tight circle of must-haves.

Appendix O

Excerpt, Dark Cove Arts Academy's Code of Conduct

Rule #35

Outdoor fires (incl. campfires, bonfires, etc.) are strictly prohibited. Contained indoor flames (e.g., a lit fireplace) are permitted only in the presence of a supervising adult. Anyone discovering an uncontained or unsupervised fire must report it immediately to a teacher.

Chapter 17

We amble across the close-cropped grass in a follow-the-leader formation. Magpie sets the pace at the helm, followed by Frankie and Rue and one of the crew heads, a quiet girl whose name eludes me. Michael and Hunter trail at the back. Kay and I are sandwiched in between. My breath comes quickly. The air tastes of smoke, adrift from some far-off wildfire. The balmy Pacific Northwest summer temperatures have decided to make a reprise, despite us being a week into the Gregorian calendar's definition of fall. This is the kind of weather that I appreciate for various reasons (e.g., not having to wear a jacket; the smell of sun-baked pine) and hate for others (e.g., increased awareness of climate change; the pangs of existential dread). I wipe dripping sweat from my brow as we enter a tunnel of trees. The path becomes overgrown with weeds and bushes with thorns that nick my legs here and there.

"Why did we agree to do this again?" I hiss at Kay.

"Because Frankie asked so very nicely?"

"More like we didn't have a choice." A crow swoops past me as if to remind me of the curse, of everything I have to lose.

"Ready to be initiated?" Kay laughs at my pained expression. "Oh, come on, it won't be so bad. A chance for you and Frankie to make nice?"

I shrug. They already know my opinions of cast bonding (it's weird and separatist), but if I have to be here, I might as well use the situation to my advantage. I'm supposed to be obsessed with Frankie on stage, so it might help if I at least understand her in real life. Plus, if I want to stay in Blake's good graces—and on this island—I better follow in the footsteps of his favorite students. Figuratively and literally, I guess. I indelicately straddle a moss-coated log, stumbling on the dismount.

"Man, it's beautiful out here," they sigh. "See the arbutus trees? They're starting to shed their bark."

I look up from the carefully memorized patina of my loafers and examine our surroundings. A few smooth, burnt-red tree trunks are exposed, limbs reaching up to the pale sky in a gorgeous stretch. Above, the crow follows us, flitting from perch to perch. It makes an almost extraterrestrial sound. Another calls back from a distant trunk in the same dialect, then another and another. They're all around us, ushering our group forward. *Where do the crows go at night?* I wonder. Disoriented, I realize I've no idea where on the island we are, how little of this rock I actually know. It's a rare occurrence that I leave the rose-trellised confines of Accolade South. Dark Cove is theoretically the perfect place to explore the beauty and mysteries of the natural world, but there's never any time to do it.

I recall a line from one of our assigned summer readings, the journals of Henry David Thoreau "The question is not what you look at, but what you see."[68]

"Pick up the pace, we're missing sunset," Magpie shouts.

"It can be dark when we do it," Frankie responds softly.

"Do what?" I whisper to Kay. They shrug.

"Do what?" Hunter calls out.

Magpie huffs. "It's a Dark Cove Theatre Society tradition!"

"What is?" asks the crew head whose name I still don't know. This is the first time I've ever heard her speak, and her voice is extremely squeaky.

---

68 Fourteen of the twenty featured authors on the reading list were white men. Five women writers were included: Ursula K. Le Guin, H.D. (Hilda Doolittle), Mary Oliver, Charlotte Brontë, and Toni Morrison. Morrison was among two writers of color, the second being Langston Hughes.

"Every new recruit must pledge allegiance to the Society by sunset on the last day of September," Rue explains.

"But it isn't the last day of September yet," she squeaks again.

"And the sun's already setting," Hunter adds.

Magpie starts into a jog. "Exactly. Hurry up!"

"There's no rush," Frankie coos. "The bonfire's the highlight, anyway."

"Did she say blood oath?" Michael asks.

"Bonfire," says Kay. "Which sounds nothing like blood oath, by the way."

"Starts with a *b* . . ."

"But bonfires aren't allowed," I remind everyone.

Frankie turns her rosy cheek to me. "We do this every year, don't worry." Of course she isn't anxious about getting caught; her looks purchase indemnity for every misdemeanor. Oh, and she's rich. And her mom's on the Board.

I cast a worried look at Kay.

"It'll be fine," they say to me, "punishment for low-level stuff like this is only detention. When Mr. H gave me that slip for wearing eyeliner, I only had to spend one lunch period with him. We organized his desk. Wasn't bad . . . a little weird. He had this drawer stuffed with, like, a trillion Twinkies. He gave me one, though, so that was pretty—"

"Did he have any condoms?" Hunter interrupts from behind us, closer than he was just a minute ago.

Kay gives him a disgusted sort of look over their shoulder. "No."

"Detentions are kept on file," I mutter.

"Aren't you used to breaking rules by now, Call Log Lady?"

A laugh bubbles out of me, my worries eased a little by my best friend. Up ahead, I see Frankie attempting to do the same for hers. "Mag, we can skip the sunset part—"

"We can't *skip* sunset!" Magpie insists.

And yet, the sun has already sunk below the watery horizon by the time we arrive at Fleck Beach, the sand tinted blue in the last of the light. The temperature drops with every passing second. The juniper trees shiver in the ocean breeze. The half-face of the moon glows dimly. A large murder of crows descends from the treetops down to the water.

Mag swats away a gnat. "I can't believe these slowpokes screwed up our tradition—"

Kay guffaws. "Slowpokes?"

"Now that's an insult I haven't heard since the second grade," I mumble.

"We gonna give each other noogies now?" says Kay.

I recoil from them as they reach for my head, cackling.

"Shut up, newbies. Someone start building a fire," Magpie commands. "First, fire, then our Treasurer of Secrets will lead us in a transference of the lore—"

"Ghost stories, in layman's terms," Rue explains.

"—and finally, we'll set intentions in the sand," continues Magpie. "Technically it isn't the last day of September, so it should be okay . . ."

"No one's grading you on this, Mag," Frankie says airily.

Magpie looks unconvinced. "The Society keeps record of these things. As Vice President and stand-in Secretary, you should know that."

"We won't tell anyone if you don't, El Presidente," says Hunter. He begins digging a shallow pit where we'll soon build our illicit fire. Kay and Michael join in. Their six hands move quickly and eagerly through the sand. Rue, Frankie, and the squeaky girl collect small scraps of wood. Mag stands, hands on hips, overseeing the operation. Everyone, old guard and new, has a part to play, even out here. Even out here, I struggle to understand mine. The laughter of others fills the late-summer air.

I brush sand off a birch log, kick off my shoes, and cop a squat. *Make nice*, I tell myself. "So . . . thanks for the invite."

"Don't flatter yourself. This is a member initiation," Magpie declares. "Attendance is required for Society council and all new members."

Without looking back, Hunter throws a cool fistful of sand behind him. "What about the other first timers?"

"Penelope couldn't make it," says the squeaky girl.

"Aight, that's one," Hunter says, "but a few of the carp guys are—"

Mag makes a sour face. “Nobody at *that level* is invited. They may *technically* be Society members, but only in the eyes of the faculty. The *actual* Society is principal cast and crew heads only. This is a sacred tradition. *Secret* and sacred, I’ll remind you.”

“What about Margaret?” I ask.

Frankie looks around. “Yeah, where *is* Margaret? Mag, you told her we rescheduled, right?”

“*You* were supposed to tell her!”

“No, I—”

“If people would just *listen to me*,” Magpie mutters furiously, then takes a moment to collect herself. “Whatever. Who even is Margaret. There’s no time to go back and get her.”

“What about that other dude?” Hunter asks. “The guy who fucked off at the portra—”

“Kemsley forfeited his place in the Society when he didn’t show up to the Welcome Ceremony,” Magpie snaps. “I’m going to get kindling.” She struts away. Frankie follows her, Rue on her tail. The Gaykeepers have a heated discussion at the treeline while Hunter pulls out a matchbox to light the fire.

“So,” he says, a match between his teeth, “that makes Kemsley the cursed one?”

How does everyone know about this curse? “No, the cursed person drops out of school altogether. At least, that’s what I’ve heard.”

Hunter pulls the match out from his bite and presses it to the striker on his matchbox, one hand cupped around his vulnerable flame. The small dash of orange makes me nervous.

“*I’ve* heard it’s pretty much always a girl,” says Michael. “We’re safe, dude.” I wonder if he looked at the portraits, too, or if that’s just common knowledge.

“Who’s to say curses abide by the gender binary? Ghosts live in the liminal, after all,” Kay muses. “Then again, ghosts and curses are very different enchiladas … and if the curse is a metaphor for—or manifestation of—the patriarchal forces at play on th—”

Magpie, who has just gotten back in earshot, makes a hawk-like screech. "We aren't talking about that tonight!" She throws a fistful of moss at the fire. The flame diminishes a little, almost dies out.

"Not talking about what?" Hunter teases. He smiles and strikes another match.

"Don't make me say it," replies Magpie.

Rue gives Hunter a warning look.

"The Dark Cove curse," the crew girl chimes in in an extra-high frequency.

Magpie groans, face up to the darkening sky.

"Wait," I say, "Mag, weren't you the one who said I was cursed just a week ago?"

"Yes, *Violet*, but that was at school," she retorts. Her golden locket catches the firelight. I notice her neck is splotched with cherry-red frustration. "Not here. This place is . . ."

"What? Haunted?"

"We don't talk about *that* here. Or in Wincroft. End of discussion."

"Says who, cult leader?" Hunter teases.

Magpie murmurs something under her breath before saying, "First of all, it's a society, not a cult. But if you want to be a dimwit and ignore our cardinal rule, go ahead. Your funeral."

"It's like saying 'Macbeth' in a theatre," Frankie elaborates.[69] "Or 'good luck' instead of 'break a leg.'"

Michael breaks a stick over his knee. "Come again?"

"Bad luck," squeaks the squeaker.

"Right you are, Edie," says Rue. I guess the squeaker's name is Edie.

There's an awkward silence. An agitated Magpie flips her hair from one side to the other.

---

69 Shakespeare's masterpiece, believed to be cursed, is referred to only as "the Scottish Play" by many. The only way to avoid the curse after uttering the play's true name is to perform a cleansing ritual (which usually involves exiting the theatre, turning around a few times, spitting, swearing, reciting the *Midsummer* line "if we shadows have offended," and humbly asking to be allowed back inside). Thespians are a superstitious lot.

"I get it, Mag," says Kay. "Don't wanna rustle up the dark spirits."

Another hair flip. "Thank you."

My knee quivers involuntarily. I remind it that I don't believe in the supernatural. None of this stuff is logical, just good fun. Faux anxiety to don and discard. Horror movies, horoscopes, and scary stories may be Kay's bread and butter, but I consume the stuff like popcorn. Entertainment. That's all. Still, I decide not to press the subject.

"Now," Magpie starts, "if you'll all get in a circle, we can commence."

Hunter scratches his head. A flash of bicep peaks out from his polo sleeve. "I dunno, this is all a little too culty for me."

"For the trillionth time, we're not a cult, we're a *so-ci-et-y*, and the Society prides itself on tradition."

Hunter pokes at the fire with a long stick. "And ghost stories are a part of this tradition? 'Cus I'm, like, ninety percent sure I saw the Dark Cove Ghost at orientation last year." Another match hisses to life in Hunter's hands. He tosses it into the fire. "I don't think she likes me."

"What's there not to like?" Magpie remarks sarcastically.

Hunter's laugh skips across the water. Everything is funny to Hunter Kinsey. "Is that the dead you guys are so afraid of waking up? 'Cus I can't blame you, she seems like a bitch."

"Our ghost is a good ghost," Magpie snaps. "You'll understand if you just *listen*."

"All right, El Presidente, please, don't let me screw up your epic tradition." Hunter, Michael, Kay, Frankie, Edie, and I form a small ring around the young fire.

She gives us a dignified "thank you," and the red in her complexion calms somewhat, or maybe it's just a forgiving effect of the blue hour. "We invited you here tonight to welcome you to the Dark Cove Theatre Society, a club of legend. Once, members were hand-selected, by invitation only. These days, it's up to the teachers and directors to decide who's in"—she squints at me—"unfortunately. That said, tradition's tradition. Tonight, you'll hear a few of our stories. Nothing we speak of on this beach is to be repeated to the others, do you understand?" Magpie waits for us all to nod. "Good. Now, Rue, our Treasurer of Secrets, will begin by telling the tale of the Dark Cove Ghost."

"It would be my pleasure." Rue bows graciously before stepping up to the crest of a white sand dune. Her backdrop: a melange of dusky rose, purple twilight, and seafoam green. "Our story begins in the early 1900s—"

"Wait." Hunter raises a hand like it's a class discussion. "I thought the Dark Cove Ghost was that homecoming queen chick who went missing in, like, the eighties?"

"Nineties," Kay corrects. "Prom queen."

"True," Rue continues plaintively, "the island hosts nearly as many ghosts as it does students. These spirits are drawn here for all the usual reasons, *unfinished business* chief among them. The island is their anchor. Here, they became themselves. Here, they lost themselves. The island has seen more cruelty than its rosy-faced children can imagine. But it all began with the island's first undead resident: Gwendolyn Wincroft."

"As in Wincroft Theatre?" Hunter asks.

"Oh my god," Magpie yelps. "Let the girl talk."

"Yes, Gwendolyn Wincroft, as in Wincroft Theatre. Wife of Dark Cove Arts Academy's founder, Gwendolyn was a typically timid woman, as most women were expected to be. Gwendolyn's demure personage was rooted in her fear of her husband, who was a mean drunk and controlling to the extreme, but he was a legendary director. Everyone in the industry clamored to be a part of the legacy he was building out here. And while he taught at the school, his wife was relegated to the chapel in which the couple lived. The only time she was permitted to leave was to run errands—laundry, foraging, fetching mail, and other shipments from the mainland, and so on. Gwendolyn's was a woefully small existence, and Dark Cove was her cage.

"Naturally, she sought freedom wherever she might find it. She befriended the crows. Her laundry loads stayed light, her trips to the river were frequent. Her greatest rebellion, however, was her letters." Here, our storyteller pauses for dramatic effect. Behind her, the open sky is blotted with darkness like ink. "See, Gwendolyn Wincroft—like every resident of Dark Cove—had a secret. One that, in the end, would cost her life. Gwendolyn had a pen pal, a woman she knew in another life on another island: Great Britain. Exiled from the world with no one for company but a cruel academic and a handful of his pupils, Gwendolyn relied on her letters as a lifeline.

"It was inevitable that her feelings for this off-shore woman would become romantic. Certain as the crashing tide, she fell in love. The letters, over days, weeks, months, evolved into things of intimacy as Gwendolyn and her paramour revealed mutual feelings for one another. Together, the women conspired an escape plan for Mrs. Wincroft. She would steal a modest sum of money from her husband's safe and bribe the ferryman to take her back to the mainland. From there, she would venture home to her true love." Above, stars join our audience in tight, curious clusters. "It was on the eve of her planned escape that Gwendolyn's husband intercepted a letter. Appalled by its contents, Wincroft scoured the island for the sinner, his wife. He scaled cliffs, searched caves, left no stone unturned, before he found Gwendolyn at the mouth of the river by Raven Lake, dutifully cleaning his shirts. He ambushed her, pushed her down, and held her head underwater until her body went limp."

The night air chills.

"Wait, he drowned her?" Hunter asks, pulling on a hoodie as Magpie shushes him. He ignores her. "How do you know that?"

Rue bows her head gravely, her eyes magnified like an owl's through her lenses. "There's no proof of her death; only the stories passed down by the Society, here on this beach, can preserve the truth. Gwendolyn Wincroft's corpse drifted out to sea, leaving no lasting legacy nor evidence of existence other than the tombstone behind the dining hall, which marks an empty grave next to the skeleton of her keeper and killer. Mr. Wincroft, conversely, has been honored as one of the Academy's brilliant founding fathers. To this day, Gwendolyn's ghost is tethered to Dark Cove by the force of her final act and the unfulfilled longing for her lover, doomed to wander this island forever. It's said that where she drowned, the water runs cold, and that you can hear her cries where the river meets the sea, right here on Fleck Beach. Several Society alumni have also reported seeing her floating in the rafters of the theatre that still bears her husband's name."

At this, everyone seems genuinely disturbed: Hunter has retreated into his sweater, Edie's all blanched, Magpie's brushing her arms to hide her shivers, Kay and Michael are tangled in a fearful embrace, and Frankie, sitting in the sand at my feet, shakes like a leaf.

"Rue, that was amazing, and heartbreaking, and seriously messed up," Kay says. "Well done."

Our storyteller gives a small bow.

"Like, I'm legitimately uneasy right now," they continue.

"Same here," Edie agrees.

"No need to be afraid, loves," Rue says calmly, tracing the outer edge of our circle. "The ghost of Gwendolyn might wander the island, but she's said to be our protector."

"Who's 'our'?" Hunter asks.

"The girls of Dark Cove."

"*Your* protector, then," he mutters.

"Male privilege stops just short of ghostly guardians, I guess," Magpie says dryly.

Hunter, unfazed, presses on. "Why just the chicks?"

Magpie ignores him, turns her head to Rue. "*How* are you friends with this guy?"

Rue chuckles and places a kind hand on our resident himbo's hooded head. "Gwendolyn protects us from the thing that resulted in her annihilation: the greed of man."

"But if it's always a girl who's the *cursee*," says Hunter, "it sounds like y'all have a pretty useless guardian."

"Deadweight ghost!" Michael throws his head back, laughing, high on summer air. "So, wait, does that mean Gwendolyn's behind the curse, or—"

"Of course she isn't!" Magpie leaps to her feet. "And how many times do I need to tell you that you can't talk like that here?" A crackling quiet befalls our bonfire, the Society President standing there like a bolt of lightning frozen in place.

"Maybe we should take a pause on the stories and skip to the swimming?" Frankie suggests, trying to ease the tension.

Magpie shakes her head swiftly. "Swimming isn't a thing, Frankie. It goes sunset pledge—which already didn't happen—bonfire, stories, intention setting, and then—"

"Why, though?" Hunter asks.

"What, do you want to, like, inspect the presidential handbook, nimrod?"

Hunter takes the second middle-school insult of the evening in stride. "Sure, hand it over, Mag."

Rue raises a cautionary hand to him. "It's all for cast unity," she says with her mouth, as her eyes say, *Stay out of this, Hunter.*

"You get that this is exactly the kind of stuff that makes people think you guys are a cult, right? Maybe that's why that Kemsley guy bowed out," says Hunter, goading Magpie. He winks at me, like I'm getting a kick out of her distress. Even though I should find it funny—after all, I do hate Magpie Black—I can't find it in me to laugh.

She's about to take the bait when Frankie says, "*My* intention is to go swimming. Is that cool with everyone?"

"I don't see why not," Rue interjects, now petting Magpie's hair. "But I'll stay back with our President and resume the ceremonies as planned."

Flustered, Mag throws her hands in the air. "But, you're my—fine, whatever, tradition's just totally out the window tonight, I guess. Vice President Frankie can do anything she wants whenever she wants. But the rest of us will be setting our intentions right here."

"Anyone wanna join me?" Frankie asks, unmoved by her friend's reprimand.

I find myself between a rock and a hard place. To "set intentions" with Magpie, who's spitting venom in all directions this evening, or go for a cold dip with Frankie Lin. I look to Kay for help, but they're busy lapping up all the drama.

Make nice. "Sure, I'll tag along, Frankie."

Magpie juts her chin out. "Good riddance."

"Come on." Frankie uses my knee to push herself up. I brush off the flecks of sand left behind by her unexpected touch. She runs ahead, kicking up sand as she goes, and then I'm following her down to the old sailboat house, thrust into some moonlit dimension in which Frankie Lin and I go swimming together. The boathouse is eerily tall and has a long clapboard dock stretching out beside it. Frankie walks to the spot where the land meets the dock and pauses there. She looks back at me with a beautiful, bug-eyed affectation, waiting. "Wasn't that story so sad?"

"Um, sure," I say, trailing behind her down the soft slope of the bank. "It's a complete fabrication though."

"Well, all these legends of the Dark Cove Ghost have to come from somewhere."

"A place of boredom, most likely," I suggest, which makes her laugh.

She says something, but I can't hear it. It sounded almost like she said . . . "I'm the cursed one?"

"What?" she shouts upshore to me.

"Did you just say 'I'm the cursed one'?"

Frankie laughs. "No, I said, you're so contrarian!"

I feel the corners of my mouth turn upward as my feet sink down the slope to her. "Okay, I admit that I can be a little skeptical—"

"I'll say."

"—but it's a made-up ghost story. I mean, how would anyone know that's how she died? And if we did know that, why would they name our theatre after a murderer?"

"Let me answer your question with a question, Violet: Doesn't almost every city in the world honor a terrible man in some way? A street name, a statue, a park . . ."

I shrug. She's right.

"And another one: How are you so sure ghosts aren't real?"

"Um . . . because they aren't?"

Frankie rises onto her tiptoes and walks along the clapboard over the water without looking at me, her steps quicker now, her body language altered.

"Oh, come on. Are you seriously mad at me for not believing in ghosts? Is that really your issue with me?"

"*I* don't have an issue with *you,*" she says simply.

Crickets. Hollow canoes clunk against one another in the boathouse like drunken lovers.

I glide past her comment. "Prove that ghosts are real and I'll admit I'm wrong!"

Almost at the end of the dock now, she takes off her polo, stripped down to a tank top. "Prove that they *aren't* real and *I'll* admit *I'm* wrong."

Touché.

That's when the sky suddenly turns a deep merlot and the wind picks up, almost toppling me over into the ocean. I stagger back. The incoming slough pushes forward with a low and accelerating moan from somewhere far across the mysterious tangle of water. Waves crash lapping up and over the dock. My skin crawls. Though there ought to be a logical explanation for the sound—the howl of a coyote, maybe—I've never seen such a sudden change in weather. *It's just wind,* I think. But this wind carries with it the undeniable, terrifying stench of death. It infiltrates my nostrils for the briefest moment, just long enough to know the smell wasn't merely a whiff of sea rot, before the howl softens to nothing and the scarlet sky blackens in a second.

I look to Frankie for answers. She smirks, not a trace of fear on her face. Cocky.

"Was that you?" I gasp.

"Maybe it was Gwendolyn." Frankie's molten eyes look different than I've ever seen them, gleaming with something dangerous. "And, by the way, I wasn't mad at you for not believing in ghosts. I'm *mad* because you talk to me like I'm an idiot."

I swallow down a riposte and sit in the terror of this moment. "You seem . . . totally not fazed by what just occurred."

"Why should I be? Gwendolyn's not gonna hurt us."

"Right, *our protector*. Well, I didn't feel too protected just now," I say, infuriated by Frankie's perpetual sense of calm and togetherness. "And you're the one who—how are you so sure of everything?"

"Like what?"

"According to you, the ghost is real, right? The ghost is our guardian angel. But also according to you, the curse is bogus?"

"It's easier to believe in something good, isn't it?"

A heavy something hangs in the air between us like an invisible fog. When the weight of it becomes unbearable, I break our silence. "The curse only goes after the weakest link, if we go by what Magpie says. So, even if it was real, you'd have nothing to worry about. I, on the other hand . . ."

Frankie's blank face curves into a simper. "Ignore all that curse talk from the other day, okay? Magpie . . . she's all bark and no bite."

"Yeah, you said that before," I reply. Emboldened by the rush of whatever just happened, I ask, "Why are you friends with her again?"

Frankie considers this. "I don't let any of her snide remarks get to me."

"Oh? Why not?"

"I see what's underneath them." With that, she turns, dives, and slices the placid water with her slender body, making a clean incision that casts out just one thin ripple. I watch her fluctuating figure under the dark glaze of sea. She is so slim, her movements so certain. She's the foil to everything that I am and a persistent reminder of everything that I'm not—of everything I can't have. When Frankie Lin emerges, jet-black hair made blacker from the water, she calls out, "Are you coming?"

I take a step forward, fold my toes over the edge of the dock, and look down. As much as I'd love to be the kind of person who can plunge themself off the seat of infinity into a murky pool of unknown depths without a care, I tell her no. "I'm scared . . . of the cold."

"You? Afraid?" Frankie asks with a lilt in her voice, and I'm not sure if she's mocking me for my perpetual fear or if she sees a bravery in me that isn't really there. "It's only bad for that first second!"

"I'm sure you're lying."

"When have I ever lied to you?"

I pause. She confessed to lying to herself mere moments ago. *Isn't everything she does a lie?*

She treads water. The soft sounds of lapping waves almost tempt me to dip a toe in. Before I can give in to any temptation, Frankie says, "Have my clothes ready for me?" Then she's gliding underwater back to the dock, pushing herself up on the wood with surprising strength, laughing easily, panting, collapsing, shimmering in the evening glow. Stupefied, I toss Frankie the crumpled uniform from a safe distance, which prompts a breathy "thanks," and I can't tell what the feeling is behind it but tell her that she's welcome anyway. She cloaks herself in the coarse cotton, wrings out her hair in a brutal sort of way. Then, she pads barefoot toward me saying, "This is everything I needed tonight." She's so close I can smell her luxury perfume mingled with the sour scent of kelp.

"This was everything I needed too," I say to fill the once-again treacherous silence, even though I didn't swim and I'm not sure what I needed. *Know thine enemy*, says Sun Tzu, but no one ever iterates the risks of that; in my attempt to wrap my mind around Frankie's allure, she's managed to start wrapping me around her finger, just like everyone else is. For the first time, that doesn't seem like such a bad thing.

Frankie turns her face to the star-smudged sky. Her laughter breaks the moment up into something I can swallow. We make our way back to the now-dying campfire together. I don't say much. Frankie tells me about the water and how dark it was and how cold it was and how she actually was lying, just a little bit. She looks up at me as if for forgiveness, or permission, maybe. She fills the night air until her voice blends into the campfire chatter. Like a confession meant just for me, she tells me that that sound in the wind was nothing like she's ever heard before. I agree with her, which makes her eyes crinkle with a smile. She settles into a spot on the driftwood log between Michael and Kay, who sings like a night bird as they play a folk song on the guitar. They move from one chord to the next, each one unexpected and perfect. No one else mentions the wind-moan or the dark-red sky. Hunter waves me over. When I sit down beside him, my arm brushes against his like a whisper.

"You're freezing," Hunter says, unzipping his hoodie. He drapes it over my shoulders.

"I'll give this back to you tomorrow," I assure him, wondering if he'll be okay without the sweater but too glad he gave it to me to offer giving it up. It really is cold out, and my complaints of heat have been vaporized by the night.

He smiles. Straight, clean teeth. "Whenever. I *intend* to let you keep it as long as you need."

This boy's charm is enough to give me whiplash. Why is he suddenly focused on directing every modicum of it at me? I look away from his still-there smile. Across the charred embers, Frankie wears crystallized sea salt like it's body glitter. I try to catch her eye, but Magpie's whispering something in her ear.

Kay yawns dramatically. I do the same, Edie squeaks in a way that I think is also a yawn, and soon we're a chorus of drawn-out exhalations rising like smoke from the fireside. The resounding, faraway ring of the bell tower brings us back to the reality of midnight and the looming early morning, the necessity of sleep. Magpie declares the end of the ceremony. We douse out the embers, brush the sand from our feet, and slip our oxfords back on before wading through the hazy undergrowth. Now, the branches are darker, their shadows longer. In any other context, the nettled path would be threatening, but tonight, with Rue leading our group of not-quite friends by lantern, it feels safe. The murmur of the sea gives way to the whispering leaves of the tall black oaks. We wordlessly weave between trunks to the soundtrack of the night. Waves break in the distance. Crickets chirp. The boys eventually split off, and the rest of us sneak back into the girls' dorm one at a time. I'm the last to enter, tiptoeing, full stealth mode, holding my breath for fear of getting caught.

Once I reach the top floor, I find Frankie lingering in the infinite expanse of hallway between our rooms.

"Good night," I whisper across the abyss.

"I'll see you tomorrow," comes her barely audible reply, clipped by the door closing behind her.

"Good night," I repeat to the empty hall.

My limbs feel loose when I climb into bed—Frankie Lin has disarmed me. Instead of counting sheep, I just keep turning what she said over and over like a stone in my hand:

You? Afraid?

A current of sleep pulls and recedes at the sound of Kay's voice, raw with exhaustion.

"How'd I do tonight?"

"What do you mean?" I ask, coming out of a deep stupor, trying to decipher whether this is already a dream.

"Nothing. Never mind. But the vibes were ... like, better than expected. Right?"

I roll over to face them. "I was surprised, honestly. It didn't feel weird at all. And there wasn't any hazing or any real drama even?"

"*I* was surprised you said yes in the first place. Especially with Frankie's aggressive invitation." We whisper-laugh beneath our sheets. "You going for a swim with her wasn't on my Dark Cove Theatre Society bingo card."

"I didn't actually swim, just wanted to avoid the intention-setting riff raff," I say defensively. "How was that, by the way?"

"It wasn't bad. How was your tête-à-tête with Frankie?"

"Also not bad. She ... surprised me."

"For real?"

I sigh. "Maybe you were right. Maybe it's not all an act."

"I'm always right."

"I said maybe."

"*Always*," they insist. "Also. Hunter giving you his sweater?"

"I was cold. He offered."

"That's all?"

"We both know he doesn't like me. He's just ... flirty by nature."

A small yawn. "We never ended up pledging allegiance to the *So-ci-et-y*."

"Curse talk must've thrown Magpie off her game."

"She was freaking out, eh?"

"Seriously," I say, and then remember Kay's first question. "Everyone loved listening to you play, roomie."

Their shadowed form relaxes under their quilt. I reach my hand out into the inky space between our single beds, Kay does the same and we touch our fingers for a moment. Our little bedtime ritual. Kay's soft snoring starts just moments after our hands part. Then, to the sullen murmur of the evergreens, I drift into sleep.

Chapter 18

As if carried by lightning, a thought occurs to me: My period is due, isn't it? The biological premonition only marginally precedes its manifestation. 9-1-1. I launch my hand into the air, catching the attention of a mid-sentence Mr. Blake, who is currently explaining *psychological theories of character development as they pertain to our upcoming examinations.* He registers my hand, appraising it like a bug. To swat or not to swat? "Yes, Violet?" he asks.

I lower my arm slowly, so as to not scare my professor into his fight state. "May I please be excused to the washroom?"

"Class ends in ten minutes. You can wait."

I shuffle in my seat. At least I'm wearing black trousers today. "Yes, sir."

When Mr. Blake turns away from the class to write something on the chalkboard, Frankie sneaks an eyeroll in my direction. It's an *oh-my-god-he's-annoying* eyeroll. She smiles at me. I smile back. Mr. Blake turns forward to reveal what's been written on the board: *Midterm Assessment* and several lines underneath. He adds in more words as he speaks.

". . . it will have both written and oral components: a three-page character description and a defense of that character"—he writes "description" and "oral defense"—"I'll remind you, this will make up twenty-five percent of your final semester grade, as indicated in the rubric. You will be marked on format, content, grammar, and creativity. I know many of you are busy with *A Midsummer Night's Dream,* but do not let it pose a hindrance to your exam performance."

Midterms always take place on the same week as the Halloween Play, which coincides with the IASA evaluations and, this year, the Board visits. It's a dreaded time at which teachers are most high-strung and Covies are most strung out. Students call it Hell Week.

"The headmaster is wont to pop in on the presentation portion, and he will most likely be bringing in some of the Board, so be prepared. Originality is paramount. For the love of god, do not choose one of your professors or classmates as a character—"

"So, we shouldn't write about a whiny sixteen-year-old who needs to go potty?" Magpie whispers to Rue. I clench my jaw so hard it gives me an instant headache.

"'We have two ears and one mouth so that we can listen twice as much as we speak,'" says Mr. Blake. "Can you tell me who said that, Miss Black?"

"No," she replies quietly.

"It was the great Greek philosopher Epictetus." The professor regards his apprentice with a chill distaste of which I'm used to being on the receiving end.

Magpie quails, understanding she's just been told, in a fancy Grecian way, to shut up.

I don't let the satisfaction I feel show on my face.

Frankie places a consoling hand on Mag's back. She shrugs it off. "I'm fine," Mag snaps in a whisper.

A roar of thunder, a corresponding flash of purple lightning, and Mr. Blake throws his hands in the air. "Since all of you are determined to derail my explanation of this assignment, I will leave it to you to review the rubric yourselves. You'll be evaluated in class and will be expected to defend your work as per the rubric. Now, you're dismissed. To those of you in the Halloween Play, I'll see you this afternoon."

"He's letting us go?" Margaret asks me in astonishment.

I answer by heeding his atypical instructions with haste and running to the nearest bathroom to grab a tampon. Surely, I must have some sort of guardian angel, because there is nary a drop of blood on the fabric of my pristine (inaccurate) day-of-the-week underwear. My flow only begins once I have safely arrived in the stall.

I don't believe in luck. But if I did, I'd say mine's changing.

Finally, the stubborn golden leaves have begun drifting off of trees and the temperatures are descending in solidarity, but whoever's in charge of turning on the heat in Wincroft Theatre hasn't gotten the memo. I march briskly down the aisle, rubbing the gooseflesh on my forearms. The first to arrive, I choose a front-center seat.

"Pleased to see at least one of my students has retained my lessons in punctuality," Mr. Blake says, stepping out from the wings onstage.

This semi-compliment from my professor brings out an involuntary smile. "Good afternoon, sir!"

"Good afternoon, Violet."

"I'm here!" Ms. Spry hollers from behind the curtains. "Just give me a minute. Trying to fix this damn—darn—boiler thingy."

Mr. Blake sighs exasperatedly and strides backstage once more.

I pull Hunter's sweater out from my satchel and slip it on, enclosing my hands in the sleeves for extra warmth.

"I'm not getting that back, am I?" the sweater owner quips, plopping himself in the seat beside me. He still smells of the woods.

"Later. I didn't expect this rehearsal to be an arctic expedition."

"Keep it, I don't mind," he says. I try not to read into his generosity.

The stage curtains rustle, and Ms. Spry rushes into view. "See, this is why every theatre needs a ghost light.[70] Guys, I'm so sorry it's an icebox

70 A ghost light is a bulb that is left on whenever a theatre goes dark. Its uses are debated among theatre folk; some argue that it's to ward off evil spirits, others that it's to keep tenanting spirits happy. Less superstitious people might argue that the ghost light is just a safety measure.

in here. I called the maintenance folks to fix the heat. Tried to do it myself but . . ."

"Let me give it a go!" Hunter hollers, vaulting onto the stage and vanishing behind the cover of velvet just as Mr. Blake reappears.

"Thanks, honey," Ms. Spry gushes.

"Isn't it nice when a boy heroically offers to do a boy task?" Magpie says stonily. I didn't even hear the girls arrive, but they find seats a few rows behind me.

"Miss Black. You're late," says Mr. Blake. "Need I remind you that you are to lead by example?"

I wave feebly in the Gaykeepers' direction, but only Rue gestures back. Magpie's eyes are down and Frankie makes no show of acknowledgment. My heart sinks a little, and I am alarmed by the power of Frankie Lin's attention and how it feels to be deprived of it. My mind sinks into a spiral of desperation. *Was our Fleck Beach détente just a late-night fluke? Or worse, all in my head?* I try to read her for an answer, a sign, but she gives me nothing, and before long, the whole cast has arrived. Ms. Spry wastes no time.

"Since our Lysander is busy, why don't we get started with our fairies? Are we all here?" Rue and the dancers leap up from their seats at Ms. Spry's question. "Beautiful. Act 3, scene 1. Allons-y! Will someone turn on the stage lights?"

The play is a welcome distraction. In just a brief passing of moments, the scene blazes into life before me. I am mesmerized. Most of the fairies are played by ballerinas, who shimmer onstage like miracles. This kind of perfection both amazes and frightens me; I'll never be that dainty, precise, or pretty, and the expectation that anyone should be is kind of devastating when you really think about it. I glance back over my shoulder at Frankie. She was looking at me, I'm sure I saw—or felt—her looking at me, but she darted her eyes away when I looked back. Or maybe I imagined it. *What is happening to me*? I wonder.

She fusses with the satin bow atop her head, tying and retying until it's exactly how it had been in the first place. She doesn't look at me until she has to. After the fairies finish a quick and flawless run of their scene, we move right into act 3 scene 2 to rehearse a mini fight sequence that we've had a bit of trouble coordinating. In it, my character curses everyone else out. When Lysander and Demetrius profess their adoration for Helena (at this point, they've been enchanted by the fairies), she thinks that they are pranking her. Hermia is mad at Helena for stealing her man, and Helena takes this as Hermia being in on the lark. There's a choreographed hair pull and even a slap. It's quite a fun bit, but it's imperative we get it exactly right to avoid any accidents or injuries. Fortunately, the fight choreo has never gone smoother than it goes in this run. I'm out of breath by the end.

"Helena, what do you want in this scene?" Ms. Spry asks inquisitively.

I know this one! I think. Between huffs and puffs, I tell the director that I want to make Hermia and Demetrius take me seriously, to get them to admit that they're conspiring against me.

Ms. Spry presses further. "Do you really want them to admit that?"

"I just want to know what's going on." I look to Frankie, again fiddling with the green strands of ribbon in her hair, avoiding my gaze. "I'd love it if Demetrius's affections were real, because my overall objective is for Demetrius to love me."

"But look," Mr. Blake says from his post at the back of the theatre, the first time he's spoken in this rehearsal, "there Demetrius is, declaring a great love for you. If that's your super objective, why don't you accept this love?"

"I suspect that Demetrius's love is a lie. I won't accept that. I need to know that Demetrius loves me for who I am." Another bow adjustment by Frankie. Determined to seize my scene partner's attention, I drag her into the conversation. "Demetrius, what's *your* objective here?"

She flashes her smoky eyes at me. "It isn't much different from what you're after, Helena."

Blake gives another one of those satisfying good-book nods before whispering something to Ms. Spry before leaving. She murmurs something back and then addresses the cast. "Amazing job, guys. I can really feel the tension here. But let's do it again to get the blocking down."

We run it back. All the movement heats me up so I can hardly feel the cold anymore. Equally heartwarming is the excuse to yell at Magpie. I spit my lines at her: "Have you no modesty, no maiden shame, No touch of bashfulness? What, will you tear Impatient answers from my gentle tongue? Fie, fie, you counterfeit, you puppet, you!"

Mag appears to be flummoxed, which is a character choice, I think, but it gives me a total rush regardless. For a half-second, I feel as if I've really bested my enemy. Then the scene is over and Magpie readopts her trademark sneer. She walks offstage, leaving just Frankie and me under the stage light.

Though I'm still bent over with exhaustion, hands on my knees and short of breath, I recognize that I have a shrinking window of opportunity here to make conversation with Frankie Lin.

"All that lunging sure takes it out of me," I say, but she goes from adoring Demetrius to ice queen in no time, already turned away. Ms. Spry declares an early end to rehearsal on account of the below-room temperature. Frankie exits briskly, flanked by her court. It feels like a real gut punch. Winded, I retrieve my satchel from the front-row seat, still wrapped up in Hunter's sweater (he insisted I keep it again). Romeo tugs at one of the overlong sleeves. As I extricate the fabric from the dog's clamped jaw, there comes the flapping sound and guttural croak of a crow above. I peer at the shadowy rafters. They carry dust like clouds. And through the fine particles, I see a crow sitting, calm as ever, as if it belongs there. As if the wood beams were trees rising up to a murky sky. It calls again, speaking to me.

A sailor's knot ties itself in my stomach. I almost forgot about the curse. It had become, for a moment, a vague singsong in my ear, very painful and crushing but only half intelligible.[71] *Just until Halloween*, I remind myself. *I just have to make it til—*

"Violet." Ms. Spry hovers by the theatre doors, watching me. Everyone else has left. I look back up at the rafters. The crow is gone. "You okay?"

"Yup," I lie quickly and easily, swinging my satchel over my shoulder and walking up the aisle to the exit. "Great rehearsal."

---

71 This is stolen from Charlotte Brontë's *Jane Eyre* (1847).

"I think so too," she says softly. "You know, you're uplifting the performance of everyone around you. Mr. Blake agrees."

"Really?"

"Really really." She flashes a retro-red, old-Hollywood starlet smile, holding the theatre door open for me.

My heart jumps. There's a fluttering inside me, and for once, it isn't a symptom of fear.

The sunset makes a rosy path on the lake. I watch it sink down, down, until it almost kisses the water. The light squiggles across the water like a line on a graph. I am reminded of a diagram Mr. Mitchell showed us in class the other day; there was a line just like this, climbing wonkily up the *x* and *y* axes of a graph. It read, "Oscillating hope, mystery, and suspense on the curve of rising action." I think it was supposed to tell us something about plot, but it stuck with me because that's just what living is for me . . . this constant state of flux between hope, mystery, and suspense on what I can only trust is a curve of rising action. Sure, I've been getting good grades this term so far, but there is a more profound sort of progress here. Even though my emotional life feels like a game of competitive Ping-Pong. I'm on my way up. Somewhere.

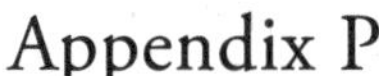

Appendix P

Diagram, Plot Devices: A History of the Suspension of Disbelief
by Leland Polluck

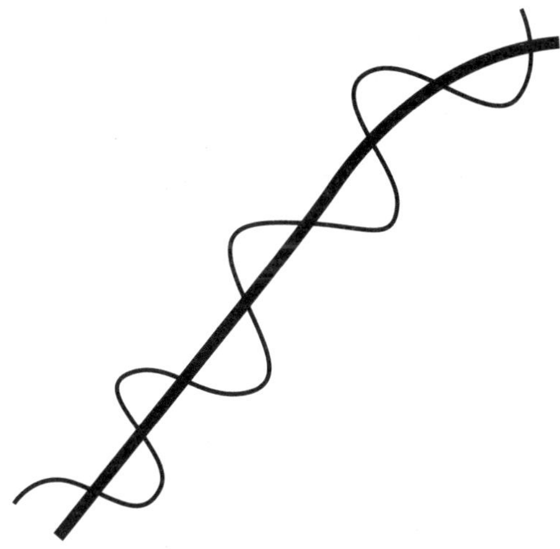

Figure 3. Oscilating hope, mystery, and suspense on the curve of rising action

Chapter 19

Twenty-odd hours later, Hunter is on his knees at my feet, looking up with those emerald eyes, once again professing his love to me—to Helena, rather. "I love thee. By my life, I do. I swear by that which I will lose for thee, To prove him false that says I love thee not."

"I say I love thee more than he can do," Frankie shouts, shoving Hunter away and placing her hands on my shoulders . . . but there's still a distance between us. I've developed a theory since last night that maybe she just feels weird performing in a theatre named after a rumored murderer, which would be very valid.

Ever since we talked about the history of this place, it has a certain air of consecration. Today, at least, there are no ghoulish crows to be seen in the rafters.

"Can we stop there?" Ms. Spry interrupts. "Guys! This is supposed to be fun! What's going on?"

Crickets. A beep as Kay hits STOP on their video camera. Along with the show designers sketching on their pads, Kay is sitting in on rehearsals again so they can sync up the music with our blocking.

Our director gets up from her seat and approaches the lip of the stage. "Demetrius, how do you feel right now?"

Dropping her hands from my shoulder, Frankie says, "Fine, I guess."

"I mean more how does the character feel? You're in love, right? Both you and Lysander are into Helena."

"Yeah, or, like, mega infatuated." Hunter's green eyes linger on me.

Ms. Spry taps a drumroll on the stage with her hands. "That's a wonderful distinction you just made. Let's explore it."

"This play isn't about true love," Mag says. "This isn't *Romeo and Juliet.* In *Midsummer,* Shakespeare's making fun of how love makes people act. It's idiotic."

Mr. Blake, who had heretofore appeared to be paying little attention at the back of the theatre, interjects. "Do my ears deceive me? Did I just hear my apprentice call the Bard *idiotic*?"

"No, sir—I didn't. I-I was saying *love* is the idiotic thing," Magpie stammers, but Blake appears already to have stopped paying attention to the goings-on onstage. "Like, the love between Hermia, Lysander, Helena, and Demitrius. It's closer to lust. It's fleeting."

Rue pipes in from offstage. "But then, isn't all love intrinsically fleeting? As Mary Wollstonecraft wrote in *A Vindication of the Rights of Woman,* 'Love from its very nature must be transitory.'" Classic Rue, expecting a gold star for reciting literature off the cuff. It would usually bother me, but I can't blame her for deploying some Wollstonecraftian wisdom when the opportunity arises. She finishes the quote: "'To seek for a secret that would render it constant would be as wild a search as for the philosopher's stone or the grand panacea: and the discovery would be equally useless, or rather pernicious to mankind.'"

"I don't disagree with you, Rue." Magpie looks to the back of the auditorium where Blake had just been, but there are only shadows. "Everyone's on the same page here. The love in *Midsummer* develops too fast."

"'Cus of the love potion," Hunter adds.

Magpie rolls her eyes. "Yeah, we got that."

"I wonder . . . what could the love potion symbolize?" asks Ms. Spry. "What are the forces behind infatuation—or crushes, flings, et cetera—that come up in your lives?"

"Tequila?" Hunter suggests. "Or, I guess if we're not going for literal liquids, jealousy's gotta be a big one."

"Possessiveness," says Frankie.

"Rational thinking?" Margaret offers from her seat in the audience. "Like, kind of talking yourself into liking someone because you think you should?"

Ms. Spry pushes her bottom up onto the edge of the stage, careful to smooth out the hem of her Burberry skirt. "I like that, and I think that has a place in this conversation. But when you're infatuated, does it really feel effortful, or does it feel like a compulsion?"

"It's definitely more compulsive," Hunter replies, then quickly adds, "Like, in the play."

"And in reality? How does true love differ from compulsion?" asks Ms. Spry.

Mag groans and collapses into a cross-legged position. "None of us has even ever been in love. We're too young."

"Young love is still love, though, isn't it?" says Frankie, looking off to the unlit back of the auditorium. *Does she see something there?* I squint to discern what it might be but can't make out anything in the darkness. "A crush has substantial power to it."

"A crush, or love, or whatever you want to call it, that shit—er, stuff—takes big-time conviction," Hunter says. "To see it through, win the girl."

Now it's my turn to roll my eyes.

"What do you think about that, Violet?" Ms. Spry asks.

What do I think about Hunter talking about love like it's a conquest? I think it figures, given his track record, and that's exactly why he's suddenly giving me sweaters and goo-goo eyes. But I don't say that. Instead, I turn to face him directly. "I think love is more than a stupid prize to be won at the end of a stupid game. Love isn't a game."

Hunter cocks an eyebrow, looking as surprised by me as I am. My conversations with him have up until now been pleasant, polite—cordial, even. Maybe there's something about being onstage that emboldens me to speak my mind. "Someone's feeling feisty," he says. A dimple digs deep into his cheek and my resolve melts a little—I may be emboldened, but I'm not immune to the charms of a well-placed dimple.

Frankie snaps out of her reverie. "Violet's right. If you play love like a game, it becomes a dangerous thing."

"Love is dangerous whatever way you cut it. Remember old Gwenny? Your guardian angel?" The golden boy raises two insensitive finger pistols. The joke leaves an acrid taste in my mouth.

"And I guess that brings us back to possessiveness. The male instinct to claim and mark one's territory," says Frankie.

"I didn't say anything about peeing on trees," Hunter replies with a weak, defensive chuckle.

"Neither did I." Frankie doesn't laugh. Her usually lighthearted, indifferent demeanor has changed. A red-hot glare burns between Helena's two suitors, but I'm starting to feel like this isn't about the play, that it might not even be about the ghost.

"Frankie?" I reach for her shoulder, but she doesn't drop Hunter's gaze, not until Ms. Spry interrupts.

"Francesca, why don't you try to bring some of *that* to your performance? I like seeing this fire in you. Write down what you're feeling in this exact moment! Journal break! Go!"

Frankie shrugs off my hand and steps off the stage.

"Who *are* you?" Mag asks, trailing behind. The question is a compliment. "And what have you done with Frankie Lin?"

I'm wondering the same thing. Also, why won't she look at me? Like, me specifically? And, lastly, why do I care? Frankie doesn't stop at her seat, seemingly compelled forward by something in the shadows.

"Where are you *going*?" Mag demands. "Rue, are you coming?"

Rue waves them off. "No, I'm inspired. Must write."

And here I go again, following Frankie Lin, swept up in her dark undertow.

"Hey," I call after her, stumbling out of the glow of Fresnel lights,[72] through a clump of technician guys, and deeper into the darkened theatre. "Hey!"

Mag whips around like I just threw a wet bag of garbage at her. "What? We're in the middle of something."

---

72 Fresnel lights (invented by Augustin-Jean Fresnel for use in lighthouses) are lanterns that produce soft-edged washes of light.

Frankie turns. "What are we in the middle of?"

"I don't know, you're the one being all weird," says Mag.

"I . . . I thought I saw something," Frankie explains, blinking at the darkened aisle leading to the back of the theatre. "It's nothing."

"I was just wondering, Frankie, if you wanted to run lines with me this weekend." My mouth produces these words without my brain's permission. "Both of you, actually."

Mag scoffs. "In your dreams, Cursed Girl." Just as well, I would rather be pummeled by *multiple* wet garbage bags than actually hang out with Dark Cove Theatre Society President Megan "Magpie" Black.

For the first time since Fleck Beach, Frankie fixes her black eyes on me. It isn't easy to make out her features what with the house lights being off, but I think I see a smile. "Sure, yeah. Maybe tomorrow afternoon?

I ignore the shocked expression on Mag's face and say, "I have work, but what about Sunday?"

"Around noon?"

"Sounds excellent. Sunday noon would be very excellent."

Sunday noon would be very excellent? I pivot back to the stage before I can utter any other sentences that sound computer generated and go to journal in my seat next to Kay. They snort.

"What?" I ask.

With a chuckle, they purr, "Care to explain what *that* was about?"

Through gritted teeth, I tell them to shut up. With love. "Later."

Chapter 20

It's a happy dream at first, a crisp autumnal scene bathed in gold. I'm at the bottom of the bell tower at the entrance of the dining hall, which is the same but the facade is covered in vines, ornamented by clusters of a bright flower I can't identify. I watch a bee move from bloom to bloom, gathering pollen fastidiously. Fascinated, I observe her low hum for a long while, but then it lands on one of the two tombstones that shouldn't be there, that should be behind the dining hall, but the architecture of dreams is flimsy like that. The bee on the grave becomes a crow. It pecks on the stone, etched with bold letters:

GWENDOLYN WINCROFT
LOVING WIFE

More death markers spring up from the ground like granite mushrooms after a gentle rain. Then the dream shifts and the bell tower becomes the lighthouse. Clouds gather at an unnatural pace overhead, all gray and silent like an old movie. A menacing fog creeps quickly across the field toward me, shrouding the stones so only the crow is visible, black plumage against gray gloom. It flies up to the lighthouse, and I wonder if the light will go on and show a way out but of course it doesn't—the lighthouse is out of commission, and at Dark Cove you must be your own light, or whatever that asshole Frederick Stine said, and actually now the lighthouse is the bell tower again. A woman calls from up in there. The crow lands at her feet. Standing before the gargantuan bronze bell, she's wearing a broad wedding gown with a high lace neckline and sleeves to match, red buttons trailing down from her elbows to a pointed finger. It is directed at me. Her crimson lips move, screeching something I can't understand. Something in a Latin tongue, "*Ad vitam aeternum*," but I'm only getting an A-minus in Latin and I don't know what it means. She goes on crying out in the thick, ancient language. Then, in English, "Look down." Her voice echoes in a heaven-high howl. I do as she advises. Slithering among the fallen leaves, a snake now coils around my ankles. I try kicking myself free but the creature is already fastened to my calves, binding my knees together. I look around for help but the woman is caught in her taffeta gown like a net. She fades into a dim phantasmal vapor. The crow swoops down on me as the snake makes its way up my legs. The noxious gloom-fog envelops. My body, a fly in a gossamer. The earth trembles. Trees crack and fall. "Help," I try to scream, but no sound comes out.

I don't feel like talking about it, not after that nightmare, but Kay is persistent. They followed me from the dorm room to the bathroom to the dining hall to my shift at the archives and have seated themselves on the edge of the desk, poking and prodding at everything within reach.

"Look at this." I brandish the file of a dropout. "This girl dropped out in 2001 on Halloween night exactly; she specialized in acting."

Kay rolls their eyes. "And what do you plan to do with that information?"

"Study it." I tuck the papers into the right side of my good/bad folder. "Learn about the warning signs—"

"You're gonna drive yourself crazy with this folder."

My jaw clenches. "You know, there is highly classified stuff here. I could get in trouble. Maybe you should ..."

"I should what?"

A divinely timed e-mail notification pops up. The subject reads RE: IPHIGENIA. I hit the X and close the bubble.

"Aren't you ever tempted to read those?" Kay asks.

"No." I flash them a dissuasive glance, not in the mood for their antics. I'm nervous to hang out with Frankie one-on-one, I have a literal mountain of work to do, I can't get that dream out of my head . . . and now I want to read this latest dropout file in peace.

"What's the harm in looking?" They nudge my office chair so it swivels a degree closer to the screen.

I swivel back. "I signed a contract. NDA stuff. It'd be too risky."

"That didn't stop you from keeping all those files you were supposed to shred."

"That's different, Kay."

"How?"

"It just is. If we clicked on the e-mail, Madame—who's right upstairs, by the way—would see we opened it and—"

"It's logged into Mme. Camry's account?"

"Probably. Maybe. Dunno."

Kay deflates with disappointment. "Boring."

"Exactly. Do you really care about her, like, latest book club pick or whatever? I highly doubt her correspondence contains anything scandalous."

"Beyond boring." They roll up the sleeves of a Coogi knockoff sweater that makes them look like the main character in a Nora Ephron movie. "Speaking of scandalous . . ."

"Not now."

"You promised we'd talk about the Frankie thing," they hiss from over the desktop. "You can't keep running away from this conversation."

"There is no *Frankie thing,* and I'm not avoiding any conversation. We both have work to do. Please, just let me focus."

"But I don't wanna do work," they whine. "I *want* to gossip!"

"The hard part is getting started. You always say that about making music, but then soon enough you're—what do you call it?"

"In the zone," Kay answers.

"Exactly. So just ... go get in the zone."

"It's not that easy, Violet. The zone is a sacred space. The zone is a zillion miles away from here. *The zone* is a dot right now."

I flip open an accordion folder in front of my face like the privacy screen in a limo. "Mr. Hendrix gave you a laptop! Entertain yourself."

"All the fun websites are blocked. All I can do on that thing is study and make music on this depressing second-rate GarageBand program." Their hand reaches for the mouse that's attached to the DCAAAF computer. I stop them before they can disturb the screen saver; the Dark Cove coat of arms slides across a black backdrop and changes color upon impact with the screen's edge. If left undisturbed, it would cycle through the ROYGBIV rainbow forever and ever.

"I just wanna see if the websites are blocked on here, too," Kay groans. "I bet you can access all kinds of stuff. The dark web! Or worse, Madame's dirty search history ..."

"That would all be very against the rules."

"What are you, a hall monitor?" They teasingly reach for the mouse again.

"I can't afford to lose this job, Kay. Or get kicked out of the Society."

"Someone's into the whole Dark Cove Theatre Society thing now, aren't they? Might it have to do with a certain Fra—"

"No," I snap. "I'm enjoying the challenge. Mr. Blake might actually be warming up to me, too. It has nothing to do with—"

"You being obsessed with Frankie?"

"Sh!" I peek up the iron staircase to see if Mme. Camry—or anybody—is lurking at the top. The coast is clear, but I hear the distant rhythmic thrumming of my boss's brass cane up and down the library aisles. "Don't say that name, please."

"Frankie?" Kay chuckles, playing with a staple remover like a puppet. "Sorry, sorry. Code name?"

"Call her ... Zelda."

"As in, *The Legend of?*"

"Exactly."

"Okay. I just need to know what's going on between you and Princess Zelda."

I shrug, hopefully in a way that looks like I don't care. But honestly, I've been wondering that same thing for a few days now. "It's nothing. She seemed off, so I was just reaching out as a friend—"

"And when did you two become friends?"

"I don't update you on every advancement in my social life," I say, rifling through a sheaf of paper without any real objective.

Kay drops the staple remover. It clatters on the desk. "You used to."

"Things have felt a little weird between us since Fleck Beach," I say.

"Between you and me?" they ask.

"Between me and Frankie. Something has been bothering her . . ."

Kay slides off the desk and ogles an errant stack of folders. "Maybe it's all that talk about the curse. Or the ghost? You saw how uptight Magpie got—"

"Please don't touch those." I prick my finger on a staple. Blood sprouts. "No, it's not the curse. If anyone's cursed, it's me."

Kay rolls their eyes almost imperceptibly, but I see it.

"What?" I demand. "Just because I got a bit of positive feedback doesn't mean that I can rest on my—"

"Who says you're the one who has to be cursed? Magpie?"

I suck at the finger, which is still bleeding. "Well, who's more read up on this freakin' curse than Magpie? And according to her, it's always someone who's a weak link."

"You're not weak. Seriously, babe, besides that one panic attack you had a billion years ago—which isn't a sign of weakness, by the way—"

"It was only a few months ago."

"Besides that event from ancient history," Kay continues, "what makes you think you're a weak link?"

I breathe in two lungfuls of dusty air. "I blinked in the portrait."

"Oh boy . . ."

"Listen, Kay, every year in the Society portrait, someone blinks. Every year. One blinker."

"Okay, but—"

"It's not only that. There's a crow. In the window! And I forgot, Kay, or I didn't see the significance of it, but there was a crow in the rafters that day, the day of my monologue, and then in the window, and then the other day, too, I saw it in the—"

"Try breathing, Violet. There's something like a billion crows on this island—"

"It's more than that. I've had dreams, they feel like a sign or—"

Kay bursts into a fit of laughter. "Our whole lives you've been so anti-supernatural and all of the sudden you're this occultist. I can't believe it."

"Well, glad you find it so funny," I snap. "Why don't you go not believe it somewhere else?"

The smile on Kay's face withers. "Sorry," they say coolly, "I'll get out of your way."

"I'm just on edge. It's . . . I have work to do."

"I know."

Great, I think, *just when I take care of one cold shoulder, I get another one.*

"Kay, come on, you have composing to do, anyway. So. Be good, do your work upstairs, and maybe one day soon we can rent some DVDs out to watch on that laptop of yours," I bargain. "We can stay up late, marathon it."

They give a small grin. "Make it tonight, and you've got yourself a deal."

"Um, I really have to drum my lines into my head tonight before hanging with Frankie tomorrow. Tomorrow night?"

"I have band practice."

"Right. Let's lock in a night next weekend. Saturday?"

Already on their way out, they call back to me, "You've got yourself a deal, girl." Their footsteps clang up the staircase. Then, silence. Even in the muted dark, long after my friend has left, I can't seem to get my mind back on track. My mouth still carries the metallic taste of blood.

Chapter 21

I wake up to a knock at the dorm room door, snagging a little on my dream. It lacked in continuity, the dream, set in the theatre at first, but then the theatre turned into my room back home, but Frankie was there, and—

Knock-knock.

Right. The door.

"Who goes there?" Kay grumbles.

I drag myself off my mattress. "What time is it? What *day* is it?"

"Time is a man-made construct. The Gregorian calendar is a lie. Go get the door and let me sleep." Kay buries themself further under their blankets.

I pad across the wood floor and yank the door open.

It's Frankie, straight out of my dream, except she isn't dressed in anything my subconscious could ever imagine her wearing: baggy sweatpants and a ratty tee from an old Hozier tour, both black. In fact, her fuzzy pink bunny slippers are the only colorful thing about her. There's no tint on her lips. The polish on her nails is chipped. Her perennially silky curtain of hair is swept back into a lopsided bun. She looks wan, with none of her usual luminescence.

Something is very wrong.

"I'm sorry. I can't make our lunch plans," she says at the speed of thought.

I rub the sleep from my eyes. "What's going on?" I half expect the hallway to spin three-sixty like that scene from *High School Musical 3: Senior Year* ... or that other scene from *Inception*. Is this a dream within a dream?

"I didn't sleep well. I'm not feeling well." These words spill out of her mouth like water. She runs for the bathroom. I guess I should chase after her? I brace myself for the variety of food poisoning scenarios that may await ...

Inside, a single stall is occupied. Soft sobs echo against marble.

"Frankie?" I half-whisper, and that's when the sobs turn into a heaving thing, the kind of crying that gets done when the world ends.

I splash my face with water, not taking the time to pat it dry before approaching the stall. Carefully, I rap on the door. "Let me in."

For a moment, her weeping calms. The bolt unfastens, her wordless permission for me to enter. I slink inside and lock the graffiti-etched door behind me. She sits on top of the toilet lid, face hidden inside cupped hands.

"Are you okay?" I ask stupidly, the answer obvious.

Unsure of what to do with my limbs, I place my hand on her back and crouch down, balancing on my heels at her level. I reach my other arm over her back and hold on, inhaling the ghost of her day-old perfume. I feel her ribs expand and contract with frenetic sadness. Acutely aware that this is the closest I've ever been to Frankie Lin, I go rigid.

"Everything is wrong," she wails. "I don't know what to do."

"What is it?" I whisper into her licorice-black hair, where I think her ear is.

"Everything."

"Can you tell me some of the things?"

She wipes her nose. "I don't want to."

"That's okay." I am surprised by my own softness, by the aching inside my chest. It reveals to me an inconvenient fact: That I care for Frankie Lin. That I wish to protect her, in some way, for some reason too big to be contained in this tiny bathroom stall.

"I failed my history test," she confesses, "and Mr. Norman told my mother."

Crap. "It's just one test. It's just a number," I lie, and she cries even harder. She knows as well as I do that every failing grade at this school is a strike against you, and the rules of baseball here apply. Three strikes and you're out.

The longer you live here, the more this island reveals itself to you as a microcosm of the world: its arbitrary rules, its peaks and deadfalls, its natural theatrics. Expulsion, I've learned through my trawls in the DCAAAF, isn't that conceptually distinct from fatality. Expelled students depart without ceremony. We never see them walk the gangplank. We never see them again, period. The evicted make no broadly perceivable mark on the world, no grand legacy. They leave behind a trail of foam on the water cast by the homeward ferry, and even that lasts for only a moment. Out here, it's sink or swim. Victory or defeat. Life or death.

I'm not sure which is worse: to be forced into oblivion by the faculty or to take yourself out.

"I'm not doing well in anything," Frankie says between erratic breaths. "Even in rehearsal, I'm not really in it. If they kick me out . . ."

"They won't."

"Why not?"

"Because . . ." Dark Cove wouldn't be Dark Cove without Frankie Lin. I try imagining it and come up short. Everything would be out of whack, our ecological balance off-kilter. She tops our social pyramid, like a flyer on the cheerleading squad or the angel on a Christmas tree. Sure, the structure would stay intact, but it would be missing its show-stopping fixture. Without Frankie Lin, there would be no one to compete with, nothing to aspire to.

Instead of all that, I say, "You belong here."

"I won't if I keep failing," she utters numbly, the song leached out of her voice. I watch her collapse in on herself like a wave just off the shore, face buried in her own trembling hands. This couldn't possibly be the same girl who vaulted into the darkened ocean with reckless abandon.

"Frankie, you're the most talented person I know … and I can't even tell you're not 'in it.' Besides, acting is about what people see, not what you feel."

Through the muffle of her palms still covering her face, I can't quite make it out, but I think she says, "The emotion matters. To me. But I can't—I *know* you hate me, even when you have to pretend to be into me."

I want to correct her but I'm not sure if I heard her right, and I'm even less sure if I'm ready to admit that it's getting much, much easier to pretend—that I'm not even sure what's pretend anymore.

"It's not your fault," she adds. "It's me. I can't get *anything* right."

If Frankie Lin can't get anything right, is there any hope for the rest of us? "You're brilliant. At everything. Brilliant people aren't always great at tests. Brilliant people aren't perfect. Emotions are … messy."

Finally, she raises her face to me, a raw and open wound. It's flushed, streaked with mascara, eyes haunted, bloodshot and cavernous. Tears depart from their ducts steadily, single file. "You know universities don't get all that, my mom doesn't—" and then she breaks down again, only this time she grabs onto my shoulders, hugs me fiercely, heaving into my chest. "She's on the Board. I'm shaming her."

"Frankie, your mom loves you. Everyone loves you!"

"*No one* even *knows* who *I am*. Even if I wanted to go home, I couldn't." She gasps for air. "I can't go back there. You think the teachers here are intense? Wait til you meet my mother. She expects perfection. Nothing less. No. I can't go back. I can't."

The hard silence that follows forces me to confront the truth: *I've been all wrong about Frankie Lin.* By mythologizing her, making her into the villain of my story, I denied her contradictions. Probably because they're hard for me to understand. But she is real. Credulous and shrewd. Self-critical and confident. Courageous and terrified. Like a pendulum, she goes from one end of the spectrum to another. From calm and collected to repeating the words "I can't go back" again and again. She whispers them to herself like a private incantation or a CD stuck on the worst part of a song. "Can't go back."

I have no idea what awaits Frankie in Taipei. I have no real understanding of her backstory or home life, just a hazy conceptualization cobbled together by social media posts: her enormous closet, her diving medals, her vast network of airbrushed friends, her favorite vegan recipe and go-to order at Dreamers Coffee.[73] Essentially, I know nothing real about Frankie Lin or what the stakes are for her.

"I know you hate me." She moves like an earthquake in my arms. "And I understand why you do."

I hear her loud and clear this time. "I don't hate you, Frankie," I say. But I *did* hate her, didn't I? When exactly did that stop? And why did I start? I feel a pang of guilt as I uncover the root of the feeling there in my gut: envy, jealousy, all those seeds of competition that the Academy plants in its good, good girls. "I just didn't know you. I didn't let myself know you. But I'd like to get to know you now. If you'll allow it."

My formerly sworn enemy looks up at me, face swollen, just inches between us. "You don't really want that."

"I do. I swear I do." The bathroom lights flicker and a gradual drop in temperature draws our bodies together. The mystery of this interior weather change hangs heavy above our tiny stall. "Let's study for your next test together," I suggest. "Let's run our lines later. Let's stick to the plan. I'll take you to my favorite spot on campus." The last time I was there—my hilltop reading nook under the great willow tree—was a few weeks ago, when Frankie crept up on me and everything was different. Today, the immovable Frankie Lin stares me down with big eyes full of demons, now brimming with hope. Like maybe I can be the one to exorcise her. "Can we just stay here for a while?" she asks.

"Yes, Frankie. We can stay here as long as you need." I hold onto her like this, crouched on the floor of a tiny bathroom stall, not saying anything at all, until pins and needles prick into my legs.

Nothing ever goes according to plan, does it? I think. I almost want to laugh.

---

73 A snow-mist cold brew.

Chapter 22

Frankie Lin. I can't stop thinking about her. She didn't feel up to our line run—though I foolishly spent all afternoon yesterday waiting by the willow tree just in case she changed her mind—so I haven't talked to her since the bathroom. It's as if I've been bewitched. My muscles tense up every time I see her—inconvenient, seeing as today we have intimacy training.

Thankfully, Mr. Blake isn't in attendance, so that takes a wee bit of the pressure off.

"If at any point you feel weird, you can give me a little signal and I'll stop, okay?" Ms. Spry makes a small hand gesture that she asks us to copy. "Just do that if you want me to slow down. Cool? Now, when it comes to intimacy onstage, whether that's a kiss or a handhold, we want to be super communicative about what we are going to do, right? It's like the basic rules of consent you guys already know about.[74] You wanna make sure your scene partner is comfortable with every touch, and you *never* want

---

74 There is no formal sexual education at Dark Cove Arts Academy—the school operates on the assumption that these vital lessons have already been taught—but there are pamphlets about various STIs available at the infirmary in Accolade North.

to surprise them." The teacher's wide, doll-like eyes scan the players in the audience, locking into us one at a time to make sure we're listening. "Do any of our couples feel comfortable coming up here?"

Frankie checks in with me wordlessly from the seat beside mine. I give her a small nod. "We can," she offers.

"Beautiful. My two brave young women," Ms. Spry exclaims as we walk up onto the stage. "Now, Demetrius. You really go through a journey with your affection. You aren't into Helena at first, then you're ga-ga over her, and then you're just in a sort of honeymoon phase by the end, right?"

"Totally." Frankie gives an enthusiastic head bob that I've found annoying until recently. Now, everything she does seems to hold some profound meaning, each gesture is a glyph for me to decipher.

"How could we show that journey physically, say, in Act 5, scene 1? You're out of the woods, literally and figuratively, but you're still super in love," Ms. Spry probes.

"Maybe I could put my arm around Helena's waist?" Frankie throws me a sideways glance, which I catch through her fringe of thick lashes.

"That's a good idea," Ms. Spry says calmly, script firm in hand. "Now, Helena might be fine with that, but we also want to check in with Violet here ahead of time. Violet, at this specific beat, for example" —she points to a line in the script—"Frankie could touch your waist. Are there any areas you feel uncomfortable being touched?"

A few students chuckle darkly.

"I know, I know, it can be a little weird, right?" Ms. Spry opens herself up to the class. "But this isn't just about Helena and Demetrius; everybody needs to think about this. What boundaries do you have onstage? I want you to mull over that this week, but you can also change your mind, too. Just like in real intimate situations. Like, sexually."

Michael and Hunter nudge one another like animals at a zoo. Everyone else blinks awkwardly.

"Alrighty then." Our director resumes her post in her director's chair. "Why don't we practice? Act 5, scene 1? Let's start from the lovers' entrance. Have a chat with your partner, and if you need to check in with each other in the middle of the scene, you can absolutely do that, okay? Places!"

As our peers navigate themselves to their marks, Frankie leans into me. "Is it okay if I put my hand on your waist?"

"Yes," I answer, surprised at how certain I sound and feel.

Shortly after Ms. Spry says "action," Frankie casually wraps her arm around me. She rubs her thumb lightly against the small of my back. My skin tingles pleasantly under her touch, not understanding that this piece of affection could very well be an acting choice. *Is it?* When I look at her, she's already got her dark eyes on me, and then there's that invisible tightrope connecting us.

"Still okay?" she whispers under the thunder of dialogue.

I gulp. "Mm-hmm."

Appendix Q

Poem by V. Costantino

Love hatched under ~~spotlight~~ dappled moonlight;
we mine for rubies but
the forest is looted clean.
Long and long I've sought where you might be.
A million expressions of your woman-face have drifted through
the sky like stardust
and cleared out all the scudding clouds,
those ones channelled deep with fear.
At last, here, an old corvid
shows me where you've been.
We fly beyond the grime and gore
to where you've always been.

— V. Costantino

Chapter 23

Backstage, everything starts to feel real. Yes, the air is powdery with makeup and machine-produced fog. Yes, we are in costume; I, in silky pajama pants and a lacy chemise that leaves my décolletage exposed. Yes, we are playing pretend. But the gravity of this moment is every bit as potent as the heady scent of hairspray. Just a little over two weeks out from opening night, we're preparing for our first dress-tech rehearsal. While everything's all set up, Ms. Spry arranged for a quick promotional photoshoot.

First up, there's Frankie. From the wings, I eye her side profile, backlit and defined. The hiss of the fog machine precedes the arrival of a cloud. In it, she looks like an angel. Technicians play with the light and her hair catches and refracts every color. I previously would have assumed this to be the effect of some top-shelf leave-in conditioning oil, but today it feels possible that this a glimpse at her aura. Frankie's halo. Her legs stride through the mist, the particles divide for her, bowing to a young woman so self-assured that her movements could change the weather—the opposite of how I move through the world. Out there, I am the one who bows. I make myself small in the face of a storm while Frankie dances in the eye of it. How strange it is now, holding the secret knowledge that she feels as lost as I do. She must look untouchable to the audience on the other side of the scrim.[75] I'm overcome with the sudden want to reach out and be the one to touch her.

"You are a vision," Rue tells me, interrupting my reverie.

Eager to wring as many resumé credentials as possible out of this experience, Rue has volunteered to help with hair and makeup—both the assistant and the crew head have called in sick—and is currently at work on a pile of braids atop my head. The dressing chair that I sit in faces an unmirrored wall and I'm content in this momentary oblivion. For now, my appearance is a mystery to me, which is exactly how I like it. The serenity is fleeting, as Rue spins me toward my reflection. I gape at it: my natural curls cascade from a tower of braids like fine loomwork—*who knew I had so much hair?* The costume, made to my measurements, looks like it belongs there, on my body. The makeup, though it's caked on quite heavily, is dramatic in the most spectacular fashion. My cheeks are done in a deep crimson, my lips to match. Every facial feature has been exaggerated. I could have never imagined *liking* an exaggerated version of myself, and yet ... "I love it, Rue. You're a hair virtuoso."

"If only I wanted to be a hairstylist. Unfortunately, I'm destined for a career as a theatre critic." She sighs, gazing at her work. She wears contacts for the show instead of her glasses. Her face is lightly dusted with sparkles, her makeup quite minimal. Rue is such a beauty, I had always assumed she'd wanted to be an actor. "I prefer analyzing art to creating it," she explains simply.

"Why don't you come on over here and philosophize about art criticism and whatever while you do *my* makeup?" Magpie whines. "Literally where is Carlotta?"

"Carlotta?" I ask.

"The little hair, makeup, costume, whatever girl. I've been waiting for my turn for ages."

---

75 A scrim is a gauzy screen of cloth that looks opaque until lit from behind. This one has the picture of Dark Cove's forest woven into it, which vanishes when backlit. It creates a dreamy sort of storybook illusion. Though I doubt this is the designer's intention, I read it as a metaphor: a forest is just a pretty scene until you spend some time within it.

"Her name is Edie and she's got that flu that's going around," says Rue.

"Flu is just another word for lazy."

"No, flu is a euphemism for 'projectile vomit in the girls' bathroom.'" Rue moves on to Magpie's luscious plume of hair. "Fret not, love. You hardly need any work done here. You're a natural work of art."

"So's Violet," Frankie says nonchalantly, brushing past me as she joins us backstage. "They want you for photos now, V."

V. I take a beat to savor the new nickname.

In *Romeo and Juliet*, Romeo has this monologue where he asks what's in a name. The implication is that names are irrelevant, but I disagree. The common names of flowers telegraph information about their color and history. The names of places can honor even the dishonorable. And nicknames ... nicknames are intimate.

Frankie smiles sweetly, her cupid's bow painted hot pink. Her arrow aimed right at me.

"Violet! You ready?" Ms. Spry calls from the other side of the curtain, yanking me out of my daydream and onstage as if by a cane. I trip out over the hem of the stage curtain, falling over onto my hands and knees in an accidental cow pose. In front of everyone.

Reflexively, I tilt my head up to the rafters, looking for a crow or some portent of the supernatural, but it's empty up there. Dust and shadows, no birds, none of the undead. I crane my neck down again, expelling breath as I go from cow to cat. Magpie gives a hearty laugh; Romeo barks from the back of the auditorium; the photographer, Ms. Spry, and Hunter all stare down at me in a triangular formation onstage. I couldn't be more thankful for the rouge already on my cheeks—hopefully it's concealing the never-ending blush that I am experiencing.

"Oh my god, Violet, are you all right?" Ms. Spry asks.

Hunter offers his hand to help me up. I let him. "I'm fine, fine." I dust off the knees of my PJ pants but it just rubs the dirt into the Duchess satin. The costume team won't be happy. I fix the curtain closed behind me, getting a sight of Frankie's sympathetic expression before it's overtaken by red velvet.

"Okay, you ready? *We've* been ready for a minute, so," the photographer says impatiently like he's some in-demand professional and not a Vis student. It's Nondescript Bro, Hunter's friend.

"Sorry to keep you waiting," I mumble, weaving through a maze of set pieces (lanterns, ferns, pumpkins, etc.[76]) to center stage.

"You're worth the wait," says Hunter. He gives me a roguish wink.

The aforementioned blush deepens.

"My guy," says Nondescript Bro, "why are you flirting with *her* right now?"

"Don't mind him. He doesn't get out of the dark room much," Hunter whispers as I make an effort to look stoic.

Though this allusion to my inadequate level of desirability according to NB[77] should offend me, I can't help wondering the same thing. Who is Hunter to flirt with me? Who am I to indulge it? His friends would never approve of any sort of relationship between us, and, as was evidenced by his actions at the Spring Fling, Hunter cares all too much what his friends think. I wonder if he knows I heard him that night. Maybe he's trying to prove something to me, that he's a "nice guy." He's probably just trying to prove to *himself* that he can get me.

"We're doing one-on-one pictures with each pairing of lovers for these posters," says Ms. Spry. "To hype up the love-quadrangle drama-lama, we're getting shots of each couple looking lovingly at each other and then fighting. Cool?" She directs us to sit on the floor near a potted fern and act "lovey-dovey." Hunter, without a care or thought, abruptly puts his arm around me. "Hunter," Ms. Spry urges, "remember what we said in rehearsals about asking first?"

He recoils his arm quickly. "Oh, sorry. Is it okay if I put my arm around you?"

"Sure," I respond robotically. My shoulders tense up as he jerks back into position, eliciting rapid-fire camera snaps from NB.

---

76 Maidenhair, foraged from the island. PVC, foraged from the Accolade North props room.

77 Shorthand for Nondescript Bro.

Click, click, click, click, click.

"Get a little closer," NB commands. We scooch in. "Closer! You hardly fit in the frame here." After another adjustment, Hunter is in startling proximity to my face. I hold my breath, recalling the chicken salad I ate for lunch and then wondering if he wants to kiss me. I know he's just acting, but I'm nervous that he isn't, and that he's going to forget to ask for my permission again.

Click, click, click.

With every freeze frame, it seems Hunter draws in another inch. His green-eyed gaze darting between my eyes and lips. Making me almost believe he wants me. Making me believe it might not just be a game.

Click, click.

My heart is a goddamn ticking time bomb, racing faster and faster until at risk of explosion.

Click.

Then it's pitch black. Hunter's forehead bumps into mine. Something crashes loudly. A scream erupts from somewhere backstage.

The posters are up the following Monday—and they're *everywhere.* Pasted onto lockers, disrupting the integrity of stained-glass windows, and littered on the floors of Accolade South. It's surreal, looking at these high-def, blown-up images of me, looking at other people looking at these high-def, blown-up images of me. I feel so . . . perceived, but not in the violating or embarrassing way I would have expected. Maybe a better way to put it is that I feel seen. Kay squeals as we rush up to inspect the bulletin board. To NB's credit, the photos look very professional. Every poster tells a different story, though not quite the intriguing romance our director had described. Mostly, the marketing materials focus on Puck and the fairies, since they were photographed first, and before the blackout.

It was a full hour before power was restored in Wincroft Theatre. We spent some of that time playing the "I can't wait" game in the dark, but that didn't last long because every answer eventually became some variation of "I can't wait until the lights turn back on." By the time the bulbs flickered to life, NB was jittery and apparently "running late" for some ambiguous commitment. As a result, my photo shoot was cut short, not that I minded. I got two solo stills before Ms. Spry called on Frankie and Magpie (the latter of whom is my suspect for the mystery power-outage screamer, though she denies it). Then, we took a burst of photos of the four of us and NB unceremoniously announced that that was a wrap. (We pushed our dress rehearsal to Tuesday.)

The hero image shows Rue, leg back in tendu, looking cheekily over her shoulder at the three dancers, each one frozen in mid-air. There are just a few posters of the lovers. In one, Frankie and Hunter appear to be mid-brawl. Another has Frankie stroking Magpie's cheek as the latter rolls her eyes. Then, there's a photo from my brief session with Hunter, which depicts us in a passionate stare down. I can almost feel his breath on my face just looking at it.

Kay digs a finger into my ribs when they see it. "Okay, are you into Hunter Kinsey again, or should I give you an Oscar right now?"

I squirm away. "It's called acting."

"Well *he* is *not* that good of an actor. Seriously, you guys look so good together."

We are interrupted by the sound of tearing paper—it's Magpie ripping a poster of her and Frankie off the board. When Kay gives her a look, she glares back at them. "What? Never heard of a souvenir?"

"Oh, we know all about souvenirs, don't we, Vi? Got a folder full of 'em," Kay teases. "I'm sure Magpie'd love to see it ..."

Even though I know they're only joking, my stomach lurches. "No!"

"Consider yourself lucky," Kay says to Magpie.

Magpie flips her hair. "I always have," she says hollowly. Then, turning to me, "At least you didn't blink." And with that—a smile that I'm not sure is sincere and a joke that I'm pretty sure I'm in on—she swoops off to rip down another set of posters in the dining hall.

Kay snorts. "Well, that was relatively non-bitchy. Are you and Mag friends now?"

"No way. Maybe ... cordial acquaintances? She hasn't called me 'Cursed Girl' in over a week."

"I'm so ready for this show to open, if only to never hear the word 'curse' again."

Chapter 24

I'm just three sleeps away from beating the Society curse. Just three sleeps away from the play opening on Halloween Monday. It's so close I can almost taste the candy corn.

"I can't wait for Hell Week to be over with," Magpie says when it's her turn in the final "I can't wait" game of our final rehearsal.

"Don't wish this experience away, guys," Ms. Spry chirps. "It'll be gone before you know it!"

Hunter runs a hand through his hair. "Oh, yeaaaah"—he intones the *yeah* for a few seconds—"Spry's first Hell Week. You ready for this, chica?"

"Oh, Romeo and I have our outfits all picked out for opening night." She pulls at the lapel of her Gucci blazer. "Romes wants to impress the Board, don't you, boy?"

"And the school evaluation rep people, don't forget them, Romeo," Hunter says, patting the sleeping dog. Romeo twitches, oblivious, probably chasing after a dream rabbit.

Our director chuckles. "Yes, and the school evaluation rep people, too."

"At least you don't have to worry about impressing your mother, Ms. Spry." Frankie half-smiles. "Or midterms."

Our director looks around the circle. "I'm sure you'll all spend your weekend studying your butts off. And resting, right?"

"*Suuure*," Hunter draws out the word again, looking right at me. "Studying, *right*."

"I don't know what you're talking about," Ms. Spry says, and I myself have only a suspicion as to what he's hinting at. "I don't think I *want* to know. So, I'll let you get to your Friday nights. I'll see you on the big day! Show's at six, right? But we're meeting first thing after school. Don't let any *studying* get in the way of your punctual-ness! Make sure to get enough sleep and all that. Okay. Go on, get."

She shoos us away and, as I gather my things, I feel pure excitement coursing through me. There are, of course, the standard precursive nerves, but the blocking lives in my body now. It's more than muscle memory; it's a sort of cellular certainty. I don't have to think of what to say, where to go, how to feel. The lighting transitions from warm to cool, and the whole cast moves through scenes like one season passing into the next. It's a kind of magic, and I know we all feel it running through us, like an electric current. The thought of someone dropping out feels like an impossibility; it would break the circuit. We rely on each other. We're connected. If I wave my hand and say these words, another performer knows what they must do. What a wonderful sort of alchemy it is, to make something out of just the imaginings of a group of friends.

The Gaykeepers scurry out of the theatre, snickering as they leave. "See you later, V," Frankie calls back to me, the mystery of "later" like a burst of confetti in the air.

I've never been invited to the Dark Cove Theatre Society's Hell Week Party. Honestly, I forgot it was a thing until right now. I don't know, it's never piqued my interest as it does every other Covie's. Though it's only ever whispered about, the annual event is the source of widespread rumor and envy alike. It's said to be the initiation site of many a Dark Cove romance. Attendance is by invitation only. No plus ones allowed. The location is kept secret. All that's known about the cloak-and-dagger party is its invariable timing (the Saturday before Hell Week) and its exclusivity. Oh, and there's booze. Lots of booze. Word on the island is there's a secret stash of approximately a bajillion bottles of bootleg whisky and gin stored under the floorboards of one of the cabins at the old campsite. Don't ask me how it hasn't been raided by the faculty yet—actually, don't ask me for any details at all. As I said, I've never been invited before. So, when I find a wax-sealed envelope in my mail cubby, I'm not expecting much of its contents—probably a notice of some sort from the school. But, the seal isn't forest-green DCAA official, it's crimson red and embossed with a small ring of crows. I slide my fingertips under the crisp parchment and lift open the envelope. Inside, there is a torn-out title page from *The Edible Woman* (sorry, Margaret Atwood). Scratched on the reverse side in blood-red ink is an invitation to the party. *The* party. An invitation presumably meant for me. This is a presumption I would regularly second guess, but this year, I *am* a member of the Dark Cove Theatre Society.

On the bottom of the paper, in a shade of pink lipstick I recognize immediately, there is the delicate mark of a kiss.

Appendix R

Invitation to the Dark Cove Theatre Society Hell Week Party, addressed to V. Costantino

HELL WEEK IS UPON US . . .

TIME TO WAKE THE DEAD

CABIN 5

SATURDAY NIGHT

DARK COVE THEATRE SOCIETY ONLY

DRESS TO KILL

Chapter 25

"We already have plans tomorrow, you know, the plans we've been rain-checking for a month now?" Kay reminds me when I wave our invitations in front of their face. They don't look up, dialed in on some complex recording software that makes music look like math.

"Right," I say. "Scary movie marathon. We could do that tonight instead?"

They bite into a perfect October-red apple and continue clicking away at their screen as if I didn't say anything. I wait for them to chew and swallow but their silence continues.

"Hello? Earth to Kay?"

"I'm *in the zone*, Vi. Final score's due at midnight, and it needs to sound pastoral and epic and right now every song sounds like it's performed by a loser-y, juvenile high school marching band."

"It *is* performed by a high school marching band," I counter.

"Please. Respect the zone," they say, eyes still glued on the screen.

"It's a costume party!" I press on. "You *love* costume parties! See? *Dress to kill*!"

Kay turns away from their laptop with a sigh. "Okay, you have my attention. But only for two minutes." They grab the invitations with their right hand, tossing the apple up into the air with their left, catching it without a fumble.

"Mine doesn't have the lipstick." Kay's scrutinizing stare moves up from the invitation to my face.

I shrug, reluctant to share my suspicions of what the kiss mark might mean, who might have left it there. I don't want to say it out loud without knowing for sure …

They squint at me suspiciously before returning their focus to the invitation. "Why's it written like a ransom letter?"

"I guess they just want it to be mysterious. Low-key."

"Of *course* they want this illicit boy-girl party to be *low-key*! There's going to be kegs of beer and a cabin full of obnoxious, drunk, sex-crazed teenagers. They're going against every rule there is. I'm surprised you're even considering—"

"*We* won't drink, though," I explain. Kay and I don't imbibe. Coming from a small town, we've seen too many assholes turn into even bigger assholes under the influence, and vodka's consequently lost all its appeal. "We went to Fleck Beach and didn't get caught, remember? Anyway, we signed the contract, we have to go."

"Fleck Beach had lower stakes. And we don't *have* to go. Margaret didn't go to the beach, and she's still in the Society. I mean, think rationally here," they say through a mouthful of apple, "even if we aren't drinking, being in the same room as alcohol means automatic expulsion. You know that. More than anyone, *you* know that, Miss I-Know-the-Code-of-Conduct-by-Heart-Front-to-Back-Word-for-Word."

"Yeah, but they do it every year—"

"They can afford to! If those kids get caught, their parents'll shower the school with money to keep them here! *We* don't have that financial cushion." Kay shoves the apple core into an overflowing dustbin under the desk—slam dunk.

"Frankie's mom is on the Board of Governors, maybe she'd protect us." Not even I believe the words coming out of my mouth.

"She'd protect her daughter, sure. If *we* got caught, we'd be dead meat. Two suckling pigs, roasted and served with a sprig of locally grown—"

"I get it. Jeez, I thought *I* was supposed to be the rule stickler around here."

"So did I," Kay mumbles. They glance toward their composition briefly before throwing their head back in frustration. "I could just *really* use a movie night with my buddy."

"All right," I sigh. "I get off at seven tomorrow, which gives us like . . . thirty minutes to grab some movies to rent out before Mme. Camry locks up the library. Maybe you should pick one for us?"

"You make it sound like a chore. Picking the flick is half the fun."

"Sure," I say.

"Oh, come on. We may not be puking our guts up in a cabin with Dark Cove's most wanted, but we'll have fun. Hey, we can even dress up, since you were so excited about it. Just us."

"You know that was just a selling point to get you to want to go to the party."

Kay says nothing as they fish through a complication of clips, rings, chains, and trinkets in a catch-all dish on their bedside.

"What are you looking for?"

"Inspiration." They proceed to their trunk, piling corsets, kimonos, skinny jeans, and various Spirit Halloween masks onto their bed. "Here you are." Using their pinky as a hook, they pull a pair of hot-pink heels out from the bottom of their trunk. "Try these on!"

"You know I'm not one to suffer for fashion."

"Nor do you suffer fools, and yet you just tried to convince me to go to a party with every bibulous bozo on campus."

"Bibulous bozo, nice alliteration."

"I know."

"Still not wearing those heels."

Kay chews on their lip, the shoes still dangling from their pinky finger like a Christmas ornament. "Babe, you're the one who forgot to bring *any* costumes to school."

"So?"

"So you're dressing up however I want you to dress."

"*Fifty Shades of Grey* much?"

"First you wanna go to a party with drinking, now an R-rated reference?" Kay holds their free hand up to my forehead. "Are you coming down with something?"

I bat their hand away. "Cut it out."

"No, I'm serious, I think you have a temperature. Must be . . . Bad Girl Syndrome."

I chortle. "Sure, fine, you can dress me up. I'll be your personal Barbie."

The imaginary lightbulb over Kay's head reappears with the power of a trillion watts. "That's it! You'll be Barbie!"

That was easy enough. I thought we'd have to spend hours going through that trunk before landing on a costume for our not-party. "Fine. But no heels. And I'm not wearing it outside of this room. Those are my vetoes."

"There are no vetoes during Hell Week. Check the Dark Cove Arts Academy Code of Conduct." Kay tosses the pair of fuchsia stilettos at my feet, the straps an identical shade to the lipstick kiss on my invitation. I force a laugh and wonder if Kay can tell how strained it is. If they can, they don't show it, turning to their laptop and slipping their headphones back on, leaving me alone with my thoughts.

I scan through DCAAAF files without registering the words I regurgitate into the program. The idea of the party buzzes around me. I distractedly shove a wad of discarded papers into the shredder. It jams. "Great," I mumble.

Tap tap tap.

I look to the stairs. No one is here.

Tap tap.

I check the shredder (still jammed) and under the desk (nada).

"Hello?" I ask the empty room.

No response. The tapping persists. I groan my way out of the office chair, checking between each shelf for the perpetrator of the—

Tap tap tap tap tap.

Down the center aisle, I see a crow at the window. It's large, a bald patch on one of its wings. It knocks at the glass with a thick black beak. Pale silver moonlight reflects off its bristling plumage. The bird begins a rambling sub-song in its strange dialect of rattling clicks and caws. With every utterance, its neck extends and contracts—almost looks like it's dry heaving.

"What?" I demand. "What do you want?"

After an extended final croak (which could pass for a sound effect from *Alien*), the bird tilts its small, delicate head several degrees to one side. It balks at me, *sees me*, but, I reason, probably can't understand me.[78] I shoo it away, literally uttering the word "shoo" a few times and making a dramatic sweeping gesture—this, the corvid apparently comprehends. It flies off with a few offended caws.

I reorient myself. "Where was I?" I say out loud like some tertiary character at the beginning of a horror movie who's about to get murdered. I shoo the thought away the same as I did the bird. Back to work. My last entry in the *L*'s: Sarah Lynch. The name is familiar.

I survey her file and discover a medical record for a fractured wrist. Another one reveals she experienced panic attacks semi-regularly. This must be the girl Magpie referenced when I first learned about the curse! A few pages deep, I learn Sarah's specialization was acting. Years of study: 2002 through 2004. Teachers described her as reclusive, encouraging her to break out of her comfort zone. She dropped out on the morning of the Halloween Play, supposed Dark Cove Theatre Society cursee of the year. My pulse quickens as I pull out the good/bad folder—much thicker on the good side, only a couple files on the bad—and slide Sarah's file in one paper at a time. I read them carefully as I do so.

The fractured wrist was, according to an incident report, the result of Sarah running offstage and falling in the middle of a dress rehearsal. The play: *A Midsummer Night's Dream*, directed by Mr. Blake. *And* she got a C in Mr. Blake's acting class.

---

78 Impressively, corvids do possess the ability to mimic just as well as parrots. The sound is deeper, though. Throaty.

Just like me.

A violent surge of blood pounds at my temples. A swell of nausea arrives. I swivel away from the desk, careening my head over the recycling bin. Saliva pools in my mouth, but then something else catches my attention, something compelling enough to distract from the information-overload-induced hangover. Another medical file, one of the documents with which I jammed the shredder before the crow's interlude. Though half-shredded, I can make out the name on the top: Ingrid, Nora. "How did I not notice this?" I say to myself. Nora's the girl from the nineties that Kay was talking about last month. I remember them telling me Nora fled from her aerial stunt the night before her show's opening.

Tactfully, I pluck the shreds from the bin like a delicate egg from its nest and piece them together on the smooth metal of the desk.

... professors note a shift in behavior and personality ...

They were keeping an extra close eye on her.

... student stays in dorm outside of school hours ... reclusive ...

That's a descriptor I've seen in not only Sarah's report but at least one of the other files I've compiled on the bad side of my folder—probably more, I just didn't know what to look for.

... distracted ...

An unwelcome sense of familiarity overcomes me.

... phobias growing in number and intensity ... acrophobia,[79] *ornithophobia,*[80] *thalassaphobia,*[81] *phasmaphobia*[82] *...*

Like when you're in a bad dream and you recognize the setting from another long-forgotten nightmare.

... student complains of night terrors ... a woman screaming ... hallucinations suspected ...

---

79 Fear of heights.

80 Fear of birds, or specific species of birds.

81 Fear of deep water.

82 Fear of ghosts.

My own visions come to me in an unwelcome montage, one horrific flash after the next, played under the sound of that supernatural scream that has been hunting me from one Dark Cove coordinate to the next. A creeping fog. A red sky. A lace wedding gown.

. . . environmental triggers . . . off-island treatment advised . . .

Then, just a voice—Magpie's—echoing in my ears. Those words took residence in my mind the moment she first uttered them: "Every year for the past few decades, a weak link has broken before October's end, leaving the island for one pathetic reason or another."

Nora, Sarah, countless others, and now me.

A great, convulsive trembling rushes along my spine and takes root in my skull. My suspicions haven't just been irrational fears. These supernatural encounters can't have been merely anxiety-induced instances of confirmation bias. Can they?

"Be reasonable," I command myself. "Use your logic."

Okay, okay. There could be a couple of explanations for all this:

a) Something inhuman lives on this island—is in this room—that detects my weakness, the same malevolent entity that's driven a girl away every year before Halloween night. And it wants me gone.

b) Pure coincidence.

But coincidence doesn't explain that feeling, that *presence*, still there, heavy, waiting, looming over me.

"Gwendolyn?"

"What? One sec," and that's when Kay comes clanging down the stairs. I've never been gladder for their presence in the archives.

"Thank god you're here," I exclaim, throwing myself on them in an embrace.

"Woah, there, girl." Kay peers over me to check the time on the computer monitor. It's seven o'clock sharp. "Of course I am. Right on schedule."

They pull away from our hug just as the computer produces the digital whoosh of an incoming e-mail.

From: Blake, Gunther

Subject: RE: RE: RE: RE: IPHIGENIA

We both glance at the notification before it dissolves into nonexistence. "You have better self-control than I, my friend," says Kay. "Book club or not, I woulda clicked that on my first shift. First *minute* of my first shift. Look at all those 're:'s–they've been sending e-mails back and forth forever! Think they're a thing? Mme. Camry and Blake?"

I gulp. "Are you in the mood to break the rules?"

"Wait. You're serious?" Kay smiles ecstatically, reaching for the mouse.

"No, not that!" I say, too loud. My voice echoes on the basement tile. "The Hell Week Party."

Kay's hand recoils. "Vi, come *on*, we talked about—"

"I know, but it's an emergency. Look." I frantically straighten out the pieces of evidence on my desk, lining it all up like a printed roadmap. "Look at these. All of these girls, Kay, they had the same dreams, they heard the same things, they had all the same symptoms."

Their brow knits as they approach the desk. "Symptoms? Vi, what are you—"

"The curse."

"This again?"

I point at Nora's file. "Remember her? You told me about her, and here he calls her 'reclusive'—"

"He?"

"And then look, in all of these ones I kept in my folder, on the bad side, look . . . Kay! You're not looking! These other five, they're *also* described as reclusive, right?"

Kay shakes their head. "Vi, you need to get out of here. For your own good."

"Yes! That's what I'm *saying*. I've been reclusive, just like them."

"Okay, that's so not true. You went to Fleck Beach. You *totally* came out of your—"

"That was a month ago. The rest of the time I've been in the dorm, in class, or at rehearsal. That's it. I'm subsisting, Kay. Resting on my laurels! I have to challenge myself outside of the classroom—"

"You honestly think that's what the headmaster meant? He wanted you to go to more parties?"

"I don't know! But Kay ... I am so close, two days away from beating this curse, from *being somebody,*" I hear myself whine. I hate it. "I have to go to this party. I *have to.*"

"You shouldn't be going out in this state, babe. Period," they say softly, infuriatingly softly. "Come with me. You can take a hot shower, we'll watch a movie ... I won't even make you wear the heels."

"No," I reply. " I'm sorry, but no."

Something exchanges silently between us before Kay says, "Sure this doesn't have anything to do with that lipstick mark on the invitation?"

My face burns from first-degree betrayal. "What? No! You're not *hearing me*, Kay."

"I think it's *you* not hearing *me*. You haven't been hearing me for a few weeks ..."

"It's not just the curse," I say, trying out a new tactic. "And it's not the lipstick. It's ... Finally we're a part of something, Kay."

"We've always been a part of something, Violet. Our families, this school, our friendship."

"I know that! But it's different now—"

"Now that you've got the hots for Frankie? Or is it Hunter?" they ask, not harshly. "I feel like I can't keep up with you anymore."

The basement window rattles against the twilight.

"The party's just starting, Kay, we can make it."

"What about our plans? Movie night. You've put it off so many times—"

"We can do that tomorrow!"

They cross their arms. "Sure, Vi. Sure we can."

"Kay, don't you get it? Don't you even *feel it*? She's in here right now! And the only thing that'll keep me on this island is this Hell Week Party. *I have to go.* To beat the curse. I *have to.*"

"No, Violet, you don't."

"I can't believe you're not going to do this for me—"

"No, *I* can't believe *you*, Violet!" they shout, then lower their voice to a library whisper. "I'd be more concerned if this were out of character, but, I mean, I feel like I don't even know who you are these days."

I'm nobody, I think, but what I say is, "I don't know what you're talking about." My voice sounds far away.

"Do you hear yourself? Like, do you notice you ask me no questions ever? At all? No 'Hey, Kay, how's it going?' Vi, I'm on my own here. I'm the only—" They cringe. "I'm a black sheep. This year was a big deal for me. You should be here for me. We're supposed to be best friends."

"You *are* my best friend, but . . ." at least Kay knows who they are. At least they're on their way to being somebody. Somebody who will be known as a great artist. I, on the other hand . . . "I've been busy."

"I am too, Vi! I have band practice, plus the sit-ins on your rehearsals, which suck for me, by the way. When we're with the Society kids, I might as well be wallpaper to you. Every social situation is *so* spiritually draining. I'm completely empty by the end of the day, and all I have to fill myself up with are your reports of your crush du jour, no offense, and a curse that conveniently exists whenever you feel bad about yourself or want to bail on me, just like the rules that can only be broken when it works for you . . . I get that you got that letter, and you've got this whole queer awakening going on, and I love that for you—I'd be *happy* to be there for you—but you have been *such* a bad friend."

I blink at them. My mouth opens to explain that they don't get it because they've never had a crush before and no one's ever had a crush on them, but I know that would be a cruel thing to say. I hate myself for thinking it. I wish I could unthink it. I wish I could undo everything and turn back time to before everything was all ruined. Trace it back to the point of origin like a long trail of red yarn that I could just re-spool. But it's too late. The only way I can fix it, the only way I can save myself, is to beat this curse.

"Don't you have anything to say?" they ask.

Words fail me, as they always seem to when I need them most. "Can't we just . . . go to the party together?" I say, and know immediately that I said the wrong thing.

"You're not who you used to be." With wintry finality, Kay turns to go up the iron staircase. "Have fun at the party."

And that's where the conversation ends.

Their words bounce around my head like the Dark Cove logo on the computer screen. "You're not who you used to be."

Who was I? I wonder. *And who am I now?*

Appendix S

End-of-Year Report, S. Lynch, Acting I

Student Name: Lynch, Sarah
Class Participation (25%): C
Written Assignments (40%): A+
Performance Presentation (35%): D
Final Grade: C-

Notes: Sarah is punctual. She is cooperative but not collaborative. She is unintrusive to the point of reclusive. "*Lessons deeply taught lead man to paths of righteousness.*" I worry if I do not state it clearly, the lesson may not sink in, so allow me to do so here in writing: I would advise Sarah to either overcome her shyness or else consider other creative and academic pursuits.

Supervising Teacher: Blake, Gunther

Supervising Teacher Signature: *G. B.*

Appendix T

Excerpts, Dark Cove Arts Academy Code of Conduct

Rule #8

Dark Cove Arts Academy maintains a strict dress code:
i. During school hours (8.30 a.m.–3.30 p.m., Monday–Friday), students must be in uniform.
ii. There must be no alterations made to any uniform garment (i.e., skirts must be worn at knee length).
iii. Students must take pride in their appearance when wearing any item of the school uniform.
iv. Hair should be worn tidily and at a manageable length (for boys, no longer than shoulder length).
v. Facial hair is not allowed.
vi. Visible body piercings, other than a single pair of ear studs, are forbidden.
vii. Students may wear discreet makeup.
viii. Student appearance must be generally tidy and smart, even when not in uniform, including during after-school hours and weekends.
ix. Any student considered to be inappropriately dressed will be required to change and may be requested to purchase a new uniform.

Rule #11

There should be no inappropriate displays of physical affection or intimate relationships between students.

Rule #41

No alcohol, cigarettes, or drugs of any kind are permitted on school grounds. Any students who have consumed or are found to be in possession of these items will be subject to immediate expulsion.

Chapter 26

In a blitz, I rushed from my workstation in the catacombs out into the pure blue hour of the evening. Swathed in my school cloak, hood flipped up against the bitter October chill, I ward away the thoughts pounding against my skull. Beyond Accolade North, the territory is uncharted: overgrown with weeds and knee-high witchgrass, blanketed with rotting plant matter, scat, and animal bones. No path to follow, every step disturbs the natural order of the island. At the edge of a cliff, opening myself to even a slight breeze could mean a thousand-foot fall. So strange to be this close to my own demise. I consider turning back, giving up, going home.

I trudge on. Alone, bound for the party that could either save me or do me in.

It's pitch black by the time I arrive at the campsite. There are just ten cabins and two old outhouses, all clustered tightly together a short distance from the shore, all in a state of disrepair. The windows smashed open, the steps collapsed in, vines crawling up porch railings. I follow the dull thrum of chatter and stereo—S Club 7?—until I arrive at the innermost cabin.

The Hell Week Party's already in full swing. Through the screen door, I scan the room. The layout isn't dissimilar to our dorms, just with some camp-appropriate adjustments: pine instead of cherry wood, bunk beds rather than twin four-posters, mosquito screens on the windows, and an old boombox on the nightstand. Its blue buttons (play, pause, rewind, eject, etc.) are faded from decades of hegemonizing hands—everyone at Dark Cove Arts Academy thinks they have the best taste in music and I guess they always have. Some slow song gurgles under a thick sonic barrier of static ... hard to make out what it is. A stack of CDs from the early 2000s leaves few hints. I train my ears and decipher that, yes, it is indeed S Club. "Never Had a Dream Come True," I'd venture to guess, but it's just background noise at this point.

I let myself half inside, standing in the doorway because there's nowhere else to go. The air in here is eighty percent dust, twenty percent sweat, windows all fogged up. Almost the whole Society has already arrived in their sundry costumes, and there isn't a square foot unoccupied by bodies. A portable heater works overtime in the center of the room, humming loudly over the stereo's crackle. Someone smacks a kerosene lamp. It swings madly from a hook. No flame inside. The only light comes from an electric lantern, a few flashlights, and a retro blow-mold jack-o'-lantern that produces a dim halo from the foot of one of the beds. Its plastic smile comprises one square orange tooth. I'd call the quality of light romantic if it didn't highlight the oil and sweat on the face of every person in attendance.

Xander, Salma, and a cluster of others topped with witch and warlock caps appear to be playing a game of spin the (Evian) bottle between bunk beds. Margaret's hat falls off when she kisses one of the stage carp guys at the center of the circle. There's a string of spit between them as their lips part. Unlabeled mickeys of questionable gin and magnums of cheap wine are passed between hands. More mystery liquor is carefully measured in cups. People say when. Edith, dressed like Audrey Hepburn, shuffles a tarot deck with difficulty, the cards sticking together from the humidity. Where the desk would be in my dorm room, Mag stands alone on a metal cot swaying sort of solemnly to another early-aughts ballad.

"Freja, you won't let me dance without a partner, will you?" the President whines. Freja says something too low for me to hear and walks away. Mag flushes, wobbles a little. Bodies shift. I let the screen door slam shut behind me. Heads turn.

"Look who got all dressed up," Magpie shouts at me, commanding the attention of the room, instantly exposing herself as a mean drunk, stumbling off of the cot, and kicking over the stack of CDs in the process. She wears a men's dress shirt (stolen from the Theatre Department, I'm sure) and no pants. She phoned it in—Uma Thurman from *Pulp Fiction*, supposedly. I'm surprised she didn't even *try* to upstage anyone, even if she has been less competitive lately. But who am I to judge? I've come to a costume party with no costume on. Lowering the hood off my head, I survey the room for a mirror. No dice. I take off my cloak before wrapping it around the good/bad folder—which has apparently been clutched to my chest this whole time—and place it on a pile of coats.

"'Evil things, in robes of sorrow, assailed the monarch's high estate.'"[83] Rue recites, her lips curling under a pencilled-on mustache. I didn't see her when we walked in, but now, she's lighting a row of stubby candles on a shelf by the door from which I just entered. There's a plastic raven fastened to her shoulder.

"Did you just get here?" I ask. If Rue and Magpie have already arrived, where's Frankie?

"Only Rue could quote Poe after taking shots," Hunter bellows from the top of a bunk bed, straight-cut-jeaned legs dangling off the ledge. He wears a biker jacket. The sight of him out of uniform feels taboo, like walking in on someone getting changed. "You look good, Vi," he says.

"I wear this every day."

"You look good every day." He gives me a drunken wink with both eyes.

There are those evil butterflies again. I pivot to Michael, who's wearing a vaguely Trekkie ensemble. "You boys have clearly had a few."

"*In vino veritas*,"[84] Hunter says, and I'm too stunned to say anything back.

Michael, making his way over to me, trips over something (himself?). "Where's Kay-for-brains?"

---

83 A line from Poe's forty-eight-line poem "The Haunted Palace" (1839).

84 Translated from Latin: In wine, truth.

See? I told you it was gonna be like this, my best friend would say if they were here right now. *Everyone's already shitfaced.*

"They stayed back tonight," I say.

"Yeah, not their scene." Michael uses his foot—he's wearing sneakers that don't go at all with the space-age look—to slide a cooler out from under the bed. "Want a beer, dude?"

It takes me a beat to register that I am dude. "Got any Coke?"

Michael only laughs, fishes a (very expired, judging by the olde-worlde red eagle label) Bud Light from the beer-only cooler, and cracks the can open. A small mist of fizz. "Come jam with us."

"Um, I might check out the campsite first," I lie. Really, I just want to find Frankie.

"Suit yourself."

Michael turns, stumbles onto the mattress from whence he came, and proceeds to play an air guitar with unexpected virtuosity. Meanwhile, on the top bunk, Hunter gives me a nod. His golden waves are slicked back with a generous amount of gel, a single curl falling onto his face.

"Sure you don't wanna jam?" he crows, drumming out a basic beat on his knees.

I shrug, trying to look blasé, breezy, insouciant—there, that's my costume: the cool girl[85]—and consider the invitation. "Thanks for asking—"

"That's not a no," Hunter interrupts.

Mag's laugh comes coarse and harsh. She clings herself to the metal poster of the bunk bed. "Anything for Justin Bieber."

"I was being polite," I retort, my voice overlapping with Hunter's as he says, "I'm not the Biebs! I'm Greased lightning!"

"Not a character," Mag says dryly.

"Sorry, Hunter, just gonna check out the grounds." I head for the door just as Frankie enters wearing a sequined dress under a long, reflective windbreaker.

---

85 "A person should always choose a costume that is in direct contrast to her own personality," so says Lucy in *It's the Great Pumpkin, Charlie Brown* (1966).

She shimmers in the moonlight spilling in from outside. "Leaving already?"

"Oh, hi! Um, not yet ... Rainbow Fish. Gonna explore the grounds a little," I repeat. (Have to stick to my lie now.) Frankie purses her peony lips, a poorly hidden smile. She's pleased that I correctly guessed her costume. A party balloon swells in my chest; I'm getting better at reading her. She threads manicured fingers through silk hair. I identify her nail polish as OPI's Lincoln Park After Dark and OPI's Do You Sea What I Sea?, alternating in color from pinky to thumb.

"Well," she says, "find me when you're done. And ... be careful out there." I think I detect a hint of genuine worry in her voice.

"The coyotes tend to keep to themselves," I assure her (and also myself).

"What about the murderers?" Mag shouts—way louder than necessary—over the music. She weaves her tipsy way between bodies toward Frankie and me. "Better watch your back. We'd all be, like, totally inconsolably devastated if you died."

Right. This place is the alleged site of a killing spree. Or disappearance. Or whatever it was.

"Exploring Camp Murder solo dolo?" Hunter sucks his teeth. "I don't think so. Let me be your bodyguard."

"She doesn't need a chaperone," Frankie sniffs, throwing her windbreaker onto the coat pile.

"You can never be too careful. She is *cursed*, after all," Magpie remarks.

Muscles contract. I mask my fear with annoyance. "We're still on that?"

"'The wind *is* chilling and killing.'"[86] Rue throws away the poetry, fully committing to the bit.

Hunter cocks an eyebrow in that overconfident way he has. "Chaperone don't sound like such a bad idea now, does it?"

The air feels thick and hot, like porridge. "I don't believe in that curse," I say, mostly to Magpie, again partly to myself. "But, sure. You can come, Hunter."

---

86 A line from Poe's last complete poem "Annabel Lee" (1849).

"You're not just being polite?" He smirks. I punch his arm lightly, awkwardly. He gives a princely grin and gestures for me to lead the way. "M'lady."

Before I leave I say, "Frankie, if I don't die, I will find you upon my return."

She manifests a lollipop out of thin air and waves it like a wand. I can tell she's a little sloshed too. "You better," she says slowly. "Hide and seek?"

Mag bats a thick fan of falsies. "I'm sure finding you in this two-hundred-square-foot cottage won't be too much of a challenge," she jeers, draping herself onto Frankie in a languid embrace that reminds me of a grapevine on a trellis. "Even for someone as oblivious as Violet."

So much for my *cordial acquaintance* theory.

"Don't miss the Ouija board," Frankie insists, peeling away from Mag. "It's a Dark Cove Theatre Society tradition."

Before I can answer, Hunter cuts between us to go outside. A rush of minty-cold air slices through the stuffy cabin. "Vi, Camp Murder awaits," he declares, already tramping down the wood-plank steps.

Frankie's eyes are glistening, almost pleading, daring me to stay.

"Be back soon," I promise. The flimsy metal-frame door slaps shut behind me. White moths against the black mesh screen in the near-Halloween darkness. The shoreline lies like a sleeping woman under a blanket of fog. Out here, the quiet turns the sound of your own exhalations into a racket. Hunter's voice comes like cannon fire. Something flies from its perch nearby.

"It's fuckin' insane thinking people were macheted, like, right here." He wields an imaginary weapon, slashing through an empire of weeds between two cabins. "Do I make a convincing Michael Myers?"[87]

"You mean Jason?" I correct him. "Thought *you* were supposed to be the film guy. Michael Myers kills with a chef's knife. Machetes are *Friday the 13th*."

Hunter drops his pretend weapon. "Why not both?" He wiggles his eyebrows. "What's your slasher weapon of choice?"

---

87 The killer from John Carpenter's *Halloween* (1978).

"Chainsaw. Always chainsaw."

Hunter grins. "Show me."

"What?"

"Show me your chainsaw!" he commands, but I still don't get it. "Make a chainsaw noise."

"No way."

"Why not?"

"I'd startle the wildlife."

"Ah, so this hesitation stems from concern for the local fauna, not out of self-consciousness?"

"Okay, Mr. Vocabulary. Where'd all those big words come from? A cereal box?"

"I'm a pancake man. And don't change the subject." He looks at me expectantly. "Go on, do your best chainsaw!"

If only to make him stop, I blow raspberries and do my best Leatherface[88] impression. It's bad, but Hunter enjoys it, at least.

"Excellent," he says, as though appraising a work of art at the Louvre.

"Thank you, thank you." I give a small bow, then pause. "Did you hear that?"

"What?"

"Thought I heard something."

Hunter wiggles his calloused fingers like tentacles. "You scared?"

"No. Well. People did die here. Maybe our slasher impressions are in poor taste."

"You think that story's, like, legit?"

"Dunno. There are fifty versions of it in circulation. Probably all—"

"Bull," he shouts. Another animal scares off. "Well, I'm sure their spirits appreciate a little graveside comedy nonetheless." Hunter, jester to the restless dead, resumes his murderer bit with a confidence that unsettles me. We walk in silence wrought with a peculiar sort of tension, full of static atoms and jilted ghosts. I think we both feel it, so we

---

88 The killer from Tobe Hooper's anti-capitalist masterpiece, *The Texas Chain Saw Massacre* (1974).

don't stray far from the party, walking just outside the safe, second-hand glow of the cabin's picture window. Hunter tucks himself under an old spruce tree out back. There's muffled laughter, voices chanting "Ouija! Ouija!" inside, in a whole other dimension. Above, a patch of cloud glows weakly against the breast of the blackening sky. My eyes strain to discern any shapes in the late night.

"I've heard you and Frankie have been getting close," Hunter says with an obviously feigned casualness that's new for him. I realize now that he may not be a bad actor, but he isn't good at lying. "Are you two . . . friends?"

Adrenaline ripples through my body like cheap talk moves across campus. "Oh. Sure. She, um, keeps me on my toes, I guess."

"Thought I saw you staring."

"I watch her onstage," I say, defensively for some reason. "That's just because, well, because . . ."

"Because she's more yourself than you are?"

"Huh?"

"*Wuthering Heights.* 'Their souls were as different as frost and flame,' or something like that."[89]

"First the Latin, then the vocabulary, now an out-of-pocket Brontë sister quote?"

"Guess I've been hanging out too much with Rue. Well, that and I'm trying to impress you." Hunter chuckles darkly. "But I'll letcha in on a little secret: it's the only thing on the summer reading list that I didn't look up on SparkNotes."

"I'm sure Emily[90] appreciates that. Probably the biggest compliment to a dead writer there is."

We draw out our laughter as long as socially acceptable before another quiet spreads over the moment like syrup on a shortstack.

"Can you see, like, anything at all right now?" he eventually asks.

"Absolutely not."

---

89 "[. . .] so he shall never know how I love him: and that, not because he's handsome, but because he's more myself than I am. Whatever our souls are made of, his and mine are the same; and Linton's is as different as a moonbeam from lightning, or frost from fire."

90 Brontë.

There's a rustling and then the click of a Zippo lighter. Hunter's face appears in a dim vision that would have sent pre-summer me into a swoon-spiral. "Hey," he says. A wry smirk, then he moves a hand up to his face. It holds a cigarette. "Want one?" He conjures a half-full pack of the kill sticks[91] from out of nowhere.

"You know smoking is the biggest con there is, right? It's the opiate of the nation."

"I thought that the opiate of the nation was retail or something? At least that's what you said before you started your seasonal employment at, where was it, Lululemon?"

"Yes, retail too. Retail, smoking. Potato, *poh-tah-toh.*"

"Retail and smoking are ... the same?"

"It's all capitalism! I'm a socialist," I say, hoping he doesn't ask me anything about socialism.

"An antisocial socialist." He laughs, throwing his head back, then reaches his arms up into an exaggerated stretch. His T-shirt raises, exposing a sliver of boyish midriff that makes the night tremble.

"I'm not antisocial."

"Well, then how come I never saw you around 'til, like, June?"

"I'm just ..."

"Reclusive?"

"No!" My pulse quickens tenfold. "I'm here, aren't I? Aren't I?"

Hunter whistles low. "Chill, chica. It's just a joke. You're not reclusive or antisocial. You're just ... selective."

I take a breath, but my heart's still pounding wildly. "Something like that."

"And I'm honored to be selected," he says smugly. Someone's gotta take this guy down a notch.

"Keep smoking and I don't know how much longer I'll be able to *select* you anymore."

He tucks the pack into the back pocket of his Guess jeans. "Come on. It's punk rock, right?"

---

91 "Kill sticks" is a term coined by Canadian playwright Judith Thompson in her play *The Crackwalker* (1981).

"You don't honestly believe that. It's the polar opposite of sticking it to the man,"[92] I growl, infuriated by his obliviousness.

Clearly amused by my fury, Hunter probes me. "How so?"

"It's handing a bunch of disposable income to the man and then dying early. It's conformity in the extreme."

"I'm not gonna die early," he says without a shadow of doubt. The cigarette still dangles casually from his mouth. He takes a drag. In his leather jacket, he looks like something out of *The Outsiders.* It's a cheap imitation of cool, but as much as I hate to admit it, I will never not swoon for anything Patrick Swayze adjacent.

I make a mean face to remind myself that I'm pissed off. "You're only kidding yourself, Hunter Kinsey." He laughs again, louder this time. Sick of everyone not taking me seriously, I don't have to play at anger anymore. "Stop laughing at me, I'm not joking. I'm not just here for your amusement. Not everybody's a player in your comedy of who-gives-a-crap. I know you have fun, you know, messing with me, but just cut it out."

An apologetic look spreads across his stupid, boy band–worthy face. "I'm not addicted or anything, Vi. And I'm not messing with you."

"If you aren't already, you're just a sixteen-year-old moron *bound for* addiction. And expulsion," I add curtly, surprised at myself. I'm braver at night. "And you have been known to mess with me."

Hunter tosses the cigarette onto the sand and pinches it out with his foot. Not quite dead yet, the sad stub glows dimly. "That was my last smoke then, no messing around," he says, and you can tell he really believes what he's saying. "And I'm seventeen." Winks. God.

"I didn't mean—don't mean to act crazy or whatever. It's just . . . it's a personal thing I have, I guess. I am trying to say that—"

"No, you're right. It's stupid. To look cool at parties." And there it is: that wide, Abercrombie smile. Hunter takes a step closer to me. The leaves underfoot are matted and wet, rotting. I smell the smoke on his breath when he says, "Trying to look cool for you." He stands, boring his

92 The punk-rock reputation is considered by some scholars to be a mere residual effect of a 1920s publicity campaign that marketed cigarettes to suffragettes as "the torch of freedom."

eyes into me all serious like I've never seen him, like all the games are over, like he wants me for real. "You don't drink, either, I gather?"

"No. I don't judge it. I just don't do it myself."

"Me neither."

"Yeah, right."

He puts his hands in the air where I can see them. "I'm just high on life, ma'am, I swear."

"You're a bad liar."

"I know, but that's part of my charm."

"Shut up.

"Make me." His eyes flit down to my lips, then back up to my eyes. I'd recognize that look anywhere. It's in every Meg Ryan rom-com and countless episodes of *Sex and the City*: the moment before the kiss. I spent way too many nights imaging different permutations of this scenario, my first kiss, and for the longest time, I pictured Hunter initiating it. In my head, he looked almost exactly like he does right now . . . but I moved on. I got over him. But here he is, he *wants* me. The golden boy. Just a few moons ago I knew that I wanted him too. But, but but. Everything's changed too quickly. Back then, it was simple: I hated Frankie, I loved him. Now . . . I need to say something, anything to fill the dwindling space between us before it closes completely.

Hunter does it for me. "I love how intense you are about stuff."

"What do you mean?

"I *mean* you have strong convictions. It's hot," he whispers, his mouth just inches away from mine. "Like, I can totally see your gears turning right now. Always thinking . . ."

There's a squelching sound as I lift my feet out of the muck. There's some suction that keeps me in place. "I wish I could stop. The thinking."

"Maybe I can help with that . . ."

He can't, not even as he leans in further, not even as he places his lips lightly on mine. Not even as I kiss him back. With our mouths smoldering against one another, worlds expand and collapse on the shore. This one tastes of tobacco and everything else I stand against. His hand moves to my waist, the warmth of him like the sun, like summer in mid-October. It doesn't belong. A crude gravitational force pulls me in, but it feels all wrong. Heavier, like we're on a different planet with a higher mass. A cosmically incorrect occurrence. I let myself fall against the rough bark of an old spruce tree under the weight of a million stars and a trillion questions. *Do I even want this anymore?* The answer comes to me a second too late.

I experience the following passage of time in fragmented panels, like a comic book—this happens, then this, then this:

I push myself off of Hunter's chest, breaking our complicated orbit. Hunter steps back, the cigarette at his feet still smoking like a gun. Behind him is Magpie, wearing a satisfied expression, holding a red Solo Cup that crinkles loudly in her drunken, pinky-up grip. With her other hand, she holds a lantern up to Hunter and me like a searchlight. His green eyes refract the electric glow like an animal's in the dark.

"Well, well, well, what have we here?" Magpie asks. Next to Magpie is a shadow in the shape of a person. Synapses fire and tell me it's *her*. Frankie, lollipop lowering from lips in slow motion, face obscured by the late hour.

"Sorry." I say this to Frankie.

"We didn't mean to interrupt." Frankie hiccups. She backs deeper into the shadows. "I'll just—"

"Frankie, we have every right to be here. We don't need to go," Mag slurs. "Violet doesn't own every make-out spot just because she'll flirt with anything that has a pulse."

Brain. Not. Processing. "You guys were going to make—"

"No, we weren't," Frankie croaks.

"The Ouija board told us to find you. We thought you'd be dead, Cursed Girl, but looks like we didn't get that lucky. You two, on the other hand, are all about getting lucky, apparently."

"Excuse me?" I say.

Frankie takes another step back. She's barely an outline in the darkness. "Let's leave them be."

"It was only a kiss," I stammer.

"It was only a kiss," Hunter whispers, and I don't know if he's agreeing with what I said, disappointed in what I said, or just quoting the Killers.

Magpie grins evilly. "Aw, trouble in paradise?"

"We're not—" I can't think. "Why don't you just mind your own business, *Megan*?"

She snarls. "Oh, I see, *that's* why you're sucking face in the shadows. You don't want everyone to know you're *actually* just straight."

"I'm not—"

"What? You're not straight? Coulda fooled me, Cursed Girl. What are you, then, bi-curious? Flirting with my *best friend* for fun, as a little experiment, and then wearing Hunter's nasty hoodie by day? I *told* her you were just making eyes at her to turn *him* on. That is, if you can even call what you do flirting. Maybe that's just how the socially inept make friends? Don't get too close, Frankie, she might start having a p-p-panic attack."

Hunter throws himself into the closing distance between me and Mag. "Friends, Romans, countrymen, why don't we all just take a step back?"

I see the whites of Mag's eyes rolling in the dark. "Gladly," she says before flipping her flat-ironed mane and strutting away. "Let's go, Frankie."

But Frankie's already gone. And the plummeting of my heart tells me all I need to know about its allegiances. Now I'm left in this mess of post-kiss emotion with my ex-crush standing there, studying my expression like I'm a book and there's a test tomorrow. "You good?" Hunter asks uncertainly. I nod, but even he can sense that all the dominoes have fallen and no one's in the mood to play again. "You sure you're good?"

I shrug.

"You wanna leave?"

"Yeah."

"I'll go get your jacket."

"Thanks. It's the, uh, school cloak," I say numbly, then remembering, "it's wrapped around a folder."

Hunter starts into an easy sprint to the cabin. The screen door slams behind him with all its many white moths begging to go in with him and I'm alone. The temperature drops a clean ten degrees. Goosebumps splatter across my body.

Hunter returns with the cloak after a few minutes inside. "Couldn't find the folder."

"Oh"—*shit fuck dammit all to hell*—"okay."

"You wanna go find it?"

I shake my head. The good/bad folder can stay in that cabin with all the refuse and unlawful litter, an archive of my being here. The evidence of my curse.

Hunter offers to head back to campus with me. My mouth makes a sort of "mmm" sound in agreement and he thumbs the sparkwheel of his lighter to guide us back. We walk over crushed stone without touching, a careful foot apart, the island's quiet nocturne and the crickets in the bush and the glow of his Zippo as our only accompaniment. A sleepless dark carrying us wayward for however long. At the fork in the footpath by the lake where we first met, we stop dead in our tracks, looking at each other like neither of us knows our lines until he finds his: "Was that kiss . . . okay?"

I watch my sigh transfer into a small, cold cloud. It evaporates in the space between me and Hunter. Hunter and me. "It was really nice," I admit. "Really nice. But. I don't know if it is something that should happen anymore."

"I get it. Let's focus on the show for now, all right?"

"Yes. The show," I say, voice warbling with the knowing that I might not make it to opening night. "But, yeah, it was . . . really—"

"Nice. I agree."

"I'm sorry I ruined it. It's just . . ."

"I get it, Vi. Seriously. G'night." His face dimples with a farewell smile that tells me he doesn't get it. As he walks away, he doesn't get that I'm frozen in place, that I was basically in love with him for months, that he broke my heart at the Spring Fling, that he's been messing with my feelings since the first day back, that I finally see now that I never wanted him, at least not since that night on the dance floor, and it took this devastatingly perfect kiss for *me* to get that it was only that I wanted him to want me.

If a guy like that—this very normal, windswept internet-boyfriend type of guy—could like me, could like "the fat-ish one," the questionable queer, the Cursed Girl, then that would prove something. That I'm also normal and *worth* liking and not just some defective weakling.

Of course, believing a boy could prove all this to me was idiotic, just like believing the Hell Week Party could save me from the curse was idiotic . . . a convenient denial of reality.

Because here we are, in the raw dead of night, and this guy, this stupidly good-looking guy, kissed me, and all I feel is a gathering terror in my stomach that I can't even begin to analyze. Not now. Because it's too late, too late for me to realize the beautiful, complicated, impossible thing that's been staring me in the face all along, the beautiful, complicated, impossible thing of the girl who I can't even bring myself to think the name of right now.

I've ruined any chance at that. I wish I could talk to Kay about it, but I've ruined that too. And in this moment I realize how right they were, that I only think of them when I need them. All these things that can't be dissolved, miles of red yarn and I'm tangled up in it.

I look up at the dark for a clue of how to fix this. There's only the ghost of the waning moon wearing the same old-man face that we've got back home, held by the same stars I used to wish on with everything I had to get here. Dark Cove. I try to imagine returning to my small town, with its single-screen cinema, sad sports bar, and gas station, where the only thing to do is go to the outlet mall the next town over, where the politics are as dated as the ripped-up vinyl in the greasy spoon diner, where it's quiet and pristine and everyone's mean if you're different. The gridded streets may as well be a jail cell. The summers are a scratchy, sweltering suffocation. The winters are spent jamming hands in your pockets, dreaming of elsewhere ... anywhere ... here. But the size of this place isn't much greater than where I came from. It's just a speck of rock in the middle of the hungry ocean.

The old man vanishes behind a wall of thunder-heavy clouds. The starchy collar of my cloak chokes at me like a phantom-hand.

Alone, without the flame from Hunter's Zippo, I decide to try moving after what feels like a few minutes but may have been an hour or more; my limbs are stiff cold. I take a slow step forward, then another like a dead woman walking until, suddenly, or ages later, I'm at Raven Lake.

It's as if the world has been set in slow motion or fast-forward and on mute. An unearthly quiet has settled over the island. A barred owl descends onto a pine tree without so much as a decibel of sound to accompany its movement. Small insects rest on the tension of the water, waiting, waiting, their wings luminescent. The dread network in my midsection sparks alight. Hairs across my body perk up. Then, at once, the insects buzz away and the volume of the night slowly rises. Rain pitter-patters on soft earth. Another tine of red lightning heliographs off freshwater in a phantasmic pattern. A long delayed clap of thunder crescendos and transmutes into static. Static like a radio dialed between two stations. An adjustment on the dial, tuning into an old, immortal broadcast: that wretched and sinister cry from Fleck Beach and a legion of half-forgotten nightmares. It echoes impossibly from every direction, closing in on me. *She* is everywhere. *Gwendolyn.* The Dark Cove Ghost.

The Society's got it all wrong. She's no protector—she's here to remind me my hours left on this island are numbered; that, like her, I'm a ghost on this island. Cursed. Hell, maybe she *is* the curse, a devil carried by the thin night air and red sky and heavy rain. God, it reeks of rot. She couldn't leave this island, but she's going to make sure I do. Another flash of white like the twirl of a wedding gown. She smothers a scream. It dies somewhere inside me.

The midnight tempest whips my hair like strands of seaweed. Wind slashes at my cheeks. I start into a sprint and the world is blotted out by a terror and storm like I've never known. It's a violent struggle to keep pace with the night. I wish in this moment that I were a better runner, that I'd made better use of that damn Tartan Track, that these lungs of mine weren't on fire. My heart pounds in my ears, the beat of it discordant with the low, guttural moan of the invisible dead chasing after me.

Appendix U

Ouija Board Session Notes

To Michael F: IMMEDIATE GOOD BYE

To Rue: YES, L - K - D - F - I - M - D - G - Z GOOD BYE

To Mag: NO NO NO NO NO GOOD BYE

To Frankie: G - O - F - I - N - D - H - E - R

Chapter 27

"You awake?" I ask the dark dorm room. My breath is heavy, ragged. My cloak sopping wet from the relentless rain. Through the lace curtains, I see the sky has gone back to black.

The absence of snores and rustling of bedsheets tells me Kay isn't asleep. I flick on the lights and my roommate shields their eyes. "Do you *mind—*"

Then I see it: the Barbie costume, laid out on my bed, no heels.

Even after everything they said, everything I didn't say, Kay did that. They believed in me—that I'd come after them and apologize and be the friend they needed. Instead, I left them alone all night. Waiting.

Every set of footsteps in the hall must have been another disappointment, another opportunity I missed to show up for the one person who's always, always shown up for me.

And here they are, still awake, lying across from an unworn Barbie dress. Waiting for me, the one person they never could count on, to let them down one last time.

When my ragged breaths turn into sobs, Kay drops their hand from their eyes. Their expression of anger transmutes to worry.

"I'm sorry," I say, the words shattered by devastated gasps. "Kay, I'm so, so sorry."

"What happened. Are you okay?" They roll quickly out of bed, rubbing their puffy eyes. "Babe, you're soaking . . ."

"Kay, you were right. I ruined everything. I've been such a bad friend. I've been so caught up with—"

"Take a deep breath, Vi."

I try to, but it's hard.

"What happened?" they ask calmly.

"I'm—I'm going to change. I just. Kay." I choke back another sob, my throat aching with it. "I don't know what I'm going to do without you."

"I don't know what you'd do without me either." The corners of their mouth curve up a little. "Can you *change* into some dry clothes, maybe? So I can hug you?"

As I peel off the myriad layers of wet clothes, Kay fetches my (their) *Mario Party* tee. An olive branch. I wring out my hair onto the already warped wood floors before slipping into the dry cotton.

Kay flicks off the light, stretches like a cat across their bed, and pats the mattress. An invitation for me to sit. My eyes adjust to the dark as I climb into bed with them. Slowly, my breath levels out. We smile at each other, but theirs is drooping already. "Tonight sucked." A long-held sigh surges from their chest. "It's been sucking, Vi."

"I know. I'm sorry."

"It's just hard to be out of place *all the time.* You know how I fought to feel like I even belong in my body, my community . . . now here. And I'm not even sure how to articulate it. I'm not as good at words as you, but . . . I guess I just want you to know that I'm not just fine all the time, you know? Like, I know you struggle, and you've been worried about this curse thing, and when you're anxious or freaking out I'll always be there to hold your hand. But I have my own stuff, too, and I need you to be the person that holds my hand sometimes, too."

"I'll be that person. I promise." We lock pinkies under the covers. "I'm here for you forever, Kay."

"I know I keep a good composure on the outside—"

"That's your Libra rising."

They burst out laughing, and even their laughter sounds like music. "I love you."

"I love you too. So much." I relax a little into the warm sheets, our heads sharing the pillow.

"Okay, now that we're friends again, I will ask a third and final time: What happened? Where the hell have you been, loca? Spare no detail."

With great difficulty, I walk them through the terrible and unbelievable events of the last four-ish hours. By the end of it, I'm shaking again.

"Holy shit," Kay whispers. "You saw a ghost? Like, just now?"

"I don't know. I don't know how to explain it or even describe it . . . never experienced anything like it. Well, except at Fleck Beach. I heard that sort of howling sound. Then in my dream. I don't know . . . I think it *was* her. Gwendolyn."

"Well, if I knew old Gwenny was gonna show up, I would have come with," they say matter-of-factly. "It *is* Samhain. The veil between worlds is lifting. I bet she's trying to tell you something."

But, *what*? "Why does she want me off the island so badly?"

"We don't know that she does."

"Either way, I only have a day left here."

"What?"

"It's obvious I'm the cursed one."

They sigh. "It's never been obvious to me."

"Why not?"

"Because you're my best friend. You're not allowed to leave me on this island alone." Their logic is enough to make me feel safe, at least for tonight.

"Thank you. For . . . just, thank you." My days here might be numbered, but I'll always have Kay. This—our friendship—is forever. They're my family.

"Soooo," they say, "how was the kiss with Hunter, my dear emotional harlot?"

"It was . . . almost perfect, but—"

"Nothing will ever be perfect."

"That's not it. I don't expect perfection—"

"Ha!"

"Okay, okay. I'm *trying* not to expect perfection *anymore*, but ... it felt wrong. If I'm being honest, things feel wrong most of the time. Except ..."

"Except when you're onstage? With a certain someone?" Kay gives me an exaggerated wink. "Starts with an *F*?"

I don't need a mirror to know my face is the color of a hothouse tomato.

"*F* as in Frankie." They smirk knowingly.

"*F* as in Frankie," I confess. And it feels so good to say her name.

"Are you going to tell her?"

"No."

"Why not?"

"I ruined any chance of that."

"I mean, she's just down the hall, you could go right now ..."

"No. I don't even know what I'd say."

A long quiet. "Should we go to sleep?" Kay whispers.

"Is that code for *get the hell out of my bed*?"

They laugh. "You can stay with me tonight, if you want."

"That sounds good," I whisper, still trembling a little with residual fear. "But there's no way I can sleep right now."

"If only someone had the forethought to rent some physical media ..." Kay leans over the side of the bed and rises again, flourishing a DVD.

I squint at the label. "*Young Frankenstein*?"

"It's pronounced 'Fronkensteen.' Couldn't watch it without you, babe. Anyway, I had a feeling we'd make up."

They reach for their laptop tucked under the bed and pop in a DVD. We stay up past three in the morning in fits of laughter, doing Dr. Frankenstein impressions until someone down the hall shouts at us to quiet down.

I wake up on the wrong side of the room with Kay's elbow in my face and their soft snores in my ear. Gray light filters through the curtains and casts a floral pattern onto the far wall. Hard to tell if it's early or just overcast. There comes a steady tapping sound at the window, coaxing me out of consciousness.

Tap tap.

I wonder . . . *could it be . . .*

Tap tap tap.

I don't want to disturb Kay's sleep, so I just lay there like that, listening to the tapping sound, coming to terms with the idea that last night wasn't just a nightmare. A particularly loud rap at the window wakes Kay. They almost break my nose with their elbow.

"What *is* that?" they say hoarsely.

"I don't know, it's been going for a while."

"Vi, your *breath.*"

I cover my mouth with the comforter. "Sorry . . . didn't brush my teeth last night."

"You better do that," Kay groans. "It smells like something died inside of you."

"I will."

"No, like, now. It's urgent."

I chuckle and slide to the foot of the bed. "Fine."

"And find the source of that annoying sound. And kill it."

I check the clock (already noon), pad to the window (overcast) and see the crow on the sill. *You again,* I think. It's nearly identical to the one last night at the archives, feathers missing from the wing, its coloring stark against the pale backdrop of the dreary autumn day. It pecks its fat beak at the window in a stochastic rhythm. At once, it stops tapping, looking right at me, trying to communicate something. I look right at it, trying to decipher its message. It flies off before I can.

"What was that?" Kay asks.

I blink at the crow, now just a black speck in the thick mist. "Not sure."

There's only one more sleep until the Halloween Play. One more sleep until . . .

Kay sits up. "What are you staring at?"

"Just a crow," I say, and my mouth *tastes* like something died inside me. Eager to wash away the horrors of yesterday evening, I grab my toothbrush and head to the lavatory.

There, I find Magpie hovering over a stone sink. I hesitantly step up to the faucet beside her as she ties the satin bow at her collar. She's already dressed up. Without making any sudden movements, I turn on the tap. It runs furiously, as cold and hard as ice. Water ricochets off my toothbrush and splatters Magpie's white cotton blouse. She makes no move to retaliate. I twist the squeaky knob to shut off the tap, bad breath forgotten, waiting for her next move.

She opens her mouth, and I steel myself for a fight scene:

Beat. MAGPIE *locks eyes with herself in the mirror. A sharp intake of breath.*

MAGPIE: Just woke up?
VIOLET: Yeah. You?
MAGPIE: Didn't sleep.

Beat.

MAGPIE: Frankie's not talking to me.
VIOLET: *[Taken aback.]* Oh?
MAGPIE: For last night.

Beat.

VIOLET: Oh.

MAGPIE *takes a tiny comb out of a cosmetic bag and brushes her brows.*

MAGPIE: She says I embarrassed her. And you.
VIOLET: Well, yeah.

MAGPIE *tucks the brush back into some sub-compartment of the tiny bag and whips out a wand of lip gloss. She puckers her lips, still looking only at her reflection.*

MAGPIE: I didn't. Like, not really.

A dripping faucet fills out the dialogue VIOLET *should probably insert here.*

MAGPIE: Listen, I'm not a good person. I'm a bitch for no reason. You just need to know that about me.
VIOLET: Is that . . . an apology?

Beat.

MAGPIE: I'll see you later.

MAGPIE *shrugs, adjusts a padded headband that belongs to* FRANKIE. MAGPIE *blinks into the mirror. She doesn't move to leave. She stays glued to the spot.*

VIOLET: Are you . . . okay?
MAGPIE: I'm not a good person.
VIOLET: You said that.
MAGPIE: My whole thing is I'm not a good person but I am a talented and capable person.
VIOLET: Okay.
MAGPIE: But apparently I'm neither of those things. Talented, capable. I'm not special. I'm just a raging bitch.

Beat. MAGPIE *takes the manilla folder out of her purse.* VIOLET *grabs it.*

MAGPIE: [CONT'D] I didn't read it.

KAY *enters the lavatory.*

KAY: What the hell are you doing in the bathroom day and night? Why don't you get out of there and give someone else a chance.[93]

93 A reference to *Young Frankenstein* (1974).

VIOLET: Sorry, Kay, I'll be done in a minute, just wait for me in the room?
MAGPIE: Don't worry, go ahead.
KAY: [*Uncomfortable.*] Didn't mean to interrupt.
MAGPIE: It's fine.

MAGPIE*'s lip quivers. She reapplies lip gloss. Her eyes well up with tears. She blinks them away.*

VIOLET: Oh. [*Beat. Goes to awkwardly hug* MAGPIE, *hands* KAY *the folder.*] Magpie, we've had our differences, but you *are* talented. And capable.

KAY *opens the folder.* MAGPIE *shrugs off the hug, composes herself.*

MAGPIE: I don't need your pity.
VIOLET: I'm not—
MAGPIE: Under my care, every single Dark Cove Theatre Society tradition has been broken. Like, that's not even an exaggeration. There isn't one person who doesn't think Kemsley should've been elected President.
VIOLET: That's not true.
MAGPIE: Ms. Spry doesn't think I'm any good. Even the party last night. [*Beat.*] I don't deserve to be here.
VIOLET: Magpie . . .
MAGPIE: Tomorrow he's evaluating us—
VIOLET: Mr. Blake?
MAGPIE: Our character descriptions.
VIOLET: Yeah.
MAGPIE: I can't do it.

Beat.

VIOLET: Because of all the pressure with the Board here? The headmaster always makes a bigger deal of it than it is.
KAY: He did make an extra big deal of it, though . . .
VIOLET: Kay . . .

MAGPIE: I just can't! I can't face him! Whenever I do, I feel it.
VIOLET: It?
MAGPIE: Reality. The fact that I'm, like, not special. Blake can see it. I'm sure you can too.

RUE *enters.*

RUE: Everything okay, loves?

KAY *shrugs.* MAGPIE *looks back to the mirror.*

VIOLET: I don't know. Mag, are you okay?
MAGPIE: [*To her reflection.*] Literally when will you stop asking me that? It's totally irrelevant. It's not enough to be okay!
VIOLET: What do you mean?
MAGPIE: Stop acting like you don't get what's going on here. Just stop! Rue sees it. Hell, Kay probably even sees it. At least Mr. Blake—are you really that dense? You know as President, I'm his apprentice, right? He puts a lot of trust into me. It's a rare honor and I'm squandering it. Majorly. Which means, not only am I a bad person, but I'm also a total failure. A nobody. And I have nothing to compensate for . . . [MAGPIE *sighs, deflates.*] You can't just be *okay,* Violet. You have to be special to survive here.

A long beat. The tap drips. KAY, *feeling awkward, looks through the folder.*

VIOLET: I get it, Mag. We're all in the same boat. At the end of the day, we're all the same.
MAGPIE: Violet. We might be in the same boat, but are you a captain, are you a passenger, or are you some random who throws themself overboard?
KAY: Yeesh . . .
VIOLET: Um . . .
MAGPIE: Do you get it?
VIOLET: I think so?

MAGPIE: Frankie told me about the spiel you gave her. Your little motivational speech in the bathroom the other week.

RUE: Mag, perhaps let's not—

MAGPIE: What? She tells me everything. Well, she did. And you were right. Frankie *is* special. Capable. But I'm not Frankie. I'm not Rue.

RUE: Mag, please, love.

MAGPIE: Don't lie to me, and don't be all cute about it, and don't act like you all won't throw a little party when I'm gone. *Yippie, none of you guys are the cursed one! Magpie's been the weak link all along! Isn't that a laugh?* So don't tell me I belong here. I don't. I know that now. Pretty much got the truth right from the horse's mouth.

VIOLET: What horse?

MAGPIE: Oh my god, keep up! Mr. Blake! It's a waste, me being here. I have to stop wasting my own time. [*A devastated gasp. Shallow breaths. More lip gloss.*] That's basically a direct quote. That's why I have to leave.

KAY: [*Horrified.*] Blake told you to leave?

MAGPIE: Well, no. He didn't *tell me to leave*, it's my decision but that doesn't matter.

VIOLET: Then I'm sure he's just—

MAGPIE: I'm trying and trying and for what? Like, seriously? For what fucking reason? To go out into the real world and fail out there like I'm failing here? I'm wasting my own time and effort and energy. Honestly, I'm so, so tired.

VIOLET: Mag. Those are fears we all have. Trust me.

MAGPIE: You're not listening.

KAY *and* VIOLET *exchange a look.*

MAGPIE: This isn't something that's, like, in my head, okay? He *told* me.

VIOLET: Okay. What exactly did Mr. Blake say?

MAGPIE: I don't know, I don't, like, transcribe all my conversations! Something about me burning at both ends, that it might all be for naught, or whatever . . . [*In a Blake voice.*] That my fate is in my own hands, but perhaps I should consider putting "an end to this toil without meaning."

KAY: Wait. "Put an end to this toil without meaning"?
MAGPIE: Yeah ... something like that. Why?

KAY *leafs through the folder quicker now.*

KAY: Well, I just read that somewhere in this ... [*They unsheathe a paper.*] Here! One of the students who dropped out. Blake ended their report card thingy with that quote. See? In italics.
MAGPIE: [*Nonplussed.*] It's probably from some play or whatever.
RUE: It is. I recognize it. The words of a tragedian, likely Greek. I want to say Euripides? However, the exact play escapes me. If only I could ...
KAY: There are quotes like that in *all* of these drop-out files.

VIOLET *grabs the good/bad folder.*

VIOLET: How did I not notice this? The quotes aren't in any of the star students' files?

KAY *shakes their head.*

VIOLET: Here's another.

RUE *leans in. The group huddles together over the bathroom counter, the contents of the folder now spread out in the gaps between sinks.*

RUE: "A straight path is always the right one." That must be a Euripides quote, too. [*She grabs a page.*] The same play, most likely. This is going to drive me to insanity ...
VIOLET: [*With a gasp, realizing ...*] I had a quote too.
MAGPIE: What?
VIOLET: Just like these. In my report card last term.
RUE: What did it say?
VIOLET: I remember it word for word because I thought it was so weird.
KAY: That and you memorized the whole thing ...

VIOLET: That too.

MAGPIE: Spit it out!

VIOLET: It was right before he told me to change my specialization. "Then you called me into council. What shall I do?, you asked me."

RUE *snaps her fingers, triumphant.*

RUE: "What shall I do? you asked me. What scheme, what strategy can I devise that will prevent the stripping-off of my command and the loss of my glorious name?"

KAY: How do you …

RUE: It's from *Iphigenia in Aulis* by Euripides.

VIOLET: Iphigenia …

KAY: Oh shit. Isn't that—

VIOLET: The e-mail …

KAY: But why would—

MAGPIE: What are you talking about?

VIOLET: In the archives … I work on a computer that's logged in to an e-mail account, I assumed it was Mme. Camry's, but …

MAGPIE: Whose is it then?

VIOLET: I don't know, I'm not supposed to touch it. Anyway, the little notifications come up. And a few times … there's been one from Blake with that name in the subject line. Iphigenia. I never thought …

MAGPIE: Thought *what*? People need to start finishing their sentences!

VIOLET: Rue, what was the answer? In the play. What strategy, or whatever …

RUE: It was a sacrifice on the altar. The sacrifice of Agamemnon's daughter, Iphigenia. That's the premise of the play. The daughter had to be sacrificed to appease the goddess Artemis in order for Greece to prosper. This was all prior the commencement of the Trojan War.

KAY: The sacrifice of a daughter. Anyone else thinking what I'm thinking?

VIOLET: The curse …

MAGPIE: What does *this* have to do with the curse?

VIOLET: There's only one way to find out.

KAY: [*Thrilled.*] No. Way.

MAGPIE: *What?*

VIOLET: We have to read that e-mail.

KAY: The one from Mr. Blake to we-don't-know-who.

MAGPIE: How'll *that* do us any good?

VIOLET: There's gotta be something going on here. [*Shrugs.*] Don't you want to know what it is before you leave?

MAGPIE: [*Shrugs back.*] Sure. Why not.

The former enemies smile at each other.

VIOLET: All right. So it's already logged in, as I said I can go to the archives and—

KAY: Let's go!

MAGPIE: I'm coming with you.

RUE: Me too.

MAGPIE: [*Touched.*] Really?

RUE: Mag, I'll not allow you to leave this island. Besides, this riddle is far too intriguing to leave unsolved. But we'll have to wait 'til tomorrow. The library is closed on Sundays. Unless, Violet, perhaps you're in possession of a key?

VIOLET: [*Dammit.*] Nope.

MAGPIE: I do.

VIOLET: What?

MAGPIE: I have the master key.

KAY: How?

MAGPIE: [*A little proud.*] Stole it. It's in my room.

VIOLET: Oh my god. This is too—

KAY: Don't say risky.

VIOLET: I wasn't. I was going to say perfect.

KAY *whoops, gathers the pages back into the folder.*

KAY: It's bad-girl hours!

RUE: We still have to wait. At least until nightfall. We can't storm the library in broad daylight.
KAY: One does not simply walk into Mordor.[94]

VIOLET *laughs.* FRANKIE *enters quietly. No one notices.*

MAGPIE: We'll go tonight.
VIOLET: [*Nods.*] Midnight.
MAGPIE: Just us?
VIOLET: We should ask Frankie to come, too.
KAY: Ah, young love.
VIOLET: Kay!
RUE: Love?
MAGPIE: Wait, you *actually* like Frankie?
VIOLET: It's not just that. [*Sighs.*] She doesn't deserve to get hurt. I mean, any more than I already hurt her.
MAGPIE: And me.
VIOLET: If we're doing this, she should be there.
RUE: I agree.
VIOLET: She's a part of this.
MAGPIE: [*Nodding.*] She *is* the Vice President.
VIOLET: Yeah. And she's . . . it just wouldn't feel right without her.
MAGPIE: I'll go ask her to . . .

MAGPIE *turns to* FRANKIE, *who takes a few steps into the circle. She nods at* MAGPIE, *then locks eyes with* VIOLET.

FRANKIE: Where are we going?

Heads turn. A plan is plotted. Later, night falls.

94 A reference to *The Fellowship of the Ring* (2001).

We sneak out of the foyer of the girls' dorm as soon as the grandfather clock's hands meet. The atonal gong is our cue into the night as if onto stage. Hoods up, wind biting, no rain, the clouds cried it all out yesterday. Last night feels faraway—the party, the problematic snogging, the supernatural storm—but the grass is still slick with droplets, evidence of its recency. How quickly things change. Kay, Magpie, Rue, Frankie, and I: mortal enemies, now allies, or at least co-conspirators. United by something larger than ourselves: a play, a club, an insurrection. Quiet as smoke, none of us speak a word as we skulk across the fields, shoulder to shoulder, like a pack of thieves. Mostly, this is a practical silence one to ensure our stealth—but it doubles as a cheap way of avoiding the things we're all too proud to say out loud. *I'm sorry; I'm scared; I don't want to leave; how can I stay?; I was wrong; you were right; I don't like him; you're all I can think about; I'm so happy; that terrifies me; you look beautiful tonight; what happens after this?; what does any of it mean?*

The air is electric with it all: rebellion, mystery, potential. A great wind blows through the trees. We throw caution to it. Frankie trails at the back of our diagonal phalanx with Magpie. They made up somewhere between then and now with the help of Rue, the peacemaker, the Treasurer of Secrets; she leads the way this time. Kay and I are sandwiched in the middle, belonging here. A crow overhead flies with us, keeping our pace, the clever thing, a feather or two missing from its left wing. I wonder if it's the same one from the window.

"Are all the crows molting?" I say to Kay in a low voice.

"It's molting season," they whisper.

I think about that. The trees shedding leaves and bark, the birds discarding feathers like an outfit after a long day, the patchwork of all these old memories on the scarred earth, everything on the island, all of us changing on our own accord and, somehow, in perfect synchronicity.

"Tell her," Kay urges me, always reading my mind.

"Not now. No time."

"She came for you, y'know," Kay says as we make a low sweep up to the library entrance, past the two tombstones—the crow finds its perch on Gwendolyn's.

I glance back at Frankie, chin tucked against the cold. Frankie Lin, my ex-nemesis, my now-crush, my what-if. Did I mess this up? Could we really go back to being just strangers? Kay, Ms. Spry, the Society—yes, even the bloody Society—and these girls … they're my community now. I can't stand to lose them. Clustered together under the stone archway, we arrive. Magpie retrieves the knobbly key from her pocket and holds it up like a talisman. Ancient, significant, powerful. The exterior door unlocks with a clunk that echoes throughout the courtyard. It startles our crow off, and we scurry inside. Once through the Art Deco door, a small relief comes.

"We're in," Frankie says in a breathy voice that sounds surprised.

Rue creeps forward. "The inner sanctum."

"But will we make it out?" Kay's joke falls flat and another church-like silence comes over us.

Tiptoe to the back, down the familiar iron steps with deafening clangs, into the dusty crypt of the Dark Cove Arts Academy Archival Facility. Frankie takes a whiff of it through the nose. The rest of us hold our breath as I approach the still-on computer. It buzzes at the center of it all like a satellite in a black hole. The armory slides across the screen in green, now blue. I wiggle the mouse and click on the envelope icon that Mme. Camry ordered me to "ne touche pas" a billion years ago. Loading, loading, a staticky sound as the zeros and ones fire off.

"We're in," Frankie says again.

Welcome back, Renfield.

Renfield? I run through my mental Rolodex of faculty members but come up short. *Renfield.* Couldn't be a Board member. *Renfield.* Then I remember: the office, the horse-head paper weight, the *R* on the nameplate.

"This is the headmaster's inbox."

Appendix V

Digital Correspondence Between R. Henley and G. Blake

From: Blake, Gunther

Subject: RE: RE: RE: RE: IPHIGENIA

Date: October 29

Renfield,

I hope this finds you well. Apologies for the weekend interruption. A brief update on the Iphigenia project, which, I assure you, has been top priority. I did not mean to convey otherwise. I understand your concerns about the timeline given the upcoming Board visit and International Art School Association rankings, but your faith in me mustn't waver now. Good god—of course the top spot will be ours. It is always ours.

Recall when you first invited me onto this island to restore the Academy back to its former esteem ... A quarter century I have dedicated to the image and excellence of this institution ... your institution ... do you think I would let you down now? The Iphigenia project has been one of my greatest achievements to date. The children call it a curse! We have created something so powerful that it is perceived to be supernatural. We are gods on this island, Renny, and that, my dear friend, we can hang our hats on.

The cause for delay is our change in target. I did not wish to bother you with the minutiae; opportunity came knocking and I have pivoted from our initial mark. This has pushed our timeline, yes, but it is nothing for which I was not prepared ... this girl's even weaker than the last, though it may surprise you to learn I have selected Megan Black as this year's Iphigenia.

Every day, it seems, the poor creature fails in a new way; how she secured the presidential title baffles me. Her status among the student body will make for higher visibility and greater impact. I admit, it has taken time to break her. You see, I have had to be meticulous, given the Blacks' fortune (heaven forbid she find her way back to the island after a change of heart). That said, I have crushed her beyond a shadow of a doubt; our usual tactics are proving most effective despite the change in structure. Her departure from the island is imminent ... it will indubitably remind our students of the standard to which they are beholden.

As for that Spry woman ... I have heard rumors of her tenure here. I must ask ... is it I who should be worried, Renfield?

Our guest director has not favored the student enough to bolster her confidence. The child's ineptitude borders on the absurd and Spry lacked the foresight/experience to cast understudies ... a bad look for our guest director. Of course, I have prepared an alternative. Kemsley is ready to step in at a moment's notice. He may be the wrong sex for the role, but the move will gain us "diversity" points with the Board and IASA at the very least, as you mentioned already below.

Regardless, you and I will be positioned to regain control of this year's production and I'd wager next year's as well ... the Board will see for themselves that capable hands are the right hands. Once all is in order Halloween night, I say we celebrate after curtain call with that Scotch the wife sent.

Best,
Gunther

From: Henley, Renfield

Subject: RE: RE: RE: IPHIGENIA

Date: October 26

Should I be worried?

You've gone quiet on me Gunther. Cutting it close. Not appreciated. This is top priority. Don't care how you extricate student from island, not within my purview. Make an example of her. You've five days. Get. It. Done.

R. Henley

From: Henley, Renfield

Subject: RE: RE: IPHIGENIA

Date: October 22

Gunther,

Confirming Board + IASA will arrive on Halloween morn. Tickets booked for all. Received word DCAA will host IASAs Marybeth Markin for annual eval. Remind department. Top spot should be ours. Female director will align better with new "gender diversity" parameters. Absurd.

You have Spry under control yes?

She has a bad effect. Students getting softer, skirts shorter, excuses longer. Performance is slipping, DC star pupils included. Must scare them into proper behavior. Must reflect standards of institution re: IASA rankings.

Which leads me to the matter at hand. The student. Updates? She will leave on schedule yes? Apply extra pressure as needed.

Rgds,
R. Henley

Chapter 28

We stand locked in a semicircle around the computer, half a ring of petrified wood. My hand lies frozen on the mouse. There it is: evidence, finality, proof of the curse and its origins. The *Scooby-Doo* monster-in-the-mask reveal—*it was the headmaster all along, with the help of his trusty sidekick Blake*—and yet, it feels anticlimactic, the answer disappointing, so ordinary. A microcosm of the world. *How did I not see it?* The big twist isn't a twist at all; it's just the patriarchy, an answer that only pries open a chasm filled with even more hopelessness. It's too big.

Magpie is the first to speak. "So, I'm, like, a sacrificial pawn in their weird power play? This is just some majorly fucked-up game between Blake and Henley?"

"Renfield," I whisper, the name numb on my tongue.

"It would appear that way," says Rue.

Frankie is blanched, arms wrapped around herself like a sheet. "The signs were all there."

"But why?" Magpie whimpers.

"To improve the school's ratings, it seems." Rue's still scrutinizing the e-mail, glasses balancing on the tip of her nose, looking for nuance where there is none.

I release the mouse from my grip, extending my rigid fingers. "By scaring the students into shape."

"Twenty-five years ago, Blake was hired," Frankie mutters. "They've been doing this to us for twenty-five years."

"But Dark Cove has ranked as *the* top art school *in the world* since then. Like, hello, that's why I even go here," Magpie exclaims. "There's no way a Grecian-level sacrifice is still necessary."

"It's worked for them this long," I say bitterly, "why stop now?"

"Because they like it," Kay scoffs. "These asshats are everyday sadists. That's probably why they became teachers in the first place. For power. I mean, look at this. Blake's e-mails are, like, jovial. He finds it funny."

Rue backs away from the screen. "Kay's right. It's likely at least partially for sport. Tradition."

I could almost laugh. "Dark Cove *loves* tradition."

"What I am having difficulty with is this 'change in target' bit," says Rue. "Who did they have their sights set on initially?"

Kay sits in the chair. "It must have been Violet, right? Her report had the Sophocles quote."

"Euripides," Rue corrects.

"Right. The old white guy's *other* favorite old white guy."

"But why change it from me to Magpie?"

"Because, other than Hunter, you're Ms. Spry's favorite," Mag says sharply.

"Magpie . . ." Frankie sighs.

"I don't mean that in a bitchy way! Violet was, like, good, or whatever, and Ms. Spry kept praising her in rehearsals. On and on and on, *great job, Violet, nice choice, Violet, I love you, Violet!*"

"We get it, Mag," Frankie interjects.

Kay turns to me. "You were getting more confident. Anyone could see that . . . Blake probably knew he couldn't take you down."

"Well, Mag's always seemed pretty confident to me," I reason. "Why pick her?"

The President gives a barking laugh that quickly fades into a whimper. "Blake knew my weak spots. He figured out how to tear me apart from the inside out."

"*And* they wanted a student with status, to really pack a punch," says Kay. "No offense, Vi."

"None taken."

They chortle. I laugh, too.

"Well, if I'm the cursed girl, it's not like I can do anything to stop it," Magpie says, slumped over the desk. "They want me gone. End of story."

Kay sits on the desk next to the computer, elbow propped on it casually. "You can break the curse by *not* dropping out."

"If I don't leave now, I'm sure they'd just expel me. Or Blake would keep making my life a living hell. Literally, I'm so done with it. I'm not playing this game anymore."

"What if we *can* stop it?" says Frankie.

"How?"

"Blake's already on the back foot, you saw that. My mom's on the Board of Governors. We could show her these e-mails, she could show the rest of the Board. There's no way they'd let this slide."

"The evidence is irrefutable," says Rue.

Magpie takes a sharp breath. "You're sure about that?"

"One hundred percent! Think about it. It was the Board that put Spry forward to direct the show," Frankie elaborates enthusiastically. "It's a diversity move."

"In my personal experience, the ol' B-O-G aren't all stellar allies," Kay mutters.

"Fair, but they like the *appearance* of diversity at least, right? My mom only joined the Board this year, but she's got a lot of pull."

"So you'd just, what, forward the e-mail to your mom?" Mag asks.

"No, my mom doesn't read my e-mails. But I know where she's going to be tomorrow . . ."

I put two and two together. "The Board visit! It's perfect!"

"*Too* perfect," Kay interjects. "We have to be forgetting or missing something. It *can't* be this simple."

"It can be and it is. This isn't a curse, it isn't supernatural. It's just a couple of old white guys, like you said." Frankie starts pacing the length of the archives. A look of determination on her face. "Old white guys who are afraid. Afraid of the Board, that's clear, and Ms. Spry. IASA. They're afraid of losing control."

Kay smirks. "If it bleeds, we can kill it."

"Nietzsche?" Rue asks.

"Schwarzenegger."

"Twenty-five years," Frankie reiterates, this time like a rallying call. "They've been doing this to us for twenty-five years!"

"And they would have gotten away with it too, if it weren't for us meddling kids," I add.

Frankie laughs. "Trust me, guys. We can do this. The ferry gets in tomorrow. The Board is going to sit in on some of the midterms. It's all set up without us even trying. The only thing left for us to do is overthrow the two biggest powers on this island." There's a flicker of fire in her dark eyes that I haven't seen since Fleck Beach. It excites me.

"I'm in," I say, hand hovering readily over the mouse. "What do we really have to lose at this point?"

Magpie slams her hands on the desk. "*I* don't have anything to lose. *You guys* do. Violet will get fired, first of all. Frankie, it could hamstring your mom's career. Kay puts one toe out of line, I bet they could get sent back to Accolade Dicksville. Please. It's not worth it. Don't do this for me."

"Okay. Then we won't do it for just you," I say steadily.

"For who, then?"

"Well, for one, if you leave, Ms. Spry's set up for failure."

"And if Ms. Spry fails, Dark Cove's stuck with the Odd Couple in charge," Kay adds.

"Do it for her. Do it for Nora Ingrid, Sarah Lynch, everyone who came before us, and everyone who comes after us. This is about all of us, Mag," I conclude.

For a while, there's only the faint buzzing of the computer. A deep, dark silence, just long enough for instinct, or at least a sense of justice, to predominate over fear.

"Okay, fine, if you guys are, like, positive . . . then, yeah, thanks, or whatever." It's the closest I've seen Magpie to sentimentality. She hates it. “But if we’re doing this, can we just do it already? This place gives me the creeps.”

Frankie beams. “I like it here.”

“Is it the dust?” I ask her, the first words I’ve addressed to Frankie since last night, and they come out sounding like a dig at her. “I mean, you like dust, right?”

Frankie laughs lightly. Kay laughs too, and I’m pretty sure they’re both laughing at me but I don’t mind. I start laughing too.

Magpie shakes her head. “*What* has gotten into you people?”

“I don’t know,” Frankie replies in a breathy voice, darting her molten eyes to me, “something about getting everything out in the open.” She leans across my body, her hand grazing mine as she reaches for the mouse and hits print. An electric field alights. The old machine churns out a sheet of evidence, then another.

Kay laughs a mad-scientist sort of laugh. “Oh, it’s game time.”

Chapter 29

On Monday afternoon, Rue, Mag, Frankie, and I discuss the hasty details of our planned coup in quick whispers as we hurry from the dining hall up the crooked hallway to 13A. Kay isn't in this class so they can't join us, but honestly, they don't need any more points against them in the scenario that this goes south. We all agreed that Playwriting class was the most befitting setting for mutiny, what with Henley and a few of the Board members sitting in on our evaluations today.

The headmaster ushers in three of them: two white-collar men, neckties elaborately knotted, noses red from the October chill, and a tall, gorgeous woman in a fuchsia three-piece pantsuit. Mrs. Lin looks so much like Frankie, it's striking. She nods at her daughter politely. Frankie nods back from her place at the table. It's a cold reunion, but there isn't time for any niceties before Mr. Blake curtly welcomes our esteemed guests and Magpie is called to stand for her presentation. Already, her neck is splotched with red. I try to give her a reassuring look, and I see Rue and Frankie do the same.

Our professor doesn't mince words. "Did everyone read Megan's character description?" He knows she hates that name. "What did we think?"

Whether due to day-old hangovers or general pre-exam burnout, no one seems eager to contribute their opinion this morning. I stay quiet. It isn't time. Not yet.

"No need to be shy. All criticism is valuable." Mr. Blake strides over to the blackboard, a stubby piece of chalk in hand, poised to pontificate. "Not much to discuss, I suppose. Rather unremarkable work. Utterly uninspired. I am disappointed, Megan, but not surprised, that you submitted such a clichéd character. The misunderstood, whiskey-loving workaholic with nary a redeeming quality."

"I wouldn't really—" Magpie takes a shaking breath. "I was trying to challenge myself."

He flashes a set of nubby incisors, that glint of pirate's gold. "How so?"

Magpie doesn't meet Mr. Blake's foreboding gaze. Rue and Frankie look at her expectantly, wondering probably, the same thing I am. *Is she losing her nerve?* Mag's valley-girl voice comes out in a sad sort of warble. "I took inspiration from a … complicated relationship from my own life to craft a—"

"Ah, I see," Blake interrupts. "You wrote a character description of your absent father? Well, I'm sorry he's too busy making millions to care for you, but you can take that to the counselor. This is playwriting."

Magpie, nonplussed, makes no moves to save herself. I decide to toss her a life preserver.

"I found this character quite intriguing, actually," I interject.

Mr. Blake's bushy brows dart far up his forehead, like two poisonous caterpillars startled off of a leaf. "Tell me what drew you to this character then, Miss Costantino."

"He's an anti-hero," I say. "He does possess some clichéd characteristics, yeah, but they're based in reality. This is a real man, a man I'm sure I'd despise if I met him, but reading this page, I empathized with him—"

"Do you understand the meaning of empathy?" Blake asks without waiting for an answer. "I think the word you're looking for is *sympathize.*"

"No, actually, that's not the word I was looking for. I *empathized* with this character because he exhibits a great deal of fear. He's afraid to let people down and afraid that people will let him down. I can relate to that."

Frankie, Rue, and Mag look over at me. Our President's eyes harden. "Thanks for your feedback, Violet."

"Of course. Maybe our professor just had trouble with this one because, well, I reckon it takes a person to be emotionally intelligent in the world they inhabit before they can empathize with a character in worlds imagined."

For a brief and blissful moment, the great Mr. Blake says nothing, and I know I've just guaranteed myself a failing grade in this assignment. My damnation is certain, and yet, surprisingly, I don't really care. At least not right now. Right now, I'm too busy reveling in the shade of burgundy on my professor's face; it deepens by the second. The Board members murmur amongst themselves. Headmaster Henley sits as still as a wax figure, but I note a bead of sweat melting off his forehead.

"Violet is reading far into a character that lacks real depth." Mr. Blake unblinkingly re-aims his dagger stare at Magpie. He supposes she might be easier prey, but she isn't going to cower away this time.

Tongue sharpened, back straightened, she resumes her presidential manner. "I'm sorry you feel that way, Professor, but I'm sure we can agree there is room for different interpretations of a single work of art."

"Excuse me?" Mr. Blake folds and refolds his hands, turning to the headmaster for intervention. Henley only sits there.

"She said she's sure you can agree there is room for different interpretations of a single work of art," Frankie repeats, her angelic smile so perfect, so proud. Mrs. Lin shoots Frankie a look I know all too well—she's fuming—but Frankie's zoned in on Mr. Blake.

He's purple with fury, cornered, and right where we want him. We know it's time to go in for the kill.

The headmaster rises to his feet. "Someone is feeling brave with their mother in the room, hm? If you'll allow me—"

"'Before this man is heard, I have the right to speak,'" Rue says boldly. "That's Euripides. A quote from *Iphigenia,* but you knew that, didn't you?"

Mrs. Lin's look of anger transmutes to confusion. Headmaster Henley chokes on something. Between coughs, he says, "It would appear, Miss Sandhu, that you, like many students in this class, are sorely unfamiliar with the Academy's standards—"

"Not me," I say before I can think. "I know *exactly* what the Academy expects of its people. Through my work in Dark Cove's archival facility, I've learned *a lot* about the standards here. 'Keep your place, or you'll pay for it in pain,'[95] hm?"

"What is the meaning of this?" Blake rasps.

"Yes, what *is* the meaning of this?" Mrs. Lin says finally.

"Mrs. Lin—pleasure to meet you—I've been asking myself that same question all semester," I say, "and I only recently ascertained that the meaning of it, all along, for twenty-five years, has been *sacrifice* for the greater good of Greece—I mean, Dark Cove. Isn't that right, *Renfield.*"

"You have no idea what you're doing," Mr. Blake hollers, Headmaster Henley still hacking up a lung in the corner. "And I'd stop right this second before you—"

"Oh, Professor," Frankie says blithely, "we've already done it."

Blake guffaws. "Is that so?"

"My mother and the Board will be *very* interested in learning more about this Iphigenia Project of yours," Frankie continues with a sweet smile and a flourish. It's the big reveal: she places the printed papers on her desk. None of the students pick up on what's going on, but I note the color slowly draining from Mr. Blake's spherical head. Headmaster Henley similarly appears to have seen a ghost, his jaw gone lax as a skeleton's. In a flash, Blake lunges for the papers, knowing immediately what they are, it seems, and tearing them in a tantrum. The halves all drift to the floor in a haunting pas de quatre.

One of the white-collar men goes to investigate the fallen papers.

Mrs. Lin stands in a flash of fuchsia. "What is this, Francesca?" Her voice is strong, resonant, just like her daughter's.

"I have another copy, Mama, don't worry," Frankie replies calmly.

"Enough!" the headmaster commands. "Miss Lin—Francesca—you will report to my office immediately. Professor Blake will accompany us." He stares daggers at his subordinate, whose threat level diminishes by the second. "You other girls will need to explain yourselves as well. But for

---

95 Another *Iphigenia* quote.

now, Mr. Duncan, Mr. Floyd, Mrs. Lin, I apologize for this obscene interruption. Might I invite you to help yourselves at the dining—"

"Do not offend us further, Renfield," says Mrs. Lin. "We have all made a long journey today; we will not be dismissed so easily. You may, however, release your class. I believe there is a show tonight?"

"Quite right, yes," Blake mumbles. "Class is dismissed."

Mrs. Lin narrows her eyes at her daughter. "Francesca. Come."

The class remains seated for a second that punctuates our professor's loss of power. Rue, Mag, and I are stunned stock-still as Frankie leaves, flanked by Blake, Henley, Mrs. Lin, and the two other Board members. Most of the students scatter like a stable of spooked horses, liberated and baffled, out of 13A. Nina Petrov lingers in the hall. Margaret is the last to exit. She leaves the door open wide behind her.

It's then that it dawns on me I should be following Frankie—I can't let her go alone—and make haste out of the building. The door of Accolade South opens into a dense fog. I dash forward, looking expectantly back at the empty cobblestone trail behind me. Where I lost Mag and Rue, I don't know—they're probably guarding the e-mail scraps from *The Covie Chronicle* vulture. It doesn't matter. The words from the e-mail are still burned into my vision, scrolling before me as I amble forward into the mist, the text like newsprint on gray paper.

I consider what the headline would be for this particular story. "Students Overthrow Dark Cove's Patriarchs"? Or perhaps "Dark Cove Arts Academy's Mass Expulsion, Halloween Play Canceled"?

Nothing beyond a three-foot radius is visible. "Frankie?" I call out weakly. No answer. I lost her. Again. I resolve to wait out her return in the dorm. The doorway appears out of the fog.

Strangely, my impulse is to use the brass knocker. I've never been here during school hours. It feels like visiting a vacant but well-endowed museum, one of those old estates preserved, scattered with belongings, only a fraction of its holdings on view. No fire in the fireplace, no scuffle of footsteps overhead. Just the lingering woodsmoke from this morning. I climb the stairwell as a guest, an observer of a life I once but may never again take part in. From this perspective, I interpret the strange and scintillating relics of my bedroom—a comb threaded with curly hair, my dirty nightshirt thrown on the floor, fuzzy slippers, crumpled script notes—and reconcile myself to the idea that *this* is the evidence of my existence here. Not the folder. Not the legend of my meltdown. It's this: my life. I contemplate packing it all up but urge myself to remember the potential positive outcomes of Frankie's meeting. I climb into my crumpled sheets, cool and coarse. I close my eyes against the already returning doubts, but moments later there comes that tapping at the window. My eyelids snap open. The crow. Sitting up, I see her beady black stare fixed on me. She readies herself for flight, almost gesturing for me to follow with her tattered wing extended. I intuit somehow that this is her final visit, that if I let her off into the fog alone, I may never see her again.

Without thinking, I barrel out of the empty dorm and pursue her. Contrary to the saying, she does not go as the crow flies,[96] but waits for me on a tree outside, then flits from perch to perch along an undefinable path. We split off from the lakeshore, over the lawn, through bramble and brush, across craggy terrain, through the fog-drenched forest. It unfolds and unfolds. After a long stretch, I hear the rustle of water. Fleck Beach reveals itself slowly through the thick mist. It is nearly unrecognizable. The shape of the shore has been altered by lunar cycles, maybe—no, that can't explain the fallen trees where there were none before, barren rock in the shapes of familiar faces, the roof of the sailboat house caved in, bluebeards sprouting from an impossible crevasse. A four-foot wave crashes into a sandy froth. It's a different beach from a different realm. I wouldn't know where I was if it weren't for the battered dock. The crow lands, trots along this runway and into dense ocean fog. I run after her to the very edge, but she has vanished.

"Come back!" I call to her. "Where're you going?" Then, in a scream so ferocious it's a roar, "What am I supposed to do?"

I train my ears to the frequency of the island, desperate for an answer. There is only the ocean thrashing before me, hard and unyielding.

---

96 This expression meaning the most direct route.

I close my eyes and listen deeply to the crash and splatter of nature's invitation. Maybe that's all it is. That old summons to let go: *You? Afraid?*

I jump. The saline solution flows in small and erratic rivers up my nostrils, the ocean floor falling away in a rush, sinking farther to the bottom of the world. Down, down to its molten core. Ice cold; the drop in temperature, a slap in the face. The hungry slurp of the ocean sucks me down deeper. Pressure accumulates. Suddenly, I understand the utility of fear. Terror burns away in my chest to a small flame, deprived of oxygen. Powerless. Everything I know disassembles, floats away, implodes, expands, dissolves, erodes, and re-forms like minerals in hard water. I don't have control. I never did. Maybe this is what Frankie was after when she said this was just what she needed. A shift in perspective. A frantic, breathless moment, a growing distance from the chatter that blends into your own inner monologue until there's this constant cacophony of criticism. Now . . . it's quiet. The answer is writ large in the glimmering black around me. Black ice. Black fire. Black feathers. Black like her endless eyes and silken hair. All I see is Frankie, Frankie, Frankie. I see her everywhere. And I'm not afraid—

Is this what dying feels like? Is this that life-flashing-before-my-eyes montage?

Death keeps the shallows. Everything gurgles, distorts, and disorients. Not quite sure which way is up, I grab at nothing, the Pacific's liquid muscle. I gasp for air where there is none. My mind is a swivel chair, my lungs a kiln; my legs churn mechanically, like the egg beaters Mom uses to make my favorite biscotti.

Then, I feel something. At the small of my back. I open my eyes to the stinging, dark green salt mass and look around . . .

Whether it's a trick of my oxygen-deprived brain, an angel, or a hallucination, something auroral slithers just below, reaching up to touch me, warm against the ocean's bitter chill. I try to discern its shape through the particles of murk. There it is: a woman's left hand, glowing, a wedding band on its assigned finger. I can't see the person to whom it belongs but I don't need to. It's Gwendolyn. Her voice comes to me, impossibly clear, a howl unaffected by the auditory physics of water. It envelops my whole being. The sensory hiccup lifts me slowly, softly up. *How long have I been under?* I'm about to break the surface. I see the sky brighten through mild ripples. Just as I feel the early sun on my face, I hear that haunting voice from my dreams. It speaks in Latin. This time, I understand it. "*Subsisto*," she tells me.

"Stay."

I wake up not with the sun on my face, but creased cotton. *Where am I?* is my first thought. I blink salt—no, sleep—from my eyes. A whiff of topsoil and expired lotion tells me I never left the dorm. Deep gulps of stale air remind me I'm a fool. Like Helena and the rest, a small player in this mad, magical place. It was just a dream. Consciousness closed the scene. And yet, I'm still out of breath. Chest heaving. I feel the weight of my body against the mattress, heavy under the things I can't understand. What brought me to this island, what connected me to these people, what draws me onto the stage, where the crow goes—these are unseen mysteries, like the pull of a tide under a moonless sky. I belong on this island. I'm meant to be up there. With her. With her, I can soar beyond everything. And still more poetry pulses to the surface of my memory, this time Emily Dickinson:

"Hope" is the thing with feathers.

Guided by this magnetic reset, my internal compass fixed, I lift my head, check the time, scramble up onto wobbly sea legs, and rush out of the dorm.

It's time to open this show.

Appendix W

Love letter from G. Wincroft addressed to Elizabeth

Dearest Elizabeth,

Do you love me still? Will you love me always? Forgive my pestering, but I fear I have been made unlovable by the horrors of this island, or rather by its keeper. There was a time when I once did love him, or at least felt that I ought to, when the island was a place of great and incomprehensible majesty. It was spring, I think, but it is now autumn and every cheerful memory has fallen away with the leaves. My husband has turned this island into a cage, though certainly there is no need for such an elaborate trap; the ring on my finger will do.

To be born a girl, we both by now know, is a prison sentence. We are handed a compass that points only to annihilation. We do not repine, nay, we curtsy and oblige to the whims of man. We bestow upon them only pleasant smiles as they degrade us. We are deceived into believing that we aspire to this sentenced subordination. Then, once shackled by betrothal, we are disillusioned from our girlish daydreams of gallant gentlemen, adoring princes, and other mythical men. Instead, man reveals the cruel instincts of his kind, and all those pink fantasies quickly expire. They rot. They fester. They grow fungus enough to induce hallucinations, mad dreams, death, and decay. Oh, how it reeks of death all around me. The corvids circle my body ceaselessly, but—you'll think me mad when I tell you this—they have become a comfort, my little companions. They threaten me not; rather they warn me of the fate that will be mine if I remain here. They have shown me the way out just as your precious letters have given me wings. Each one is a paper feather. At last, I have gathered enough to fly away from this damned island and over the ocean to you, my darling Elizabeth. My heart yearns for nothing more than your sweet words. Your blissful touch.

I can no longer sigh in vain, wishing my way to you, mourning you, hoping for you, always hoping. I cannot save the island nor its creatures, but I can save my own waning soul. And so, I must depart. Do not attempt to dissuade me, dearest. I have planned it well, and I fear if I do not leave now, I will be bound to this island for eternity. Either I die at his hand, or I will obliterate myself from my own hatred of him. This hatred . . . it is like a weed planted in my darkest parts.

Once, I believed my love for you to be the most monstrous of my aspects, but I recognize it now as my saving grace. God would not punish me to love his darling angel. My heart is full of you and your immense light. I shall follow its ever-beating glow. Elizabeth, I hope to arrive at your doorstep even before this letter. This will be my last. I will love you all my life and in death all the more.

Ad vitam aeternum.

Yours,
Gwendolyn

Appendix X

Excerpt, V. Costantino's Acting Journal

September 27

THINGS I LOVE:

1. Nonna
2. Kay
3. Mom
4. Dogs
5. Lists
6. Homemade paper, the really pulpy kind
7. Reading
8. Writing
9. Drive-in movies
10. Orchestra pits
11. Curtain call
12. Acting
13. Yeah, I guess I really do love acting

Chapter 30

Every theatre seat is empty when I walk in, save one. "Hey." My voice is muted by the lush upholstery, but a golden head turns.

Hunter waves me over, the motion like surf on the seashore. "Hey! Cutting it close, eh?"

A sigh of relief. *The show's still on.* "Yeah. Oops. Where is everyone?" I ask, walking down the aisle. "Frankie and them?"

He grins. "Back there"—*she's here*—"getting ready."

"Oh, good! Should we . . ."

"You and I go last. We got time to chillax."

"Cool." As I approach Hunter, I see he's petting Romeo, who wears a bowtie on his collar for the special night. One of them smells like wet dog.

"It's Frankie." I hear myself say the thing I've heretofore been too much of a coward to say. "I'm sorry, it's just so obviously Frankie."

Hunter gives a reverberant laugh, coming from that deep mine of gold within him: his unbruisable ego. "I know it is. I've seen you up there with her." He looks to the stage. "Wondered if it could all be an act."

I give a full-toothed smile. "Are you implying I'm not that good at acting?"

"Come on, Vi." Hunter bats a hand in the air. When Romeo looks up expectantly, the human resumes petting the dog. "You know you're a star. You shine up there. That's where you belong. Well, if that's what you want." He shakes his head, hair shifting at a half-second delay. "I can't keep up with you."

"I've been getting that a lot lately."

"So, what *do* you want? Writing or acting?"

I want to be here. I want to perform. I want to write stupid love poems. I want it all. "Why not both?" I wiggle my eyebrows playfully.

"You're quoting me now?" Hunter's laugh bounces off the theatre walls, delivered to me in surround sound. "Well, that's good. Bet you're as great at writing as you are at acting."

"Thank you."

"Hey, look, you accepted a compliment!"

"I'm learning," I whisper, eyes glancing over the unlit stage. "Slowly learning."

We take a synchronized breath.

"Ready for tonight?" he asks.

"No. You?"

"Nah."

I yawn and laugh at the same time, allowing my body to relax into the velvet chair. It smells dusty. I love the dustiness.

Hunter yawns as he speaks. "You talked to her yet? Frankie?"

"No," I whisper, "just got here, remember?"

"You gonna do it now?" he asks, curious, encouraging, like our history was so long ago that friendship is all this ever was.

"When the time is right."

"Don't wait for the perfect moment," Hunter says, almost wistfully. "Just tell her."

"Hunter! They're ready for you!" Ms. Spry leans out from behind the curtains, her chin resting on the puffed shoulder of a chiffon dress. "Oh, Violet! You're here. Hair and makeup will be ready for you in a few. Hunter's won't take long."

"Coming!" He jumps to his feet, and Romeo follows suit.

"Bring Romes with ya," the director calls back, already out of sight. "He must be hungry."

"On it!" Hunter gently tugs at the dog's collar. "Time to get you to the green room for your dinner, boy." Romeo's ears perk up into a point. Hunter casts one last look back at me. "Break a leg, Helena."

"Right back atcha, Lysander."

The two meatheads wander off into the stage set.

Appendix Y

Director's Notes by S. Spry

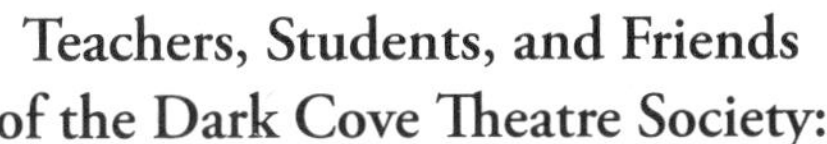

Teachers, Students, and Friends of the Dark Cove Theatre Society:

I first want to acknowledge that we are privileged to play, create, and learn on this stolen land. I only recently learned from a student named Kay Cardinal, who composed the magnificent music that you'll enjoy this evening, that Fleck Beach was once used as a campsite for hunting and gathering trips by Indigenous peoples. This island has a rich history that goes back long before Wincroft Theatre was built. We can't rewrite the school's history of violence and discrimination, but we can look forward to making art that prioritizes love, uplifts diverse voices, and celebrates community.

As you probably know, I'm new here. I came in to guest direct this show just a couple of months ago, but as I sit to write the Director's Note, I feel like I've been a part of the Academy for as long as you have. (Okay, maybe not as long as *you*, Headmaster.) My career in Manhattan feels like forever ago. A past life I attribute this weird time warp to the Dark Cove Theatre Society. Working on the long-treasured tradition of the Halloween Play has reminded me of something that I sadly forgot about in the last few years of my career: the power of community. Again and again, from the first round of auditions to this very moment, the members of this cast and crew have surprised me with their immense talent and generosity of spirit. When things got scary, which they did (hello, this theatre is definitely haunted!), these students held each others' hands. When they were embarrassed to try some of the whacky things I asked them to do, they coaxed each other out of their shells with words of encouragement—and maybe a silly dance move or two. When I asked them difficult questions, they dug deep. What does it mean to dream? What does it mean to love? And, despite the many perils, why do we choose to do both anyway?

We hope to answer those questions—in a fun way—in this Halloween presentation of Shakespeare's *A Midsummer Night's Dream* at the historic Wincroft Theatre. I like to think of the show as a patchwork quilt made up of nine fabric squares, each one a scene, woven by our highly skilled student artists. I am honored that these amazing teens have trusted me to stitch all of their patches together.

On behalf of the Dark Cove Theatre Society, thank you for joining our slumber party. Now, don your comfiest pajamas, tuck yourself in, and dream a little dream with us.

Happy Halloween!

Ms. Sophia Spry
Head of the Department of Theatre
Dark Cove Arts Academy

Appendix Z

Playlist curated by S. Spry

Playlist

THE GROOVIEST PRE-SHOW EVAA

Sophia Spry • 14 songs, 52 min 59 sec

1. [RUE] "Plus tôt" by Alexandra Streliski
2. [MICHAEL] "16" by Baby Keem
3. [MAGPIE] "Alaska" by BANKS
4. [VIOLET] "Haunted" by Taylor Swift
5. [FREJA] "Glue" by BICEP
6. [HUNTER] "Mombasa" by Hans Zimmer
7. [SALMA] "Oululee Leh" by Elyanna
8. [FRANKIE] "She's a Rainbow" by the Rolling Stones
9. [MARGARET] "Shattered" by the Rolling Stones
10. [XANDER] "Rebellion (Lies) " by Arcade Fire
11. [JAYDEN] "FATAL" by Debby Friday
12. [LAILA] "Monster" by EXO
13. [MS. SPRY] "Everything is Everything" by Lauryn Hill
14. [ROMEO] "Who Let the Dogs Out" by Baha Men

Chapter 31

Patrons file in to the warbling stylings of a musical saw. In the orchestra pit, Kay is a sheet ghost among brass instruments. I give them a thumbs-up from the wings. They're too in the zone to notice.

The incoming audience comprises the Board, teachers, students—including Nina Petrov and NB on behalf of *The Chronicle*, who appear to be something of an item—and a few dour-faced corporate types from the International Art School Association, freshly delivered from the mainland. They are greeted boisterously by Headmaster Henley, whose brow looks in need of a dabbing from the kerchief in his pocket. When I catch his eye, he gives me a strangely fearful look. *Oh, how the tables have turned*, I think. *How powerful knowledge really is.* From my vantage point, I am able to see Mrs. Lin ignore Henley's offered handshake; his arm falls stiffly to his side. He follows as she takes her reserved seat in the third row. A few places down, Mr. Blake's chair is empty.

Magpie told me that Rue told her that she saw him getting on the ferry this afternoon, trunk in hand, a mere three hours after class abruptly ended. I haven't seen Frankie since then, but rumor has it, Mr. Blake is gone. For good. I can feel his absence like a very small weight lifted.

"Last looks!" Ms. Spry calls out, her voice raw and raspy from yelling all afternoon, the bottom hem of her seafoam floor-length gown dirty already.

Edie, fully recovered from the flu, scurries up to me with a fistful of stick-on jewels. "You are perfect," she squeaks and scurries away.

The orchestra hums to life as the band kids tune their instruments. Something (everything?) stirs inside of me. House lights dim.

I turn around and fumble through the darkness, arms outstretched. My hand meets another. "Sorry," I whisper, not knowing who I'm speaking to, but sensing it, or maybe hoping that it's …

"Hey, V."

Her.

I feel her near me like electricity. I begin pulling my hand away but Frankie's grip tightens on mine.

Ms. Spry starts her introductory speech onstage, welcoming the theatre patrons. "Hello, friends of the Dark Cove Theatre Society …"

"Did you hear?" Frankie whispers hotly.

"You did it. You're amazing."

Frankie's closer now, her lips grazing my ear: "*We* did it. Together."

Her breath sends a current down my spine.

"I saw your mom out there. You look so much alike."

Frankie laughs lightly. "Yeah, everyone says that."

"Beautiful," I add.

Ms. Spry welcomes each of the Governors by name.

Frankie laughs that laugh like birdsong. "I wish you could have seen her in action, the looks on their faces …"

"You saw it all go down?"

Frankie, cut out from the backstage darkness, bobs her head. "Blake and Henley ordered me out, but Mom was all, *my daughter has a right to hear this.* It was pretty cool."

"And now Blake's gone."

"Immediate termination."

"Your mom's such a badass. *You're* such a badass."

"Henley'll take a bit more time, but my mother is nothing if not efficient."

"I bet she's proud of you."

A bright swell of applause. It reminds me of Jiffy Pop on the stove.

"Yeah . . . she is, actually," Frankie says, so tenderly, earnestly. There are the muffled raps of our director's red-bottom heels walking offstage. Cast and crew rush in a whirlwind around me and Frankie. She pulls me into an embrace. The silk of her dress draws a cool shiver across the fields of my body like an overnight frost. "You ready for this?" she asks.

"Yeah. Well, that, and honestly, a little scared."

"You? Afraid?"

I laugh into her bouquet of hair, enveloping myself in the mysteries and beauty of her presence.

"You've got this. We've got this," she sings softly.

A thousand butterflies burst out of their cocoons. "Frankie, I just wanted to tell you, quickly before we . . . well, I've just been all in my head, you didn't deserve it, but finally I'm out of it, and I know now, I know who I am, or I'm starting to, at least, and I want to know *you* better, I still want that, I want that more than anything, actually, if you'll let me, and I'm so sor—"

"It's all right," she says softly, so only I can hear. "It's better than all right."

The applause dulls, and a thin wash of gold light spills through the cracks in the curtains like sunshine through clouds. A few of our castmates begin the performance just as Frankie releases me from our hug. She pulls away with a series of electric shocks, the static of our pajamas creating a cascade of silver lightning sparks. My heart thrums fiercely, punctuating every beat of the scene playing out just out of sight.

Frankie Lin beams at me, her face illuminated brilliantly somehow in the backstage dusk of Wincroft Theatre.

"See you up there, Helena." She pauses. Her eyelashes unfurl like open sails. She knocks the wind out of me. "I can't wait to fall in love with you."

Frankie floats away and through the curtains. Hunter follows, then Magpie. The audience listens to their poetry, enchanted to a hush.

I wait for my cue, take a deep, steady breath, and step out into the light.

IN TENEBRIS LUCEM CREAMUS

Acknowledgments

"What's in a name?" I don't know! My high school theatre teacher was named Katherine Spry. I had an Uncle Frankie who instilled in me a great sense of adventure. My beloved, singular Nana was called Violet. But really, there are few similarities between the people and the characters. I just wanted to honor them and keep them close as I wrote this story.

Here are the names of some of the people I am immensely grateful to that didn't make it into the book:

The whole team at Annick, especially Jieun Lee, who saw something worth exploring in Dark Cove.

My literary agent for this project, Amanda Orozco, and my acting agents, Nigel Mikoski and Yvonne Gustafson at Connekt Creative.

My parents Elena and Lorne Riley, who nurtured my dreams since I could hold a crayon, consoled me after countless rejections, and recruited everyone they know to buy this book. Thank you for the sacrifices you made for me and for always being there. I love you!

My sister and day-one bestie Bianca, her husband Aysar and their darling son Laith Joudeh, who I hope one day (when he learns how to read) enjoys this book.

The whole family, really. My Noni Louis Di Florio, an artist; my Grandmaman Jackie Riley, an avid reader; and my Nonna Marilyn Di Florio, on whom I based Violet's Nonna and to whom I will one day dedicate an Academy Award (as per the acceptance speech we wrote together when I was seven years old).

My partner Quinn Finnigan, who has been a co-creator of this story since its inception and the co-writer of most of my happiest moments. Your steadfast love and belief in me have helped me believe in myself. And now look . . . I've got a published book!

About the Author

Photo credit: Tessla Stuckey

SIERRA MARILYN RILEY is a queer Italian Canadian actor and writer with a BA in theatre. As a kid, Sierra's dream was to become an "actor slash author." She's been putting on plays and writing stories since then. *The Dark Cove Theatre Society* is her debut novel.

Formerly an editor and library assistant, Sierra now writes and auditions from her home in Toronto. You can find her words (on pop culture etc.) in *Maclean's*, *PRISM*, *Grain*, *Serviette*, *NUVO Magazine*, and more. You can find her face (emoting, etc.) on Hallmark's *Mistletoe Murders*.